MEXICAN
Standoff

BRUCE COOK

ST. MARTIN'S PAPERBACKS

St. Martin's Paperbacks titles are available at quantity discounts for sales promotions, premiums or fund raising. Special books or book excerpts can also be created to fit specific needs. For information write to special sales manager, St. Martin's Press, 175 Fifth Avenue, New York, N.Y. 10010.

Published by arrangement with Franklin Watts

MEXICAN STANDOFF

Copyright © 1988 by Bruce Cook.

All rights reserved. No part of this book may be used or reproduced in any manner whatsoever without written permission except in the case of brief quotations embodied in critical articles or reviews. For information address Franklin Watts, 387 Park Avenue South, New York, NY 10016.

Library of Congress Catalog Card Number: 88-20622

ISBN: 0-312-92114-4

Printed in the United States of America

Franklin Watts edition published 1988
St. Martin's Paperbacks edition/May 1990

10 9 8 7 6 5 4 3 2 1

For
Gladys Cook and Janet Kaye

CHAPTER 1

Only the prospect of a job would have brought me out on the 405 on a Friday afternoon. When you join that crush of creeping traffic looping down from the Santa Monica Freeway, you suddenly remember everything that's wrong with this city, Our Lady, Queen of the Angels. The traffic? Sure. The smog it creates? Of course. But worse, hanging over everything, heavier than the smog, is an atmosphere of free-floating, brain-rattling paranoia. When I read about laid-back California in those magazines they ship out from New York, I really have to laugh—or I used to when I took them seriously enough to look at them. Laid back Los Angeles? Where do they think we get all our looney-tunes? What do they think about our murder rate?

On the freeway, you can feel the anger around you as though it were something physical. The slower the cars move, the higher the tension-level rises. By the time I got to Washington Boulevard, and we had come to our third full stop, I could feel little pings of rage zinging in at me from every side. KKGO was blasting out a jagged line of Joe Henderson jazz. Under these conditions I knew I couldn't handle that for long, and so I slipped on a Bill Evans tape and settled down as best I could for the long crawl to Newport Beach. Just into the second chorus of the first cut, traffic began to move again.

The invitation to Newport Beach had come early in the morning. When the phone rang, I was half-awake, trying to persuade myself I was still asleep. Last night's Cuervo Gold had laid such a thick coat on my tongue that I could barely manage a hello when I picked up the wrong end of the receiver, but that was all right. The guy at the other end didn't call to listen; he called to talk. He identified himself only as Thomas Jarrett's secretary, and he didn't bother to explain who his boss was. I got the idea I was supposed to know that. He informed me that Mr. Jarrett wished to see me about a matter and that it was potentially worth my while. I was to be there at five o'clock, and he gave me the address. No directions, just the address. Then the phone went dead. One thing I noticed about that voice on the telephone, though: there were traces of an accent playing around the edges of it, an accent I couldn't quite place.

I put in a call to Joe Jarasek on the business section of the *Trib*. He owes me. It all goes back to a story I planted with him for a client. It was all true—but it was more than embarrassing to a competitor who had been playing dirty pool with my client. It was Joe's first big story on the *Trib*, and he's been buying me drinks ever since.

Joe confirmed my feeling that the name Thomas Jarrett meant money, big money, and my suspicion that the source of that money was oil.

"But what's he into?" I wanted to know. "Drilling? Leases? Marketing?"

"Deals, Chico. He's into deals." He hesitated. "Only . . ."

"Only what?"

"Well, you know what the oil market's been like lately."

So Thomas Jarrett was into deals. And it was "potentially worth my while" to pay him a visit at five o'clock. I hate to admit it, but that's all it took to put me out on the 405 on that Friday afternoon. Business hadn't been so good. I like to think that my particular hustle is recession-proof. There's a lot of money in this town, always has been, and when people with money want to know things about their wives, about their competitors, about their partners—they're willing to pay for it. But lately, I'll tell you, they haven't been so curious. The month before I got that call from Jarrett's secretary, they had been so lacking in curiosity that I had begun to wonder if I would be able to make the payment on my little condo. That's why I drowned my sorrows in all that Cuervo Gold the night before the call came, and that's also the reason I was so damned glad when it did come.

I gave myself a couple of hours to get down there. That's about twice the time it would normally take, but with half of Los Angeles escaping southward to play in the sun, that seemed a reasonable thing to do. Newport Beach is a kind of billion-dollar residential marina built along Balboa Bay. In California, there are nearly as many ways of living rich as there are rich people. Nowhere are options as open to people with money. You want land? You buy a ranch. You want a mansion? You buy out on Sunset. You want to play sailor? You buy in Newport Beach and tie your boat up at your private dock behind the house. Maybe the houses are a little close together, but considering the neighbors looking in your windows are also millionaires, that's not so bad.

After wandering around the curving streets that lined the boat channel, getting lost, and asking directions at a gas station, I pulled up my slightly battered Alfa Sprint at the curb opposite Thomas Jarrett's house at five minutes till five. I decided to wait it out and lit a cigarette as I studied the house. It was redwood and glass, the biggest in sight. But the most impressive thing about it was the cabin cruiser behind the house. All I could see was part of the boat's superstructure rising up from the dock in the rear. If the hull that went with it was the size it should be, then this one was about as big as the *Queen Mary* they had docked at Long Beach. Maybe Jarrett was dealing oil just to keep it in fuel. At a minute to five, I ground out my cigarette in the dashboard ashtray, jumped out of the car, and walked across the street.

The man who opened the door in response to my ring was the same one who had talked to me on the phone, Jarrett's secretary. He looked like some kind of Arab, and he was no more willing to offer his name this time than he had been before. He didn't even make sure of mine. He simply let me in, commented that I was on time, and said, "You make a good start." Not another word as he led me through the place, which was richly furnished to masculine taste, then up some stairs and into a huge room that was about two-thirds bedroom and one-third bathroom. But where was Jarrett?

"Come over here, Mr. Cervantes." The voice was a strong bass with a ring of authority. It came from the far end of the room, where I located a face capped by gray hair, rising from the floor. Was this Jarrett? I assumed he must be. A hand appeared and beckoned to me. It was a quick, commanding motion. I walked across the bedroom area toward him. With each step I seemed to sink deeper into the thick beige carpet that covered the room. By the time I mounted the three glaze-tiled steps into the bathroom area, I saw that he was sitting in a sunken Jacuzzi about the size of a kids' wading pool. He was naked.

I stood there, hovering over him, not knowing what position I should assume. Since he made no move to offer me his hand (out of consideration?—a wet hand, after all), I saw no need to kneel down close to him. Jarrett's attitude didn't invite it. He wanted to look me over. I let him. At last he said, "Well, you certainly *look* Mexican."

"That's because I am," I said. "Mexican-American."

"Chicano."

"That means something pretty specific. It's not a word I use much."

"Oh? You're not a militant then? *La raza* and all that?"

"It depends on the situation."

Jarrett nodded. There was a hint of amusement at the corners of his mouth, although not in his eyes. His eyes were cold. Then he said, "Towel."

"Pardon?"

"Towel." And he pointed toward the wall behind me. Well, I had come this far, so what the hell. With a shrug, I turned and pulled a brown towel that was about as thick and soft as the carpet from the rack. As I turned back, he was climbing out of the Jacuzzi and reaching for the towel. As I handed it to him, I gave him the once-over, just as he wanted me to.

He was in good shape for a man in his fifties and vain about his body. You could tell that, the way he toweled himself down. He gave me a series of quick little poses, expanding his chest as he rubbed his back, flexing his arms as he dried his legs. There was something vaguely homoerotic about it. Also something subtly demeaning. With his indifference about how he appeared before me, he seemed to place me at the level of a servant. I didn't like it, but I had to pay the rent.

"Saheed!" he called out, as he pulled on his robe. "Get Mr. Cervantes a drink."

I started to ask for Cuervo Gold but caught myself. They'd expect me to drink tequila. "Scotch," I said, "on the rocks, with a splash of water."

Chivas Regal. It tasted okay, almost as good as tequila. Jarrett settled into an Eames chair and gestured toward a straight-back chair nearby. I sat.

"Mr. Cervantes," he began, "I want you to find my son's murderer."

An alarm went off inside my head. I got ready to leave. It was time for me to make my little speech: "Mr. Jarrett, I think you should understand something before you go any further. Real private investigators don't work like those guys on TV. Listen, the police—"

He cut me off with a motion of his hand. "I'm well aware what private detectives do and don't do." There was a sharp edge on each word. "I've employed them for one reason or another more times than I care to remember, and with varying results—as Saheed will tell you."

I glanced over at the secretary, who stood leaning against the wall next to the bar, his arms folded, staring at me. Saheed wouldn't tell me the time of day unless his employer ordered him to.

"This is a special situation that requires special handling,"

7

resumed Jarrett. "If you'll let me explain without interrupting, I think you'll understand. Perhaps you'd care to smoke." I nodded, and he gestured to Saheed who went out for an ashtray. Thomas Jarrett was probably being unusually solicitous. Sensing my resistance, he was trying to win me over. I lit up in anticipation of the ashtray, which arrived a moment later. Jarrett began his story.

"On April 14 of this year, my son Paul was on spring break from Santa Barbara, the university there. He had brought a girl for me to meet, a girl he claimed to be quite serious about. They were talking about marriage. For reasons we need not go into, the two of them left rather suddenly late in the evening on the day they arrived. They headed out in his car for the city, evidently up the San Diego Freeway. In any case, they had taken the Marina del Rey turnoff. It was about midnight— you can check all this with the police—and . . . Do you know that stretch?"

"Yes," I said, "I know it very well."

"Then you can picture what happened. There was a drunk driver on the road—well, he must have been drunk—traveling in their direction. As I've reconstructed it, he must have been going at a terrific rate of speed."

"They often do along there."

"Yes, well, it was right where the road narrows. It goes from four lanes to three and then to two. This drunk must have tried to pass Paul's car, swinging from behind in an arc to the left. At any rate, he must have lost control completely because he slammed into Paul's car. I'm sure you can imagine what happened."

"Your son's car was knocked into the guardrail?"

"And over it. Paul's car flipped, tumbled down the embankment there, and burst into flame. The police say he must have died on impact, or at least been totally unconscious. They're trying to be nice, I suppose, trying to tell me he didn't just burn to death."

During those last few words, Jarrett showed the first trace

of any real emotion since I had met him some minutes before. It was only an almost imperceptible tightening of the throat, a moment's hesitation, a slight thickening of his voice.

"And the girl?" I asked.

"She died, too, of course. But not the . . . the man who murdered my son. He spun around and hit the guardrail, and it held him. He was evidently dead drunk. He had to be. But when they booked him and did the standard test, he checked out as inconclusive—though how he managed that, I don't understand."

I was about to ask him what charge the driver was booked on when chimes sounded downstairs. The doorbell. Jarrett turned to his secretary. "Silverstein. Be nice to him, Saheed."

The dark, silent man said nothing as he slipped out of the room. Jarrett watched him go, then said to me, "Perhaps the best thing would be to continue this downstairs. Saheed is Palestinian, and Silverstein is what you would expect a man with a name like that to be." His mouth twisted in a smile that was close to a sneer. "They don't get on well. Perhaps if a third party were present? I'll join you just as soon as I'm dressed."

I stood up, drink in hand, and started for the door. But thinking about it, I turned back and asked, "Who's Silverstein?"

"He's the father of the girl. Bringing you in was his idea."

Bringing me in? Not yet, Mr. Jarrett. I walked quietly down the stairway, not quite knowing what awaited me. I half-expected to find Saheed and the new arrival to be squared off at the door.

But no. The two were conspicuously ignoring each other—Saheed at the bar, and Silverstein carefully considering a painting on the wall. It looked like a Frederic Remington Wild West scene. It was.

Silverstein turned to me and nodded rather gravely. "Mr. Cervantes, I assume. . . . Seymour Silverstein." He put out a hand and gave me a good, firm shake. There was something about him, quite a lot about him, that said he was from the East. Of slightly less than average height, he was dressed in a dark-gray three-piece summer suit, which he wore with a narrow paisley tie that was tightly knotted. But it was more than just his dress. His round face wore an Eastern pallor that made the wrinkles and worry lines seem almost engraved into his skin.

"I'm sorry I'm late," he said. "I rented a car and drove straight out from the airport. The traffic was just—"

"Unbelievable."

"Exactly. I suppose you're used to it, though." He fumbled into his coat pocket and pulled out a crumpled pack of cigarettes. He dug one out and lit it with a series of quick, nervous movements.

"You never get used to it," I said. "You just try to plan around it."

Saheed appeared at his elbow and offered him a drink that looked like a martini on the rocks. Not a word passed between them as Silverstein accepted it. He took a deep gulp from it and a long drag from his cigarette. Then, fortified, he settled down to the business at hand: "I don't know how much you've been told about this already."

"Not very much. Just that your daughter and Jarrett's son both died in a car crash with a driver who survived. He may or may not have been drunk at the time of the accident." I hesitated. "It . . . it must have been terrible for you."

"Terrible?" he said with sudden bitterness. "I'll tell you what would be terrible, Mr. Cervantes, and that's if the man who killed her were allowed to get away with it—to go out and do it again. You haven't heard, I take it, that he skipped bail and went back."

"Went back where?"

"Then you don't know why we want *you*, especially, to handle this. You see—"

"I was just getting to that when you arrived, Silverstein." It was Jarrett, descending the stairs, dressed in white from his deck shoes to his polo shirt. He made more than an appearance—more like an entrance. "Why don't we all sit down together and get through this as quickly as possible?"

Silverstein and I went to a couch. Jarrett took the chair closest to me. I noticed that Saheed had disappeared.

"You see," Silverstein went on with some determination, "the man who killed my Sarah . . . and Mr. Jarrett's son, was Mexican, an alien. Not here illegally, it seems. He was documented. At any rate, he *is* Mexican. He *did* skip bail. And his name is Francisco Rivera—Francisco Cruz-Rivera perhaps."

"What was the charge against him?"

"Suspicion of involuntary manslaughter."

"And you want me to find him," I put in.

"That's right," said Jarrett. He sat relaxed in the deep chair, his brown, tanned arms folded against his flat stomach. "We know he's gone back to Mexico. You find him and bring him here. I want that man."

"What about extradition?"

Silverstein fielded that one: "Not likely, from what I hear. The Mexican authorities . . ." He left the sentence unfinished. I got the idea it was out of deference to me. "Well, we can't expect too much from them. I'm with the State Department. I've been briefed on this."

"You're from Washington?" I asked. He nodded. So I was right. He was from the East. I thought about all this a moment and turned from Silverstein to Jarrett. "Let me get this straight," I said at last. "You want me to bring this guy back here to stand trial. Has it occurred to you that might be called kidnapping?"

"Only in Mexico," said Jarrett. His finger was raised to make the point. He began shaking it at me. "You get him across the border, and you're returning a fugitive."

"Look," said Silverstein, "we're not pretending there aren't certain risks involved, but—"

"But we're willing to pay for it, Cervantes." Jarrett was leaning forward, studying me. This, as far as he was concerned, was the bottom line.

"Now wait," I said, "let's not talk about that yet. You picked me out because I'm Mexican-American, right?"

"That's correct," said Silverstein.

"Right," echoed Jarrett. "I found you in the phone book."

"I hate to tell you, gentlemen, but I'm not the man for the job. You know what you want? You want a bounty hunter—some guy who's done this kind of work before. I'm a snoop. I get information for people, and I'm pretty damned good at it. But I've never done anything like what you're asking me to do."

Jarrett waved that aside. "We know all that. Just because I picked you out of the yellow pages doesn't mean I didn't have you checked out. I probably know more about you than you want me to know."

"So?" What was this, blackmail?

"So the point is, Mr. Cervantes"—Silverstein this time—"we need a man who can go down there without attracting a lot of attention, can sort of blend into the landscape. And then, when he finds Rivera, can get him up here with a minimum of difficulty by paying off the right people."

"You know about the *mordida*?"

"Payoffs? We know all about the *mordida*."

"Now, have I got this right?" I said, looking from one to the other. "You want me to go down there more or less under cover."

"That's right," said Silverstein.

"You think if I put on white pajamas and a big, floppy hat and start asking questions I'm really going to fool people? Have you got any idea how big Mexico is? How common the name Francisco Rivera is down there? Don't you know anything more about this guy?"

"We have a tip where he is," Silverstein said rather dramatically. He reached into his inside coat pocket and produced an envelope.

"Let's see that," said Jarrett, and he suddenly reached across me and made a grab for the letter.

An unsuccessful grab—Silverstein pulled it back. His eyes

12

flashed angrily just for an instant. "You told me I was crazy to do this," he said to Jarrett. "Now that I've got some results you want to take over."

Jarrett rolled his eyes in a show of exasperation and leaned back in his chair with a shrug.

Silverstein handed the letter to me. "You see," he said, "about two months ago I had handbills distributed in every city of any size in Mexico. They had Rivera's—or rather, Cruz-Rivera's—picture on them, and they offered a thousand dollars for information regarding his whereabouts. Just that and a post-office box number in Washington. I just got this Wednesday. It's why I flew out here."

The letter was tissue-thin paper in a tissue-thin envelope. I opened it up and read. It was dated only a week ago and came from an address on Calle Acapulco in Culiacan. In substance it stated rather formally (in Spanish, of course) that the person in the photograph was known as Francisco Cruz-Rivera and was sometimes seen in Culiacan. A suggestion was made that a search of the places he frequented might turn him up. No promises, just facts. It seemed like a genuine lead to me. It was signed A. Ramirez. I reread it, folded it up, and handed it back to Silverstein.

"*Now* can I see it?" demanded Jarrett.

Silverstein shrugged and handed it across to him. Jarrett ripped the envelope slightly getting the letter out.

"Well," Silverstein said to me, "will you take it on?"

"I didn't say that. Look, I don't know that part of the country at all. I've never done this kind of work before. And quite frankly, the problems in getting a man out who doesn't want to go would be incredibly difficult."

"Cervantes," said Jarrett, "I said we'd make it worth your while, and we will. We are each willing to write you out a check for five thousand dollars if you will agree to take on the job. This would be understood as a nonreturnable retainer. All you have to do is make a good-faith effort to find the man and bring him back. That's ten thousand dollars just to try and ten thousand more if you succeed."

"Plus expenses? All the *mordida*?"

"Plus *all* expenses," Silverstein assured me.

"I'd like it in writing," I said. "Put it down that you're my clients, what you're paying me to do and why."

"In writing?" Silverstein was clearly uneasy at that.

I sighed and looked from one to the other and was struck by the obvious—how different the two men were. They had absolutely nothing in common but this single purpose, which was fundamentally revenge. Oh, they could say, as Silverstein had, that they didn't want this guy free so he could do it again. But deep down, each one of them wanted to see him dead. And why not? If it had been my kid who burned up in that wreck, I'd probably feel the same way. And then I thought—of what? The payment due on the condo, and the fact that twenty thousand dollars was more than half of what I made last year. And at last I said, "Okay."

Silverstein whipped out his checkbook and produced a pen. Jarrett called for Saheed.

"Wait a minute. I meant what I said about putting it in writing. Just put down the terms we agreed on and the client relationship. Then give me a copy of the letter and that handbill, and a copy of the accident report. Along with them give me the checks and fifteen hundred dollars cash advance on expenses. I'll leave for Culiacan as soon as I've got all this in hand."

"Is this to give you time to reconsider?" asked Silverstein.

"No. I'm as good as my word. If you checked me out, you must have heard that. You must know, too, that if I say I'll give you a good-faith effort, that's what you'll get. Ten thousand dollars will buy you a lot of my time and energy."

"About the accident report," said Silverstein. "We thought it might be better if you talked to the officer who was on the scene. We took the liberty of making an appointment with him for you tonight at eight o'clock. It's his dinner break. He'll answer any questions you might have. His name is Casimir Urbanski."

CHAPTER 2

Officer Urbanski was from Detroit, or a place somewhere around it called Hamtramck. Anyway, he'd been a Detroit cop, one of the many, he told me, who got laid off in the city's first round of budget cuts. He was young, single, had a good record, and so he took off for the Coast, where he'd always wanted to live. He had managed to land a job on the LAPD, since he was on the scene when Chief Davis came under pressure to beef up neighborhood patrols in Venice and East L.A. because of the kid gangs. "I dint have to do the academy again," he said, "just a refreshing course." That was the thing about Casimir Urbanski: he talked kind of weird.

He talked a lot there at Tiny Naylor's on Lincoln. The two of us in a booth, the worn waitress paddling back and forth from the counter with the coffee pot in her hand. I bought him dinner and watched him eat—steak, mashed potatoes and gravy, a side order of fries, and finally a big wedge of banana cream pie. While he ate, he asked *me* questions.

"You a beaner? I had a beaner for my partner by the TAC force in Detroit. He was okay, that little fucker. He had a couple of years seniority on me, so he stayed and I went. He was okay, though."

"Good, swell." What could I say?

"He was okay." Officer Urbanski had what I wanted, and he knew it. His elbow rested on a file folder he had lifted from the station. I didn't expect him to hand it over for keeps, but

I did intend to get a good look at it. He had decided to make me work for it—maybe he just wanted to check me out.

"You by the cops here? I mean, before?"

Before what? Before Watts? Before the SLA shootout? Oh yes, I was there, too. Or before I got sick of being passed over how-many-times for sergeant and decided to find out for myself if it was as cold outside the department as they kept telling us? "Yeah, I was a cop. Twelve years, most of it in the Wilshire District."

"That's a pretty hot kettle of fish they got down there, like." He polished off the french fries and pulled over the pie.

"It was then. I guess it still is." Then I added, anticipating his next question: "I was on robbery and vice before that."

"Vice is nice." Was he rhyming intentionally?

"I liked robbery better."

He looked at me disbelievingly. "For real?"

"For real. The thing about vice, it gets pretty cold standing around MacArthur Park waiting to be hit on by some poor insurance salesman."

"Oh, queers." He shrugged and forked in another gooey gobbit of banana cream. "We didn't do queers in Detroit."

If he had been from anyplace else, I might have asked him what they *did* do there. But I still had a professional's respect for tough duty, and I knew that Detroit was tough, maybe the toughest.

He continued his interrogation: "You been outside long? Snooping?"

"About five years."

"You do okay at it? How is it by the bank?"

"You mean the money?" I asked warily. "The money isn't bad. I'm doing okay." Was he going to stick me for this? I was prepared to give him twenty and the price of a dinner but not much more. I didn't *have* much more on me. "Why?"

"*Why?*" He seemed almost offended by the question. "I got to look out on the future, you know? You think I want to be in a blue suit all my life? I'm looking to get ahead."

16

"As a private detective?"

"Sort of. I thought, maybe, a bodyguard. You do any of that?"

"Never."

"These big movie stars, they all got bodyguards. I read it in a magazine. I could do that." He leaned forward confidentially. His small eyes grew smaller as he frowned with intense seriousness. "Hey, you know if Raquel Welch got one? That's one body I'd like to guard."

I leaned back and looked at him, a big Polish kid from Detroit, not even thirty yet. Was he stupid? No, just terribly naive. He had been here in Los Angeles for perhaps two years, and all he knew about the place was what he read in *People* magazine. Sure, it was funny, but it was also sad—sort of dismal, really. Inwardly, I sighed. In certain circumstances, I can be as unprincipled as the next man: "Well, yes, she does. But the word I get is that Raquel isn't terrifically satisfied with the guy. You know what I mean?"

"Oh, yeah." His eyes shone. "Oh, sure. I know."

"He's sort of fat and forty, past his prime. I think, and people around her think, that she needs, well, somebody *younger*. Now, don't get me wrong. This guy she's got, he's got a good reputation, he makes all the right moves. But the word I get, she needs somebody who makes all the right moves . . . faster. That means younger, doesn't it?"

"Right." He nodded emphatically. "Right. You know her, huh?"

"Not well." Cool, understated. I guess I meant I was once in the same room with her.

"But you know the people around her?" he asked, unconsciously quoting me.

"Some of them." This was not a *complete* fabrication.

"Could you . . ." Urbanski cleared his throat and lowered his voice. "Could you put in a word for me, like?"

"I could try. No promises, though."

"Oh, no. Oh, jeez, no." The smile that spread over his face

was quite indescribable. His eyes glazed in blissful fantasy. He dropped his fork in the remains of the banana cream pie and leaned back, quite overcome by the moment.

Now, I thought, the time had come to remind him of why we had met: "You and your partner were the first ones on the scene that night when those two kids were killed, weren't you?"

He said nothing for a moment, but suddenly roused from his daydream, he nodded emphatically. "Oh, yeah, right. We was heading south on Centinela. We were practically looking right at it when it happened. We heard the boom and saw the flash."

"How long was it before you were there?"

"A minute, two minutes. Three at the most."

"And there was absolutely no chance of pulling them out?"

"You're kidding me, right? The gas tank goes, the whole car goes. Boom, like that. It already went up by the time we got there. Boom, you know?"

"I know," I told him reassuringly. "I've seen it happen just like that." And it was true: I had.

"Take a look," he said, pushing the file folder across the table to me. "It's all in here."

I turned it around and tried to look casual as I lit a cigarette before opening it up. I found a photocopy there for me along with the original. The facts were all laid out meticulously in the abstract and abbreviated language of the police report. I glanced down at the filing officer's signature and saw that it was something other than Urbanski's, maybe Kearney or Kennedy. It was hard to read the signature. I glanced up at Urbanski. "Who wrote this up?" I asked him.

"My partner then, Frank Keeney. He fucked up. The last I heard of him, he got sent out to East L.A. He fucked up out there, too."

Just like that. Although I was curious, I didn't question him further about it. I just let it hang there between us. I returned to the accident report and began going through it line by line, notation by notation, letting each little fact sink in before I went on to the next. But suddenly I came across something that almost made me jump right out of my seat there in the booth. "What's this?"

"What's what?"

"It says here that the vehicle that this guy Cruz-Rivera was driving was registered to Turnbull and Son on Ocean Park."

"That's right."

"Well, that's a funeral parlor, isn't it? An undertaker?"

"Yeah, sure, of course."

"What do you mean, 'of course'?"

"Well, when you come on the scene of an accident and one of the vehicles involved is a hearse, you expect it to be registered to an undertaker, don't you?"

"Yeah, but didn't it seem, well, sort of unusual to you? I mean, how many times before have you been at the scene when a hearse was involved?"

Urbanski shrugged. "Not often. Once."

"Really?"

"Yeah. In Detroit."

"But was the chauffeur driving under the influence the way this guy Cruz-Rivera was?"

"He'd had a few. You get all kinds in Detroit." He thought about it a moment. "Besides, who says this guy Rivera was d.w.i.?"

"Well . . . Jarrett . . ."

"The guy passed the breathalizer."

"But here in the remarks space it says, 'signs of intoxication.'"

"Oh, that's fucking Keeney. You want to know what's really going on when we got there, better ask me; don't read the report."

"Well, what *was* going on?"

"This guy, Rivera, he was screaming he was so upset, trying to get close enough to pull somebody out. As far as I'm concerned the guy's just a witness. All we saw was this car go over the side, roll, and blow up. We didn't see these guys playing bumper tag or anything."

"But in this accident report it says—"

19

Urbanski cut me off. "I know what it says." He hesitated a moment, then plunged on: "While I'm wrestling with the guy, trying to pull him back from the burning vehicle, Keeney's checking over the hearse. He sees the whole left side of the thing is bashed in."

"The left side?"

"Yeah."

"So then what?"

"So Keeney comes on like a real hardass, starts asking the guy, wants his version of the accident. Which he didn't get. I wasn't around for some of this because I was calling a report in to the CHP and the Fire Department. We had them all out there eventually. Anyway, the guy wouldn't answer Keeney—just kept saying over and over he wanted to see a lawyer."

"You think he understood what was being said to him?" I asked.

"He understood. His English wasn't that bad. He just wouldn't talk to us. You can imagine how this went over with Keeney."

"Well . . . no . . . I can't. What do you mean?"

"He's got this thing for beaners. Hates them. That's really why he had a hard-on for this guy. You ask me, that's why he wrote it up the way he did and brought him in on vehicular manslaughter. The guy, what's his name, Rivera, he could've beaten it easy, you ask me. I was surprised they charged him."

"But he jumped bail."

Urbanski shrugged. "Go figure."

"Who was his lawyer?"

Urbanski shrugged again. "It's in the court records."

"Who paid his bail?"

"A bondsman, I don't know. Who stood for it? Ask the bondsman."

It seemed we had about exhausted the matter for now. I called the waitress over and paid the check. Urbanski shuffled his feet and heaved his big, bulky body out of the booth where it had been trapped for the better part of an hour. He seemed relieved to be let loose at last. On the way out, he turned to me suddenly and said, "One thing I remember. We got the tow truck over and impounded the hearse, right?"

"Right."

"Well, we barely got the beaner booked and in the tank when these two guys from the funeral parlor show up and claim the hearse. We say, you know, forget about it. Vehicle's been involved in an accident with a fatality, we keep it and go over it, right? Well, they say, like, you can't impound the stiff inside. Give us the stiff. So, I mean, who do we argue with on that? They got the Department of Health by their side. So they unload the stiff and put it in the station wagon and drive away with it."

"So what's funny about that?"

"These guys. They didn't seem like undertakers to me. They were beaners, too, only . . ."

"Yeah?"

"Different. Sharper."

After dropping Casimir Urbanski off at the Venice Station, and swearing faithfully that I would make discreet inquiries on his behalf among the people around Raquel, I drove directly back to West Hollywood, dropped off the car at the condo garage, and walked around the corner to Barney's Beanery. It's my local. It's also maybe the only good bar in Los Angeles. The lumpen proletariat of the movie industry hang out there—stuntmen, out-of-work grips, and girls who call themselves actresses and models but aren't. It's loud and sloppy and once in a while dangerous. It feels just like home to me.

"Chico!" Stu hailed me from behind the bar. "*Cómo le va?*"

I fluttered my hand noncommittally and ordered a big can of Foster's Lager. When he delivered it, I asked him, "Is Boomie around?"

"He's here someplace." He looked up and down the bar and shrugged. "I just served him a Jack Daniel's a couple of minutes ago. Try in back."

I did, moving down the length of the bar, squeezing between

couples when I had to, nodding greetings to the familiar faces along the way. I found the man I was looking for right where Stu suggested he might be.

Boomie is not a good man for me to know. We both know that, and in general I avoid him. He understands and holds no personal grudge against me. As far as I know, he has no personal feelings at all. With guys like him, it's all business. What *sort* of business? you ask. Well, his nickname should give you a hint. I don't know his last name, and I don't want to. Boomie, a.k.a. Boom-Boom, is a gun merchant.

He was shooting pool. I stood and watched for a moment, socking back a good gulp of Foster as I waited for him to take his shot. He wasn't much with a cue. I'd taken him down a couple of times myself, but it never seemed to bother him. He flubbed a cross-table right-corner shot and lost the cue ball down the hole in the process. Turning away from the table with a shrug, he took a sip from his Jack Daniel's—straight up, no ice—and leaned back against the wall as his opponent began what proved to be a long series that ultimately cleaned the table. Tough luck for Boomie, but it gave me a good chance to talk to him.

"Boomie."

"Chico."

"You still doing business?"

"Always."

"I've got an unusual request."

He turned to me, his thin face drooping in a crooked smile. "What's unusual, man? You name it, and I get it. I got a reputation to keep. So what's unusual?"

"A tranquilizer gun."

"That's unusual."

"You know what I mean. They use them in zoos and stuff. They shoot animals with them and put them asleep."

"Man, I *know*. I'm an armorer. I know my field."

"Well, can you get me one?"

"I admit, it's an unusual item. I'll have to make some calls. It may take a while."

"No good," I said firmly. "I'll need it late tomorrow. Sunday at the latest."

"I'll do what I can."

"I'm sure you will. Just one more thing: how much is it going to set me back?"

He shook his head slowly and took a sip of Jack Daniel's. His eyes were on the table where his opponent, a cowboy in a motorcycle jacket, was on his fourth shot. At last he said, "No idea. I'll let you know."

"It'll have to be on credit."

Boomie turned to me sharply. "Come *on*, man. What're you handing me?" I had injured his professional pride a second time.

"Listen," I said, "I'll probably have to get out of town with it early on Sunday. I don't want to write you a check. You don't want to take one. You'll have to trust me for it."

He sighed, glanced back at the table, and finally came back to me. "Well, seeing it's you. You've got a reputation to hold up too, Chico."

He had me there. "I know," I said.

And that was all that happened that day, except that when I got back to my place, I checked the calls on my machine and the last one on it was from Seymour Silverstein. He was brief and to the point: "Mr. Cervantes, I am at the Beverly Hills Holiday Inn on Wilshire. I would greatly appreciate it if I could meet with you privately before I fly back to Washington. Perhaps breakfast at 9:30? I'm in room 307."

CHAPTER 3

If there was doubt in my mind that I could pull myself out of bed in time to make that nine-thirty date with Silverstein, then I had not anticipated Saheed's assistance. At seven-fifty-five the next morning, five minutes before my alarm was set to go off, the doorbell rang from down at the street entrance. In my confusion, I picked up the telephone and heard my hello answered by a dial tone. Then I stumbled out of the bedroom and over to the intercom unit on the wall.

"Yes?" I gasped. "Who is it?"

"Saheed," came the dark voice at the other end. "I have material for you."

I buzzed him in and by the time he was knocking on my apartment door, I had managed to struggle into my robe and get the coffee on. I threw the door open, and he stepped inside without a word of greeting. He reached inside his suit coat and produced an unaddressed manila envelope.

Just then a sudden, shrill, insistent tone came from the bedroom. "Jesus," I said, "the alarm clock. Excuse me." I ran into the bedroom and shut the thing off. When I got back, Saheed was standing where I had left him, his arms now crossed, regarding me as though I were some incompetent servant. It was a lucky thing for both of us we weren't working together.

Again, he extended the envelope. I took it this time and tore it open. At last he spoke: "It is there, all of it—two checks for five thousand dollars. One of them, at least, we know is good. And there, too, is the fifteen hundred dollars expense money, and the letter confirming the terms you agreed on last night." With that, he turned and started for the door.

"Just a minute," I said.

He looked back, clearly annoyed. "What is it?"

"I'd like you to stay while I read through this. Would you like some coffee?"

"Not yours."

I shrugged and went over to the nearest chair and sat down to read the letter. Saheed stood impatiently by the door and folded his arms once again. I had no idea whether he had assumed this contemptuous attitude because of personal feelings for me, or if this was simply the way that he dealt with anyone who worked for Jarrett. For that matter, I didn't care. I did know, though, that I didn't like it, so I took my time reading through the document.

Saheed was evidently right. It was all just about what I had asked for the night before. It was set out in such clear and specific detail that I suspected that Silverstein had written it. The facts of the case were summarized, my responsibilities laid out—"to make a good-faith effort to find and return said Francisco Cruz-Rivera to the legal authorities of Los Angeles County." For this I was guaranteed "a minimum of ten thousand dollars to be paid in the form of a retainer, a sum to be shared equally by Messrs. Jarrett and Silverstein." I was also guaranteed all expenses "including any and all legal costs that should be incurred by Mr. Cervantes in relation to his pursuit and execution of his duties in our behalf." Jarrett and Silverstein had signed their names. But at the bottom of the page a kind of postscript had been penned: "And Mr. Cervantes will report daily on his progress to Thomas Jarrett."

I looked up at Saheed, still standing there by the door, but now affecting an attitude of bored nonchalance. I waited for his attention.

His eyes met mine at last, and I said, "No."

"*No?* What you mean, *no?*" In his astonishment, he had dropped the helper verb. Shame on him.

"I mean, no. This shit at the end about reporting every day

to Jarrett. That wasn't part of the deal. He knows it. You know it. I know it. And Silverstein certainly knows it."

"The Jew? What does he matter?"

"It matters because he's the party of the second part, and this is between me and him and your boss—equal parties. If I report to your boss, then I report to Silverstein, too. And that's too damned much reporting. You tell Thomas Jarrett I will report to him when and if I have something to report, and at the same time I will report to Seymour Silverstein. Is that clear?"

The Third World and I had a mini-confrontation right there in my living room. I stared at him. He stared at me. In the end, I stared him down. Without a word, he threw open the door and walked out, slamming it behind him. That was nice. I had penetrated Saheed's cool. I wondered how many others besides Jarrett had managed to do that.

I got up from the chair, feeling pretty pleased with myself, and went into the kitchen and poured myself a cup of coffee. It sure tasted good.

Even with Saheed's intrusion, I managed to get to the Holiday Inn on Wilshire on time. The place seemed right for Silverstein. He was not a wealthy man, and he was here on his own business. And yet if he was with the State Department, he was used to a certain standard of accommodation when he traveled. This place, classier than most of its kind, would provide it. It was a sensible compromise. There was a lot about Silverstein I liked.

He was there in the lobby waiting for me, dressed in another dark-gray suit, only this one had pinstripes. We shook hands, and he smiled rather gravely. "I'm glad you could make it," he said. "When you speak into one of those telephone machines, you're never really sure."

"Well, I'm good about checking my messages. I'm pretty dependable."

"I'm sure you are. Shall we?" He gestured in the direction of the dining room and led the way in.

When we were seated and coffee had been poured, he nodded and began a speech that he had obviously thought out carefully beforehand: "As you no doubt have guessed, Mr. Jarrett and I are not on friendly terms. It's ironic, perhaps, because our children were on more than friendly terms. They intended to be married. Although I was not especially in favor of it, I didn't oppose it. I'd met the boy, Paul, when my wife and I visited Sarah at Santa Barbara. He was a good kid, though God knows how or why, considering the way he had grown up—that father, parents divorced. There was a sort of inherent kindness in the boy that my daughter, Sarah, must have found terrifically attractive. He was also, well, very good-looking."

His voice had thickened, and his eyes glistened slightly. I wanted to say something, but there was nothing I could think of that was right. He cleared his throat and resumed: "At any rate, they wanted to get married. I said the usual things: Don't you think you're both awfully young? Why don't you wait awhile? and so on. But I didn't say, Don't do it! I forbid it! Evidently Thomas Jarrett did. As I've been able to piece things together, on the night . . . all this happened, the two of them drove down to Newport Beach to announce their intentions. There must have been a terrible scene because Paul and Sarah left—they had intended to stay the night—and drove back to Los Angeles. And it was on the way that they . . . died."

"Where did you get your information?" I asked. "Not from Jarrett?"

"A little of it, I suppose, but no, not from Jarrett. I talked with his ex-wife at the funeral. A decent enough woman—quite well-off herself, I gather. It seems, according to her, that what Jarrett objected to was Sarah's . . . well, her religion. And that's rather ironic, too, because as smart a girl as she was, she couldn't have told you what Yom Kippur was all about. That was how she was brought up." He hesitated a moment and then added, "I wonder now if we did the right thing."

The waitress came and took our order. Often it seems that such interruptions come when they are most needed. This was one of those times, as far as I was concerned. Frankly, I wondered why he was telling me all this. Although I was certainly interested, it seemed to me that I shouldn't be burdened with this emotional baggage, that I might do a better job for him without it.

As he talked on, I began to get the point. "Look," said Silverstein, "both Jarrett and I want you to find this man Rivera, or Cruz-Rivera, or whoever he is—though oddly enough, he's been dragging his feet on this course of action with you. After talking to him last night, I'm convinced we have quite different motives or at least different goals. I truly and honestly want Cruz-Rivera brought back here to Los Angeles to stand trial. It will only be for involuntary manslaughter, and it won't bring my daughter back, but it is the system. Now, I have the feeling that this is *not* the case with Thomas Jarrett. From things that he said to me at the funeral and last night, I have reason to believe that he is planning something more personal for that man in Mexico. And I asked you here to warn you about that."

"What do you mean?" He had my full attention.

"I think that ultimately, if you manage to apprehend Cruz-Rivera, there will be pressure on you to deliver him not to the police but directly to Jarrett. He's here in Los Angeles, and I'm returning to Washington, so I won't be around to prevent it. But if you hand him over to Jarrett, I don't think you would want the next bit on your conscience."

"Let me ask you something."

"Certainly. Anything."

"You were there last night when all of this was put into writing, weren't you?"

"I certainly was. I drew it up myself."

"I suspected that."

"The bureaucratic style?"

"Something like that. But let me ask you this: did you put in a proviso at the end to the effect that I was to report daily to Jarrett?"

"I certainly did not."

"I didn't think so. But there it was, inked in at the bottom. Saheed brought it over this morning."

"And what did you say?"

"I told him no. I told him that if I reported to Jarrett, I would also have to report to you."

"I'm glad you put it that way."

"Yeah, but my point was that it tied me up, that it put me responsible to one master when there were two involved. But more than that, I didn't want the burden of reporting to anybody when I didn't have anything to report."

"Quite understandable," said Silverstein. He pulled a wallet from inside his jacket and a card out of that. Carefully he wrote out a phone number on it and pushed it across the table to me. "Here. This is my card. Now you can reach me at home or in the office, probably at any time of the day or night. I do want to hear from you, of course, but I'm not putting you on a schedule."

I took the card and pocketed it with a nod. "Good," I said, and that seemed to settle that.

We had a pleasant enough meal. Silverstein was obviously in a bit of a rush to catch his plane, but he had the good grace not to jump up and leave now that his business with me was concluded. I remember that he asked me about myself—how I'd gotten into snooping, whether I found it gratifying, all the polite questions people asked about my line of work. I answered them—politely. And then he said something interesting. He said, "Tell me something about yourself."

"I thought that's what I was doing."

"Well, of course you were. I'm sorry. No, I guess I meant I was curious about you, personally—where you're from, your background."

I looked at him. How much did he really want to know? I couldn't tell, and so with a shrug, I simply dove in: "Well, I've been married . . . once. No children, which, seeing we only lasted three years, was certainly a good thing." Was this what he wanted to hear?

"Tell me about your father."

"My father?"

"Yes. I take it he was an educated man, and not a . . ."

"An illegal?"

"Yes."

"Well, you're right. He wasn't. He and my mother came up from Mexico City the year the war ended. He came to be the managing editor of *El Diario*. That's the Spanish-language paper here."

"I know," said Silverstein, and he probably did.

"My mother was pregnant with me. I was born here, and so were all my brothers and sisters."

"And where are they now?"

"Oh, scattered. You know. Washington, New York, Sacramento. Good jobs, good careers, onward and upward. If there's a black sheep in the family, it's me."

"How's that?"

"Well, I became a cop—LAPD. I went through UCLA, but where did it get me?" I regarded Silverstein briefly. He was after something. I couldn't tell quite what. "But you asked about my father. He was a remarkable man. He was a newsman, just like the guys down at the *Times*, but he was also kind of a scholar. He read the classics—the Spanish classics—and he made sure we read them, too. Cervantes was his man. He said he was his long-lost uncle. In fact, he was a little like Don Quixote himself."

"Ah," said Silverstein, "the knight of the sad countenance."

"Exactly."

"Tilting at windmills?"

"Every chance he got. He never naturalized. He made sure we all got college educations and stayed here, and then he and my mother retired down to Mexico. They're both dead now. They . . ." For a moment I didn't know quite how to finish the sentence. "They were good people."

"I'm sure they were." He sighed. "Well, I felt I was in good hands, and now I'm sure of it. Mr. Cervantes . . . I wonder if I could have that card of mine back for a moment?" I fished it out and handed it over, then carefully he wrote out a name and number on the back of it, tracing out the block letters precisely. "I'm giving you the name of somebody to contact in case of emergency. This is the Embassy number in Mexico City. If you have any difficulty getting through to this person, just use my name and that should take care of it. Well . . . I believe I have a plane to catch."

Turnbull and Son, Funeral Directors, was in one of those grand old California Victorian houses left over from the turn of the century. As I turned off Lincoln onto Ocean Park and spotted the building, it seemed more than a little out of place with its turret and high gables towering over all the tile roofs on the block. Maybe just because it was a funeral parlor, there seemed something almost sinister about the place. Painted a deep gray with heavy drapes at each window, it looked like a haunted house in good repair.

I parked the Alfa a little down the block and walked back to Turnbull and Son. As I climbed the stairs to the porch, I had the distinct feeling that I was being watched. A glance to my left caught the movement of the drape at a window. I started to knock at the heavy, oak double-door, but then thought better of it and walked right inside.

I was nearly blinded when I did. Leaving the bright California sunshine behind, I stepped into a room that for a moment seemed as dark as a mausoleum. There was soft music playing somewhere—something very soothing. In the last of the brief seconds it took for my eyes to adjust to the dim light, I sensed movement to my left. I turned toward it, and gradually the shape of a man emerged as he stepped through a set of deep-purple theatrical curtains of what appeared to be velvet.

He was middle-aged with the sort of nondescript young-old face that is so common in southern California. He wore a dark business suit and a darker tie, short hair, and an expression of sweet melancholy. Coming to me, hands clasped at his chest, he said in a quiet, husky, almost sexy voice, "You're a bereaved. I can tell."

He had me momentarily confused. "A . . . what?"

"Oh, I know. You're new in the role. It all seems unreal, doesn't it? When a loved one goes, we're seldom prepared. We walk about in a daze, wondering why . . . how. But let me tell you, Mr. . . . Mr. . . . ?"

"Cervantes. I came—"

"Mr. Cervantes, I know why you're here. And let me assure you, you've come to the right place. Here at Turnbull and Son, we don't merely provide funerals. We specialize in grief therapy. We are here to lift this awful burden from your shoulders. We are ready and willing to take care of everything."

"Well, that's fine, but really—"

"If I may be so bold as to conjecture, sir, you are of the Hispanic persuasion. You may rest assured that we have members of your ethnic group on our staff who can attend to every last detail and make you and your fellow mourners feel completely at home with us here. Our motto has always been 'Mi casa es su casa.'"

This was getting ridiculous. "I'm here to see Mr. Turnbull," I said flatly.

His head popped back perceptibly, as though he had just taken a left jab. "Oh . . . then you're not a bereaved?" He sounded almost crestfallen.

"Not lately."

"Well, then, do you wish to see Mr. Turnbull senior or junior?"

"I don't know. Senior, I guess."

"Mr. Turnbull senior is no longer with us." He made it sound as though he had been fired.

"*Junior* then. I don't care. I want to see the *boss!*"

"Please, would you mind lowering your voice? Now, does Mr. Turnbull know—"

"It's all right, Charles," said a voice from the distant right corner of the room. "I'll take care of it."

A man had emerged through a matching set of velvet curtains. Although he was quite young—not much over twenty-five, I guessed—he was clearly in charge. He was dressed more casually than Charles but more expensively—in a silk blue blazer, flannels, and an ascot. He wore a rather petulant expression, as though he was already annoyed at my presence.

As Charles silently disappeared, I said to his boss, "You're Turnbull?"

"I'm he." Well, at least he'd had an education. "And you're . . . ?"

"Tony Cervantes. I'm a private investigator." I hauled out my wallet and showed him my state card. He barely glanced at it.

"So?"

"So I've come to ask about Francisco Cruz-Rivera."

"Cruz-Rivera? Who's he?"

"Francisco Cruz-Rivera is the individual who was driving a hearse registered to Turnbull and Son and was involved in an accident on the Marina Freeway resulting in two fatalities."

"Oh, *that*." He spoke in a tone of mild exasperation, as though he had said all he wanted to about that a long time ago. "Haven't you got any friends with the police? I thought every private detective had a friend who was a cop." He was talking about television, of course. "Couldn't you get someone to tell you all about it the way they do?"

"Maybe. But why don't you just make it easier for me and tell me all you remember?"

He sighed. "Well . . . all right. This person—Cruz-Rivera?—was simply hired on a one-time basis to pick up a deceased from Ensenada and transport it back here for embalming, funeral, and burial."

"You'd never used him before?"

"Never. And considering what happened, we employed him once too often—wouldn't you say so?"

"I guess so, yes. But tell me, how did you happen to hire *him* in the first place?"

"Oh, I don't know. *I* didn't do it."

"Well, who did?"

He shrugged, as though to suggest it was quite an unimportant matter. "One of our chauffeurs, I suppose. I believe the thought was that since the individual was going down to Ensenada, it would really be better to have somebody who could speak Spanish. Cruz-Rivera was probably hired off some street corner in West Los Angeles. Nothing special."

"But you don't *know*."

"No, I don't *know*."

"Well, Mr. Turnbull, I must say that considering what happened, I think that's kind of peculiar. If I were you and one of my vehicles had been involved in an accident with two fatalities, I'd want to find out who hired the man who was driving it and why."

"Of course, what happened was lamentable, tragic really. But you must realize that Turnbull and Son is a very big operation. I'm an executive. I'm not able to handle every last little detail myself. I've found that it's best to delegate whenever possible."

I had been trying, for the last minute or so, to fix his eye. It was not easy. He looked left, right, up and down, everywhere but at me. I drew the obvious conclusion.

"I suppose that the man who hired Cruz-Rivera spoke Spanish. He was Mexican-American?"

"Oh, I doubt it."

"Why?"

"Because we don't have any . . . any Mexican-Americans on our staff. I suppose I *could* find out who hired him . . . and why."

"Yes, why don't you do that—just to ease your mind. Oh, and Mr. Turnbull?"

"Uh, yes?"

"You mentioned that Cruz-Rivera had picked up a body in Ensenada. What were the circumstances there?"

"Well, as I recall, a man had been in a yachting party that was sailing Baja, looking at the whales or something, and he had a heart attack, died on board."

"What was his name?"

"Oh, I'd have to look that up."

"Why don't you do that? You can tell me that when you tell me who hired Francisco Cruz-Rivera."

"You'll be back then?"

"Oh, yes."

"When?"

"Soon."

CHAPTER 4

I spent the rest of the day making preparations for the trip. First I went to the bank, deposited the two five-thousand-dollar checks and cashed the fifteen-hundred-dollar expense check, asking for small-denomination bills. Then I went downtown and shopped around for the right clothes. I found them in a *raza* store down on Sixth. What I said to Jarrett and Silverstein was correct. There was no way I was going to fool anybody down there into thinking I was a native if they didn't want to be fooled. Still, if I made some effort to dress the part, I might be able to forestall the moment of recognition for a while at least. I bought a couple of tropical shirts, a Western number and a string tie, some tan jeans, a straw sombrero, and a pair of boots. Then, as an afterthought, I picked up a money belt, too.

When I got back to my place in the afternoon, I called Mexicana and booked a seat on a late-morning flight the next day down to Culiacan by way of Tucson. Then I began worrying about Boomie, wondering whether he would come through in time. I had told him I had to have that thing early tomorrow at the latest. I wondered if his idea of early corresponded with mine.

After pouring myself a drink and pacing back and forth with it for about ten minutes, I sat down on the bed and dialed DeeDee. To my mild astonishment, I got her and not her answering machine. I had been having some pretty good conversations with her answering machine lately.

"Oh, hi, Chico. I was just going to call you."

"Yeah, sure . . ."

"Chico, are you *sulking*?" Was I sulking? I didn't think so. I was just tired of her bullshit. "Because if you are, you're not playing by the rules. Now, you *know* I've been on location all week. We wrapped about noon, baby, and I came right back and got *all* those messages you left, and . . . so I was going to answer them. I was just going to call you."

"Okay, okay. Look, I have to go out of town tomorrow. I'll be gone awhile. I was wondering if we could get together for dinner and stuff."

" 'And stuff'? Oh, Chico?" She drawled it out sexily, hamming shamelessly for me. "Well, I have just tons of wash to do, but I suppose it *could* wait until tomorrow. 'Stuff' sounds so much more interesting than wash, don't you think? Just where did you have in mind to go? Shall I meet you, or—"

"That's just it, see. There's a guy I'm waiting to hear from. He could call just anytime, so I really ought to stick pretty close to home. I was wondering if you'd mind coming over here. I could pull a couple of steaks out of the freezer, and . . . you know, some wine."

At last she dropped the act: "Sounds lovely. When should I come by?"

"Oh, I don't know. About eight?"

"See you then. Bye."

DeeDee Lazarus and I had been seeing each other about six months, I guess, but in that time I don't think we'd been together many more than a dozen times. There was always *something*. I had met her when I was on a case. The television production company she works for was a partnership then—a creative guy and a business guy. The creative guy thought the business guy was ripping him off, but he couldn't prove it. The books had been audited by outside accountants, and they looked okay. I was brought in to dig up what I could. It turned out to be a kind of paper chase that led me to a firm of media consultants in Santa Monica. They were supposedly advising the business guy on new markets for their product—cable TV, foreign sales, and so on. I read some of their reports and thought they were pretty general but awfully well written. They turned out to be articles copied word-for-word from *The Wall Street Journal*, *Business Week*, and some other places. For these they had been paid ten thousand dollars a month for about a year. I found out the address in Santa Monica was just a mail drop and staked it out next time a check was sent. And who should show up to pick up the check but Mrs. Business Guy in her husband's Fleetwood? I followed her to a Brand X bank way out in Costa Mesa and even managed to get the name of the account in which she deposited the check. I got pictures and all the necessary details into my report. It gave the creative guy all the leverage he needed: he threatened disclosure to the IRS, and now he owns the production company outright. This is the kind of job I like to do. I get to use my head a little, and the possibility of violence is practically zero.

Anyway, in the course of the couple of weeks I spent on the case, I met DeeDee. She was the production secretary then. When I wound things up and she found out from her boss that the little greaseball hanging around the office was a real private detective, she thought that was pretty exciting and told me so. In the course of the last six months, I guess I'd managed to convince her otherwise. Or that's unfair, really— to her and to me. What happened to us happens to a lot of couples these days. DeeDee is ambitious. She is now assistant producer of the cop series she works on, and she wants to keep climbing right up the ladder, and so she works hard and doesn't play much. When she played, she played with me. But during the last couple of months business hasn't been so good for me, and I guess I've needed a little more than she could give. That, as they say, was the subtext of that little conversation we had on the telephone.

We were fine when we were together. It's just the times in between that drove me crazy. I usually realized that about a minute after I saw her. Like that very night, when she walked through the door looking lean and hungry in khaki slacks and a madras shirt, her blond hair bleached a shade lighter by a week up in the San Bernardino Mountains. She looked great—but there was something different about her.

She stood for a moment, posing, one hand on her hip and the other tucked just behind her ear. "You like?" she asked.

"Uh, yeah? But what is it? What did you do?"

"I got my hair cut for you, you dumb Chicano."

"For me?"

"Well, for me, too." She moved across the space that separated us in two slinky strides, wrapped her arms around my neck, and began nibbling my ear. "I figured we could both enjoy it." That was when I remembered that we were fine when we were together.

The evening went just about as I expected it would—just about, though not quite. The steaks were good, the wine was excellent, and the conversation was about what I had gotten used to from DeeDee. She's the kind of person who never leaves her job. If she's not working it, she's talking about it. She discusses it almost wholly in terms of the personalities involved, which is not wholly unjustified, if you know anything about show business. It's a constant play of ego against ego—and not unlike a lot of other businesses in that regard. I'd visited the set a couple of times, so I knew a *few* of the people she talked about. But about all I could say was "Oh, yeah, I remember him" and "Well, what can you expect?" and "Is that what she's like?" And so on. Somewhere, nagging at the back of my mind, was the thought that she'd be a lot happier with somebody in the industry. This, however, was a thought I had never expressed to her.

About the only common conversational ground we had was her private eye project. Sometime during the evening she always got around to that. It must have started about the second night we went out. I had told her a few stories—mostly funny ones—about the business, and suddenly, as we sat in the restaurant over the remains of dinner, she got a strange look on her face and said, "Hey, this could be *it*!"

"What do you mean, 'it'?"

"It could be a series—my series, *our* series."

"Oh, come on," I said, "not another private eye show. There've been too many of them already."

"Yes, but this would be different. This one would be *authentic*."

"Believe me, authentic would be boring."

No matter how hard I had tried since then, I had not been able to convince her of that. She kept pumping me for my adventures. My *adventures*—Jesus! Then, when that didn't work, she wanted to hear stories I had heard from *other* private detectives. She had this idea that if I just sat down with a writer and "spitballed" (her word, not mine) some things that had really happened, whatever came out of it would be true, and real, and authentic—and all the better for it. I tried to tell her that I don't *know* any private detectives, which was almost literally true, and that p.i.'s don't hang out together and swap stories, which was certainly true. But she wouldn't give it up. This was going to be *her* series all right. She would be the producer, and I would be—what? Technical consultant—maybe even story editor. She promised I'd have a piece of the action.

Well, this was about where we were that evening before I left for Mexico, so when DeeDee began asking me why I was going out of town tomorrow, I was prepared. I had decided to say as little as possible about it. I make it a rule never to discuss cases in progress. But rules are made to be broken.

I remember that she was clearing the table, and I was rinsing the dishes and stacking them in the dishwasher. With each trip back to the kitchen, she had another question.

"Will you be gone long, Chico?"

"I don't know. I could be."

"I hope not. You know, hiatus is coming up in a week, and I was looking forward to spending a lot of time with you, you creep."

"Well, bad timing's always been our problem, hasn't it?"

"Yeah, I guess you're right."

That was the plates. I had the steak bones and whatever was left of the rice in the garbage when she returned with the salad bowls. She said something that I didn't quite catch, so I turned down the water.

"What?"

"I said, where're you going?"

"Out of town."

"I *know* that—but where?"

"Out of the country."

"*Really?* Where?"

I looked at her. "Where do you think? To Mexico."

"Oh, Chico! This could really be *interesting*. What's it about?"

I took the salad bowls from her and emptied them, then I turned the water back up and began sponging them furiously. She got the hint and went back to the table.

She returned with the wine glasses.

"You want some more wine?" I asked.

"A *third* bottle? No, thanks. Maybe a little Cognac later on."

"Okay."

"Chico? Chico, will you please turn the water down?" I did, and she moved closer to me. "Listen," she said, "you're acting funny. Is there any danger involved in this . . . whatever it is?"

Right then I made my big mistake. I should have shrugged her question off and said no, or if I wanted to swagger a little, "nothing I can't handle." But for some reason I felt it necessary that night to play her for sympathy. Maybe I wanted a little of what I felt was coming to me because of all those missed dates and heartfelt talks with her answering machine. Whatever lay behind it, this is how it came out. "Yeah, it could be risky. I'm not looking forward to it much. But you know how business has been lately. I didn't feel like I could turn it down."

"Baby, I had no idea. And I just wasn't there for you, was I? Tell me about it. Please."

"No—well, it's a fugitive. Not exactly in my line."

"For *murder*?"

"Not for murder, but . . ."

"But what?"

And just that way, bit by bit, she got a lot of it out of me—not all of it, but more than I wanted to tell. I kept back the names and my specific destination, but by the time she stopped pumping me, she had about all I knew about the case in rough outline.

I got my reward. We were sitting on the couch, balloon snifters of Hennessey in front of us on the coffee table. As I finished my recital, I leaned forward and took a gulp of it. It helped. DeeDee moved over closer to me and leaned her head against my shoulder. I don't know if what I smelled was her shampoo or her perfume, but I know I liked it. We sat there like that, very quietly, for a couple of minutes. At last she spoke up: "It's kind of scary."

"Oh, I don't know." Now, a little late, I tried the old macho number. "If I felt it was something I couldn't handle, I wouldn't have taken it on."

"Well, I'm scared. I'm scared *for* you. Chico?"

"Yes?"

"Let's make love."

As simple as that. Together we struggled up off the couch. I paused just long enough to take another draught of Cognac, and then hand in hand we made our way into the bedroom. We were just out of our clothes, in bed, and beginning to enjoy ourselves, when the downstairs doorbell rang.

Cursing, I jumped out of bed and ran for the intercom in the living room.

"Chico! Come back. Let it ring."

"Can't. It might be that guy who was supposed to call me."
"But that's the doorbell."
"I know."

I jacked the intercom to transmit and called down. "Yeah? Who is it?"

And then to receive: "It's me . . . Boomie. Let me in, Chico."

I buzzed him in and returned to the bedroom. DeeDee was sitting up against a pillow, a sheet pulled up over her breasts. What was she trying to hide from me? I grabbed up my robe and pulled it on. "Look," I said to her, "this is important. I'm going to shut the door and what I'd like you to do is keep very quiet in here. Would you do that for me? I've got some business with this guy. It shouldn't take more than a few minutes, but it's important, believe me."

She sighed. "All right."

I looked around. "You want something to read?"

"No, I'll be all right. Don't worry."

With a glance back at her, a forced smile, and a few misgivings, I closed the bedroom door and got ready for Boomie. My eye fell upon the two Cognac snifters on the coffee table. I whisked them up, ran to the kitchenette, and tossed their contents down the drain—then into the dishwasher with them.

Back to the door just in time for Boomie's muted knock. I threw it open and there he stood, attaché case in hand, looking behind him and around me, as though somebody was after him.

"Chico."

"Yeah, Boomie, come on in."

That's what he did, charging forward, tossing the attaché case down on the coffee table, casting one last glance around him in every direction.

"I want you to know," he said, "this wasn't easy. Wasn't easy? Shit, it was probably the greatest challenge of my professional career. But Chico, you placed the order and I delivered—on what? The next day! Next day delivery! You know anybody who could do better? Did you ever *hear* of anybody who could do better?"

"No, Boomie. Really, it's more than I hoped for."

"Maybe not more than you hoped for, but more than you expected, right?"

"Right. Let's see it."

"Okay." All business now, he tripped the snaps on the briefcase, unlocked it, and threw it open. He pulled the thing out in a plastic case and opened it up for me to admire. It was larger and longer than I expected. Roughly the shape of an automatic, it was about twice the size. "What you have here," said Boomie, "is a gen*ui*ne, Sierra Club–approved tranquilizer gun. It shoots a dart about twenty-five yards with some accuracy, and it's guaranteed to put anything up to an elephant fast asleep."

He offered it to me, and I took it, hefting it in my hand, examining it carefully. It wasn't as heavy as it looked. That was because there seemed to be a lot of plastic in it. "How does it work?" I asked.

Boomie showed me. Producing a little chest of loads from the case, he explained to me that it was basically a single-shot pistol. Loading and shooting took about thirty seconds. The darts that it shot were basically syringes. They emptied on contact, but it was best to shoot down on your target. Don't expect what was in them to flow up and defy the law of gravity.

"What's in them?" I asked.

Boomie looked around again. This time it was for show. "Would you believe it?—PCP. At this time in my career I find myself dealing drugs."

"I'll never tell."

"See that you don't."

"Where'd you get it, Boomie?" Was this my conscience speaking?

"Oh, *man*, come *on*! That's a professional secret." But he was too pleased with himself to let it go. "Let's just say that Sea World will never miss it. They've got enough of these things down there to hold off a fucking army of killer whales."

"What's this going to set me back?"

"Your client, right?"

"Okay, my client."

"A thousand."

"That's a lot, Boomie."

"Come *on*, we've already established it's not your money. It's got to be a pretty special job or you wouldn't be buying equipment like this, am I right?"

"Okay, yeah, right."

"So? But listen, I got a deal for you. You still carrying around that clunky old police .38?"

"How do you know what I'm carrying?"

"Never mind. Listen, Chico, you take this fucking dart gun at a thousand—and that's what it costs, take it or leave it—but you take it, and I'll toss this in for two-fifty more."

With that, he proudly produced a flat, blunt little automatic that looked like something out of James Bond—which is to say, it looked like a Walther PPK. But it wasn't. I took it from Boomie and examined it. This one was heavier than it looked, but it fit the hand perfectly. On the side of the barrel—what barrel there was—it said "Heckler & Koch, GmbH 9mmX18." I'd heard of them, but I'd never seen one.

"State-of-the-art, Chico. It'll cost you four hundred retail, and it's not hot. You can license it if you want to."

"Why me, Boomie?"

"Let's say because I like you, or I want to establish you as a regular client. Frankly, I liked that challenge you gave me. Nobody ever came to me for one of those dart guns before. Don't worry, I'll throw in a box of a hundred 9mm for the HK. But that's not so many loads. You know what it holds? Eighteen! Outrageous! Am I right?"

"Okay," I said at last. "In for a thousand, in for twelve-fifty."

"Good man." Boomie tossed out the box of shells onto the coffee table and closed his attaché case. "You won't be sorry, believe me."

Just as he was locking it up and making ready to go, there

was a muffled, indistinct noise from beyond the bedroom door, followed by the distinct sound of a toilet flushing. Boomie stared at me in disbelief. "There's somebody here, isn't there?"

I didn't say anything, but he got his answer from my face.

"I am fucking *shocked* at you, Chico. I mean, I'll give you the benefit of the doubt it isn't a Treasury agent. It's a chick, isn't it? You had a fucking chick in the bedroom all the time we were doing business out here, didn't you? You call that professional? Man, I came to you as one professional to another. I *respected* you—and what do I get from you? A chick in the bedroom. That's it, man. That is totally it!"

"Boomie," I said, "I expected you to call first. I thought we'd arrange a meeting."

"Yeah, man, but you didn't *tell* me she was here—and you should have. You *know* that."

"I know. You're right." What could I say?

Briefcase in hand, Boomie headed straight for the door. Once there, he whirled and pointed a finger accusingly at me. "Don't forget, Chico, you owe me. I'll give you thirty days—period."

"I could pay you part of it right now," I said weakly.

"Fuck that. Pay me all of it in cash in the next thirty days." He threw the door open and slammed it shut after him.

Before going back into the bedroom, I tucked the two guns away in the utility closet behind some cans of cleaner. I was hiding them—but from whom? From DeeDee, I supposed.

In the bedroom, I found her sitting as I had left her, leaning on the pillows propped against the headboard. She had allowed the sheet to drop and expose her breasts. I sat down in my robe at the edge of the bed.

"He heard me, didn't he?"

"Sure, he heard you."

"But Chico, I had to pee."

"You didn't have to flush the toilet."

"Reflex action, I guess. Sorry."

Believe it or not, in spite of that, in spite of the interruption, in spite of everything, we managed to resume approximately where we had left off. It had been better between us on some occasions, but it had also been worse on others. We managed—for that, considering the circumstances, I was grateful.

Afterward, when we were settled, lights out, good nights kissed, and on our way to sleep, DeeDee roused herself just enough to say, "Chico, your trip to Mexico—this could be the pilot for the series."

It took me an hour to get to sleep after that. Boomie was right. I hadn't been acting professionally. I realized I had better clean up my act.

CHAPTER 5

All the way down to Culiacan on that Mexicana flight, I had the feeling I was being watched. It comes to me sometimes just like that, maybe less a feeling than a certain sense of unexpected prominence. There are no physical manifestations. The hairs on the back of my neck don't stand up. My cheeks don't burn. It's as though I'm just suddenly aware that I'm of interest to someone around me. Only that and nothing more. There's a television actor I know (not a star, not even a recognizable name) who told me that he can be in a roomful of strangers and know *precisely* the moment he is recognized by one of them—and not because he catches someone's eye or hears people whispering. He says it's because brain waves are electricity, and if you're sensitive to them, you can receive them just like radio messages. But that sounds like ESP to me, and I say to hell with it.

Whatever it is, I've learned to take the feeling seriously. I walked the aisle before and after Hermosilla and Obregón, the only intermediate stops after Tucson, studying the people around me. A few of them looked up but none regarded me with more than passing interest. But the feeling stayed with me, and by the time we had banked in for the landing at Culiacan, I had decided that somehow I must try to scramble out first so that I would be in a position to study every passenger who got off with me.

I tried to do just that, pushing, thrusting, squeezing forward, like some eager beaver arriving at LAX, only to find, when I glanced back, that they were letting them out the rear of the plane, too. Well, at least I'd have a chance to look them over at the baggage pickup.

There were not many likely candidates among them. No more than a dozen people waited with me, not quite equally divided between the majority Mexicans and the minority Anglos. The Mexicans I eliminated, probably too hastily, from my list of suspects and concentrated on the arriving *gringos*. There were four businessmen, a tourist couple, and a superannuated hippie—long hair, beard, jeans, the works. The hippie seemed to be looking my way a lot—or was it because he was aware of my studying him? I couldn't tell. I thought then that maybe I was just overreacting because of my lapses of the night before. That, after all, was a possibility.

But then, as they picked up their bags one by one, and I dismissed the last among them, I noticed that one suitcase remained unclaimed. That interested me. Had someone held back on my account? Apparently not, since I was alone. Perhaps if I disappeared? I went around the corner to a phone booth, one that was situated so that I had just a glimpse of the unclaimed bag. I held the receiver to my ear and made as though I were listening. After a minute or two a *gringo* stuck his head out of the *Hombres*, and moving quickly, grabbed up the suitcase, then glanced around him as though looking for somebody and hurried on out of my sight. He was about six feet tall, with a moustache, and he was wearing sunglasses. He had cop written all over him. Had I noticed him on the plane? Maybe, but he wasn't wearing his sunglasses then, and they made all the difference. Why would a cop be following me? Or was he a cop? Again, maybe I was overreacting.

Even so, I decided to kill some time. If he was tailing me, let him think he had lost me. I went into the *Hombres* myself, combed my hair, fixed my tie, and washed my hands, and then I changed some money and took the longest route possible to the Budget Rent-a-Car counter. And there he was, arguing with the girl, waving a letter, pointing, saying something I couldn't quite catch. When he left, I walked up and asked the countergirl if she had a Mustang left.

As she readied the contract, I inquired about the man who had been there just before me. "He looked like a man I used to know in Los Angeles," I told her.

"That one! He make a lot of trouble for me! Is he your friend?"

"Not a friend. Just someone I might know. What was the problem?"

"He try to use an American Express card that don't belong to him. When I tell him he can't do that, he show me a letter says he can do this thing. But I tell him this is too irregular. The company won't let me do this. Then he get angry and yell at me. Finally, he give me a Visa card in his own name, and I use that. If I think a card is stolen, I'm supposed to keep it and call the police. But since he has the letter, I don't think I can do that, so I let him have it back."

"Well," I said reassuringly, "if it's the man I know, he's not a thief, but he *is* a troublemaker. What was his name?"

She glanced down at a stack of contracts just out of my sight. "Francis J. Keeney. And his card is from a Los Angeles bank. Is he the man?"

He was the man, all right. Frank Keeney—with Casimir Urbanski, the first at the scene of the accident that night on the Marina Freeway. He had written up the report I had read. "Oh, yes. Keeney the loudmouth." She laughed and nodded her agreement. Perhaps I could push my luck with her a bit further: "Tell me, what was the name on the American Express card?"

She looked puzzled for a moment. At last she said, "I can't remember. I think I push it from my mind, you know? It's so irregular. The company would never let me do that."

Culiacan lies on the western coastal plain, just in from the Gulf of California. Looking east from the airport, all you can see are the mountains—the Sierra Madre Occidental. And once you see them, you're constantly aware of them as a kind of lurking presence brooding over the landscape, vaguely threatening in their nearness and size. As I drove the Mustang out of the airport lot, I turned toward the city and the mountains beyond it. By then it was late afternoon, nearly evening, and the peaks were illuminated by the lowering sun, glowing a kind of golden red that clashed sharply with the deep blue of the sky. The mountains around Los Angeles never looked like this. Nothing I had ever seen did.

Traffic out of the airport was surprisingly light, and at some point along the way I became aware that there was none at all moving in the opposite direction. About a mile farther down the road I found out why.

I joined a line of cars that was stopped at what looked like a military roadblock about a hundred yards ahead. Somewhere just beyond that something was burning. I couldn't tell what. There was black and gray smoke, now just beginning to rise up into the air. As each car pulled up, two men moved down the line checking identification. One wore the khaki uniform and peaked cap of the Federal Judiciary Police, and was carrying an M-16 perched on his hip. The other was in civilian clothes—a tropical shirt and slacks—with his badge tacked out in plain sight. He was the boss. They sauntered over to me. The sun glinted off their chrome-framed dark glasses.

I handed over my Budget contract. That would do. The plainclothesman looked it over with practiced haste, his eyes invisible behind his sunglasses.

"North American?" he asked in English.

"A citizen, yes," I replied in Spanish.

"You look like one of us," in Spanish.

"I am. My parents were born here."

"No, señor, you are North American." He tucked the contract back into its folder and handed it back.

"What is the difficulty?" I asked. "An accident ahead?"

He laughed at that. It was the kind of a laugh that would chill the heart of a sinner on Judgment Day. "An accident, yes—for them, but not for us. We planned it this way."

"With your permission," I said politely, "your meaning escapes me."

"The *contrabandistas* grow so bold they move their stuff in the daytime and think we will look the other way. When we stopped them, they tried to run our roadblock. We shot them down in two seconds. It is a good lesson for them and all their brothers. Now we wait for the gas tank of their truck to explode. When that danger is past, you may move ahead. It should not be long." He gave me a curt nod of good-bye, and the two of them moved on to the next car.

He was right—it wasn't long until the gas tank blew, a matter of about fifteen seconds, more or less. It went up with a huge *whump* and shot a ball of raw flame into the air that blotted out the smoke for an instant. Then a couple of minutes after that, cars began streaming by in the opposite lane, headed in the direction of the airport, and those ahead of me began creeping ahead. The closer we got to the burning truck, the more distinctly I smelled the high, acrid odor of burning marijuana. These days *contrabandistas* meant the dope trade. Back in the late seventies the state of Sinaloa was the site of the big drug wars, and Culiacan was the command post from which the *Féderales* and their American Drug Enforcement Agency advisors directed full-scale military operations against the local dope trade—helicopter strikes, the whole bit. They say they fought pitched battles with automatic weapons up there in the Sierra. The Mexican government pronounced the operation a success, and that was the end of that—though evidently not quite. It's certainly available in Los Angeles. I've smoked a little *mota* myself. I hadn't heard of any action down here lately against the dopers. Maybe this was something special.

The cars moved slowly past the burning truck. When I got up close enough to see for myself, I understood why. It was quite a sight—an old Dina flatbed on its side, chassis exposed, about twenty-five yards from the road. It had run down the embankment and toppled over. The two men inside must have scrambled out and been shot down on the spot, for they now lay together only a few feet away from the burning truck, their bodies slowly roasting in the heat of the blaze. It was as nasty a sight as I had seen since the SLA shootout. Just beyond it, a member of the Federal Judiciary Police, M-16 slung on his shoulder, waved me on. I stood on the accelerator and got out of there quick, glad to leave it all behind.

Culiacan isn't much. Well, it's a city of over a hundred thousand, but you'd never know it when you drive in on a Sunday. I headed for the Hotel Conquistador, where a reservation had been made for me by Mexicana. It turned out to be right on the central plaza, a kind of combination hotel-motel. The rooms were stacked, but there was turn-in parking in a perimeter surrounding the building. It looked better than I expected.

Who should be waiting for me in the lobby, behind a copy of *The Los Angeles Times*, but Frank Keeney. He saw me. I saw him. He settled deeper into the lobby couch and hid behind the paper. This was getting ridiculous. My first impulse was to go over and tell him to get lost. But this wasn't the time or place for it; I knew that. So instead I went to the desk and registered. The clerk called out for a porter and loudly announced my room to him as he handed over the key. The porter carried my bag to the elevator, and I asked him to go back to the desk and ask for another room—*any* other room on a different floor. "And please be quiet about it," I asked him. "There is a man in the lobby I wish to avoid." A wink from the porter, and in a few moments he was back with another key.

Up in the fourth-floor room I tipped him five in greenbacks—a small fortune at the current rate of exchange—and told him to keep all this in confidence. He assured me a bit too effusively that I had no need to worry. I didn't trust him, but what could I do? Alone, I unpacked and changed into my clever native disguise. The boots were a bit tight, and the straw sombrero was slightly crushed from six hours in the suitcase—but maybe that was just as well. I took the Heckler & Koch and the tranquilizer gun out of the lead-cloth wrapper I had packed them in. There was a place for the dart gun and the box of loads behind the headboard of the bed. I loaded the HK—eighteen bullets double-stacked—then tucked it away in the back of my belt right at my spine. I went over to the mirror to check it out. With the shirt out and draped over it, you couldn't tell it was there at all.

It was getting dark. I decided to wait until night to check out the address on the Calle Acapulco. All suited up for the big game and ready to play, I was restless and knew I had to get out of the room. Exploring the corridor, I found the stairway and made my way down to the ground floor. The lobby was around a corner and half the length of the building away. I let myself out a side door and left it unlocked, satisfied that I had given Keeney the shake.

Culiacan, like most cities in Mexico, is laid out around a central plaza with a fountain that is surrounded by a small park and the usual statuary. This is where the action is on weekends. Men and women, boys and girls, join there in an ancient and honored tradition—the *paseo*. They make tours of the plaza on Saturdays and Sundays, looking each other over, smiling, greeting, and flirting. They may then repair to one of the restaurants or cantinas, all quite respectable places, that surround the plaza. There they come on strong, parading and preening, saying more with their eyes than their words could tell. You can laugh at all this if you want to—and in practice it does have its comic aspects—but it's how my father met my mother in Cuernavaca, and it sure beats the hell out of singles bars.

I joined the *paseo*. It seemed the surest way to blend into the scene. Trying my best to mimic the macho walk of the male strollers, a kind of slow, chesty strut, I looked over the local talent with the rest. Although there were few beauties among them, the girls of Culiacan had a kind of staunch and solemn dignity, a quiet sense of containment that few North American women show. Their eyes were remarkable—deep, dark, and expressive. The single practiced movement of an eyebrow, a sidelong glance, could indicate a degree of interest more precisely than an open invitation. I got The Look a couple of times and was tempted to stop and talk, but having nothing to say and someplace to go, I pressed on a little sadly. About halfway around the square, I broke off from the procession and made for a likely-looking cantina across the street.

It was next door to a second-class hotel, and there were a few *gringos* mixed in with the local clientele at the bar. Or no, tuning into a conversation close by, I found out they were French—wanderers from Club Med, maybe. The bartender came over, and I asked for a Dos Equis. When he returned with it, I asked him respectfully in Spanish where I might find the Calle Acapulco.

He looked me over then and said, "I don't think you want to go there, *señor*."

"And why not?"

"They make bad business there." He leaned over the bar and said to me confidentially, "You are a visitor in Culiacan, yes?"

"Yes. I am here for the first time."

"And you are staying in one of the hotels on the square?"

"Yes, the Conquistador."

"Our finest. You have chosen well. I am personally acquainted with the night porter there. His name is Esteban. Go to him, and tell him you would like a woman in your room. He will send one to you, *gordita y bonita*, whatever you like. She will be clean, and she will not rob you. I perceive that you are a businessman, a man of affairs. It is best that you stay away from the Calle Acapulco." Having given his counsel, he nodded and started away.

"*Señor*," I called after him, "there is a problem."

He held up a finger, asking my patience, and went off to serve a pair down the bar. In a minute or two he returned. "*Señor?*"

"I value your advice and would ordinarily follow it exactly.

But, as you say, I am a businessman, and I have business of a different kind on the Calle Acapulco. The address is number 17."

"Ah! El Gallo Inmortal!" He shrugged generously. "If you must go down to the street, that place is not so bad. Matters are conducted there in a professional manner. It is three blocks behind the plaza. The street is parallel to this one. The place is a cantina much like this, but there are rooms upstairs, if you understand me."

"Of course."

"The woman who runs the place is named Concepción, and she is not a bad type, considering the life she has led. Perhaps your business is with her?"

"Perhaps." I paid him for the beer, then offered him a greenback five-spot. "I appreciate your help in this."

He took the bill and pocketed it. *"Mucho gusto, señor."*

I held him a moment more. "And I will also appreciate your confidence."

"You have it, *señor*."

With that I let him go. I felt better about the bartender than I did about Esteban—if that was the name of the porter I had tipped at the Conquistador. I glanced outside and decided it was dark enough to suit me. I was ready to get on with it now. I dropped down from the barstool and got out of there quickly.

I turned down one of the streets leading out of the plaza, and within a block I realized I was being followed. I stopped suddenly at a shop to look in the window, glanced back down the dark street, and I saw that whoever was behind me was big and was dressed American—Keeney, of course. Dammit! Had he gotten lucky, or had he been on my tail since I left the hotel? I began walking in crazy, roundabout crisscross patterns—across a block, back to the plaza, up and down, everywhere but to Calle Acapulco—but still I couldn't lose him.

Finally, in desperation, I ducked down an alley and walked about twenty-five yards inside it and came up against a high wall of crumbling adobe. I saw too late that I had come to a dead end. If I turned around and went back out, I'd land in Keeney's arms. I guessed then that it was time for us to have our talk. I reached back and tugged the HK out of my belt and then squeezed into a narrow gap between two buildings. It smelled foully of urine. I wasn't sure how long I could stand to stay there.

Keeney tried waiting me out. About three minutes passed or maybe four. The stink of the place was nauseating. From where I was crouched, I had no view of the entrance to the alley, and so I had to rely on my ears to tell me if and when he was on his way. I strained, listening. All that I could hear for a while was the angry voice of a woman through an open window above me. And then I caught the skittering whir of little animal feet behind me, and I realized I was sharing my hiding place with a family of rats. A shiver ran through me. I *hate* rats. It was all I could do not to jump up and get out of there the moment I heard them, but somehow I managed to stick it out a minute or more longer. And that was all it took.

I heard the first faint crunch on the littered surface of the alley just a few feet away from me. He could move pretty quietly for a big guy. I squatted lower and held my breath. The first thing I saw was the ugly, blunt barrel of a Colt .357, and then the hand that held it about waist high. It moved in my direction for a moment, and I debated snapping off the safety on the HK and getting ready to shoot back. The hand moved away and then the figure of a man appeared in profile about eight feet away. Slowly he turned his head and swiveled his shoulders, offering me his back.

I took a deep breath and jumped, covering the space between us in one leap. I chopped down with the blade of my hand on the wrist of the hand that held the gun and then jammed the HK behind his ear. "Move and you're dead," I said.

"Bullshit."

"What did you say?"

"I said, bullshit. I'm not intimidated."

"You'd better be." I turned the flap of his ear with the barrel of the pistol and held it pinned to his head. "I'll blow your fucking head off." That was just about as tough as I could get.

"Hey, cut that out. You're hurting my ear. Look, I asked around about you, and the word is you're gun-shy. You don't like to shoot people. I'll bet you got the safety on. Am I right?" He was right. I didn't say anything. "I'll tell you what," he continued. "I'll put mine away, and you put yours away, and then we'll talk. How's that?"

I hesitated. "Okay, put it away."

He did, tucking the Colt deep in his jacket, then bringing out his empty hand to show me. I pushed the HK back into my belt, and just as I did, his right elbow flew back and caught me sharply in the ribs, staggering me. Before I could jump back, he turned and grabbed me by the shoulders and slammed me back against the wall of the building. Then he was on top of me, jamming me flat so I couldn't get at the pistol, his big forearm pressed tight against my throat. His face was inches from mine. I could smell the nicotine on his breath.

He grinned at me. "That's for hurting my ear, you little shit. Now I talk, and you listen."

With his arm against my larynx, I could hardly breathe, much less speak.

"Now, pay attention, Chico. I know who you are. I know why you're down here. I know all about you. I even know you were probably on your way to that whorehouse on Acapulco when you made me tailing you. I'm not as good at that stuff as I'm going to be. The thing is, Chico, you don't know who I am, but we're working for the same guy. Mr. Jarrett sent me down to keep an eye on you and give you some help if you need it. It looks to me like you're going to need a lot. So just ease off, okay? And maybe we can work together—if you're a good little beaner and behave yourself. Am I getting through to you?"

I managed a nod.

"Okay then." He pulled his forearm off my throat, and took

six paces back so that he was almost the width of the alley from me, a much safer distance. His left hand rested inside his jacket where he had deposited the Colt. "Don't get macho on me all of a sudden and go for that automatic you had up my ear. I'll blow you away."

I was angry. I was gasping for breath and feeling humiliated. My ribs felt like they had been kicked in by a horse. At last, when my breathing had steadied and I had cleared my throat a couple of times and felt like I could speak again, I said, "Number one, I know who you are. You're Frank Keeney. You are, or used to be, an L.A. cop. You were there with Urbanski when Jarrett's son and Silverstein's daughter bought it on the freeway."

"Hey, you're pretty smart for a beaner."

"Number two, you're working for Jarrett, but I'm working for Jarrett *and* Silverstein. And number three, because of that, and because I don't like you, I don't see much chance for cooperation."

"Yeah? Remember, Chico? I talk, and you listen. It's only because you're Spick you got this job—for the fucking language. I tried to tell Mr. Jarrett I could handle it for him, but that guy Silverstein had this idea you'd go in like some fucking secret agent and collar this guy Cruz-Rivera. Well, I can tell you're not going to do shit without me. You need me, and maybe I'll let you help me, too. You can be my . . . my translator. I don't think you've got a lot of choice in the matter, Chico."

In a way, he was right. I really didn't have much in the way of options. He apparently had all the information I had, and clearly he would just as soon go after Cruz-Rivera alone. It was probably only because Jarrett had told him to let me make contact that he had held back this long. I didn't like it, but it looked like I was stuck with Frank Keeney—for a while.

"Okay," I said at last, "we'll try it and see how it works."

"Like I said, you're pretty smart for a beaner. Now let's go find A. Ramirez at this fucking whorehouse and get on with the job."

59

CHAPTER 6

All the way to the Gallo Inmortal, Keeney talked and I listened. I found out that he was under suspension from the LAPD. Why? "That fucking captain in East L.A., he wouldn't know what was happening unless I told him." I didn't inquire further. He considered himself a private detective now—although of course he had no license. He had gone to Jarrett immediately and offered his services in the matter of Francisco Cruz-Rivera. Jarrett had put him on a retainer as a "security consultant," and now Keeney was out to prove himself at my expense. He didn't say so in so many words, but there it was.

When we hit La Calle Acapulco, the entire street suddenly exploded with carnal possibilities. Women leaned out at us from their cribs, hissing, making loud kissing sounds, remarking upon our beauty, speculating on the length of big Keeney's *membrum virile*. It was just about standard for this part of the world, but Keeney seemed suddenly astonished by it all.

"Jesus!" he croaked. "They really let them get away with it here, don't they? I haven't seen anything like this since Nam."

"Well, you've been to Tijuana, haven't you?"

"Yeah, but I always thought it was different, you know, *inside* Mexico. Everybody said don't judge it by the border towns."

"They were right. This is just one street. Tijuana's a whole city."

"Yeah, I guess so. But Jesus, look at that." A woman in a

doorway across the street flapped her skirt up at us. "They're so fucking aggressive about it. They must be desperate."

"Oh, no. Actually, Mexican women are just naturally depraved."

"Yeah!" He nodded emphatically. "I remember . . ." Then he stopped and looked at me oddly. I stared him down, and he shut up.

If El Gallo Inmortal was the best place on the block, that told you a lot about the block. The bartender on the plaza had said it was an ordinary cantina with rooms upstairs. Well, it looked like an ordinary whorehouse to me. True enough, there was a bar where a few sullen drinkers sat at widely spaced intervals, and there were some tables, too. But the tables were occupied by women and girls in various stages of undress. They came suddenly to life as Keeney and I walked in. They began bouncing to the tired rock and roll on the jukebox. One busty *India* nearby shook her breasts at us so hard that they nearly bounced out of her chemise. It was quite a show. All it meant was that it was a slow night. When we took our places at the bar a couple of them got up and started over in our direction.

I ordered a Dos Equis, and Keeney called for tequila. The bartender shuffled off, and the girls moved in. And they were just girls, both of them under twenty, with traces of their youthful good looks still detectable under the heavy makeup they wore. One wore a teddy and the other had on the kind of bikini that was never meant for swimming. They strutted for us, did a couple of dance steps, patted us on our privates, and said, " 'Allo, *guapo*."

Keeney leaned over and asked quietly, "You think we should buy them drinks?"

"That's up to you."

"Do they take Visa here?"

"I don't think so."

"Oh." He was thinking it over. Then he was back, tapping me on the arm: "The name of this place—what is it again?"

"El Gallo Inmortal."

"What does that mean in English?"

"Literally, it means 'the immortal cock.' "

Keeney burst into guffaws at that, and the girls laughed, too, eager to join in the fun. "They sure got that right," he said.

"That's 'cock' as in 'rooster,' " I added, but he had his joke and he was happy with it.

The bartender came back with our drinks, and I leaned over and asked him if I might speak with Concepción. He looked at me inquiringly, an old man without much dignity who had long ago given up asking questions. With a noncommittal nod, he left me and beckoned to one of the girls at a nearby table. He sent the message through her, and a moment later a woman emerged from the back of the place. She was not only older than the rest, she was also taller, lighter in complexion, and had a cool, almost haughty look. She wore a low-cut black dress that reached just below her knees over a considerable bosom. You could tell she was the boss.

The bartender must have pointed me out to her, for she came directly over to me and, with a questioning look, said, "*Señor?*"

"*Sí, señora,* I understand you have working here a person named Ramirez?"

"*Sí?*" Again it was a question. "She comes especially recommended to you?"

Of course that was the way it would have to be. I couldn't say I wanted to question her on the whereabouts of one Francisco Cruz-Rivera. I couldn't even say I'd like a little time alone to talk. This was a place of business. I had to pay for her time. "*Ya lo creo,*" I declared. "A friend of mine in El Paso told me to ask for her."

She shrugged. "We have many girls here. Why not one of these two? Dorita or Maria Luz?" I glanced over at them as she pointed. They were all over Keeney. He had given in and ordered drinks for them, and now they were repaying his reluctant generosity with kisses, pats, and squeezes. Why did I feel like I was pimping for him?

"They are beautiful indeed," I said, "but why not the one named Ramirez? What is her first name?"

"Alicia." She looked at me not quite suspiciously, just sizing me up. I didn't care if she was suspicious or not—just so she let me talk to Alicia Ramirez.

"Is she now occupied?" I asked.

"No. She has . . . she has retired for the night." Concepción looked at me sharply. "You pay American?"

"You may be assured of it."

"I will get her. It will be but a few minutes. Enjoy yourself in the meantime." With that, she left me quickly, clicking off on spiked heels back toward the rear of the place.

She left me wondering. What was there so special about Alicia Ramirez that she was permitted to retire early? What was it? I glanced at my watch. Not yet ten o'clock and, presumably, she was fast asleep. What had this to do with whorehouse realities? Granted it was a slow night, but—

I felt that tap on my arm again. It was Keeney, of course. "Listen, Chico, one thing we get straight right now."

"What's that?"

"We *both* go in there to talk to this Ramirez. She's a whore, isn't she? She works here, right?"

I sighed. What could I say? "Yeah, right. Okay. So?"

"We *both* talk to her. Say we want threezies or something, okay?"

Now I knew why I felt like I was pimping for him—because I was. His face was flushed. He was aroused and ready. I couldn't imagine quite what he had in mind for Alicia Ramirez, but I knew I didn't want to be part of it. "All right," I said, "I'll work it out."

Before I had quite expected it, *Señora* Concepción was back with Alicia. Sometime before I had accepted it that A. Ramirez was a whore, but I wasn't quite prepared for what Concepción had brought to me—to us. She glided barefoot behind the tall madam—not much over five feet, her eyes big and deep, her hair black and shining, her cheekbones high but with a long, sharp nose and a well-defined chin—*una mestiza*. Quite honestly, she looked beautiful to me. And although she wore a baby-doll nightie that fell straight down to her bikini panties, I could tell that she was pregnant enough so that it was beginning to show.

The tap on my arm again. "Tell her," Keeney ordered.

With an uneasy glance at the girl, I said to *Señora* Concepción, "My *gringo* friend would also like to try her. He would like to come with me. The three of us together."

Concepción took a look at Keeney. Evidently she didn't like what she saw. "Him, too?"

"Certainly," I said with greater conviction than I felt. "The three of us. Surely such things are done here. I had been told by my friend in El Paso that El Gallo Inmortal was a place of true sophistication."

"Clearly, such things are done," she said, "but this will cost you. Anything out of the ordinary costs—and costs you more. You understand."

"I understand."

"One hundred dollars," she said firmly.

"In no way would such an amount be paid," I said just as firmly. "Fifty dollars."

"Seventy-five."

"Sixty."

"Sixty-five."

I nodded. "Agreed. Sixty-five."

"You pay me," she said. "Now."

I counted it out, three twenties and a five, wondering how this was going to look on my expense account, and then I risked a glance at Alicia Ramirez, my first since negotiations had begun. She was not looking at me but at Keeney, and her face wore an expression of mild apprehension.

We were a strange trio climbing the stairs. The girl led the way, walking with that quick, hip-swinging gait that comes so naturally to Mexican women—even my mother had it. Keeney followed, arms up, rolling his shoulders in a tough, linebacker swagger. And I brought up the rear, trudging along like a prisoner to his cell.

Her room was about cell-size. I crowded in behind them and closed the door quietly just in time to see her bless herself before the omnipresent crucifix. She tugged off the baby-doll top and tossed it on the rickety bureau, the only other piece of furniture in the room except the bed. When she turned and faced us, I saw that her belly was distended only slightly. It gave her body a childish, rounded appearance that it wouldn't have had three months before. I realized then that she hadn't said a word to either of us.

She hooked her thumbs into the band of her panties and started to pull them down.

"*Momento, señorita.*"

She stopped with them past her hips, her sparse, straight, black pubic hair exposed, and looked at me curiously.

"We have come to talk to you. It may be better if you wear something."

"*Ay*," she said—something between an exclamation and a question. Well, at least Alicia Ramirez wasn't mute. She tugged up and covered her hips and then turned back to the bureau for her top.

"Hey, what is this?" said Keeney crossly. "Tell her to take it all off."

"That's not what we're here for."

"We paid for it, didn't we?"

I looked at him with disgust and shook my head slowly—no. Not here. Not now.

"All right, we'll do it your way then." He shouldered past me, grabbed her by the shoulders, and threw her roughly to the bed.

"*Hey!*" I grabbed him, but he pushed me aside.

She bounced up to a sitting position, her dark eyes wide with fear. She glanced at me, and Keeney slapped her sharply on the cheek.

"That's just to get her attention," he said, then he pushed

his face down close to hers. "Listen, you look at me. You talk to me—see? You understand that?"

Slowly she nodded and whispered, *"Hablo contigo."*

He turned back to me with a grin. "See? She understands. I'm not going to need you at all. You can take a walk, Chico."

I folded my arms to show I was staying—but also to steady them. I was quivering. My face tingled, and I was gnashing my teeth, chewing on my anger.

He shrugged. "Suit yourself." Bobbing up, he dipped a hand into his jacket pocket, pulled out a pack of cigarettes, and lit one up.

"You think this is the way to get information out of her?" My jaws were so tight I could hardly get the words out. "We're paying for it. Remember?"

"That's between you and her. And yes, I think this is the way to get information out of anybody." But he eased off then, took a deep drag from his cigarette, and forced a smile at her. "Okay, senyorita. I want you to tell me all you know about Francisco Rivera—Francisco Rivera. Understand?"

She didn't, quite. She repeated the name hesitantly—and then a glimmer came into her eyes. "Ah, *sí*, Cruz-Rivera! You came to give me the money?" All of it in one quick sputter of Spanish, of course.

Keeney turned reluctantly to me. "What'd she say?"

"She wants to know if we came to pay her the reward."

He made a fist at her. "Listen, you don't worry about the money, baby. You worry about me, understand?" And then to me: "Tell her that."

There was no need to. Instead I explained as quietly and sympathetically as I could that we had come to learn from her what we could of this man, Cruz-Rivera, that he was wanted in the United States for a very serious crime, and that if what she could tell us would help us capture him, she would be paid one thousand dollars, as promised.

"You pay me now," she said in a surprisingly firm voice, "and then I tell you."

Well, she might be undersized and pregnant, but she had

some nerve left, didn't she? I glanced over at Keeney, who was staring tensely at the girl, and began with her again. "In no way will it be done so," I assured her seriously. I hadn't even considered conditions of payment—but I had to now. "You give me your information, and if it is good and reliable, I will pay you in full. If it must be checked out, I will pay you half now and half when it is verified. That is how it must be." I said it quietly and soberly and must have convinced her.

"Okay, I tell you. Francisco Cruz-Rivera used to come in here a lot. He doesn't go with me. He likes the ones who are . . ." She spread her hands at her breasts and moved them out three or four inches. "You know, some men like that. Anyway, he has a lot of money, and he spends it, but he is a drunk. People here call him Paco—only that. But I know that Cruz-Rivera is his name because one night he got so drunk he was unconscious, and his wallet fell on the floor, and I looked inside. I . . . I took some money, too—but I left some— and I read his name. And so—"

"What's that all about?" Keeney broke in. "Tell me."

"Quiet," I said. "Let me get all of it first." I nodded at her to continue.

"Well, he came in maybe eight or ten times, maybe more, but there were times he was gone perhaps a month. The last time he came in was about three or four weeks ago. Then right after that they passed those papers around town that had his picture on it and the promise to pay. Everybody looked at it and said, 'Hey, look, that's Paco.' He didn't come back after that."

"But only you wrote that you had seen him."

"Paco is dangerous—or maybe not him but his friends. Besides"—she patted her belly—"I need the money." She shrugged. That was evidently all she had to say.

"Does Paco live here in Culiacan?"

She considered that a moment and shook her head. "No, I don't think so."

"Where?"

She looked at me and then away. "I don't know." I had the feeling she was holding something back.

Before I could press the point, I felt Keeney's big hand squeezing my shoulder. "I want to hear it," he said. "All of it."

And so I told him, omitting only my doubts at the end. I decided I didn't want to give him anything to work on.

But it didn't matter. He had doubts of his own: "She's *got* to know more than that. What're we supposed to do? Sit around downstairs and wait for him to come back?"

He grabbed her and began shaking her. "Give us some more, dammit," he growled. "We got to have more than *that*!" He pushed her back down flat on the bed, held her there with one hand, and with the other took the cigarette from his mouth.

He was going to burn her. She cried out something to me I couldn't quite catch, and then I got a little crazy. I grabbed out the HK from my belt and brought down the short barrel just as hard as I could on his temple. He turned to me dully, merely stunned, and so I brought the butt down on the crown of his head and hit him again on the temple. At last he rolled over, unconscious, and slid down to the floor.

Alicia Ramirez struggled up from the bed and sat for a moment looking down at him. Then she spat down in his face. "*Puerco!*"

"Get dressed," I said to her. "We've got to get out of here."

She didn't argue with me.

We spent about an hour alone together. She led me down the hall to a backstairs and out a rear entrance. From the Calle Acapulco we made our way quickly to the central plaza, hardly saying a word to one another—just getting away. When we reached the plaza, it was practically empty. The strollers had vanished into the cantinas and the restaurants—or perhaps off to rooms where the bills came due for promises in the plaza.

Knowing no better place, I guided Alicia Ramirez back to the cantina I had visited earlier. The bartender waved in greeting and mugged a comment on my *compañera*. I pointed to a table in the corner, and he nodded. It had been crowded here earlier, but now, with the lights dim and the din of voices down to a hum, the place seemed to have collapsed to about half the size it was. I was surprised to notice the two burly Frenchmen still sitting at the bar, involved in that same intense, guttural conversation. Come to think of it, they didn't seem like Club Med types at all.

As soon as our drinks came to us and the waitress had left, Alicia leaned forward, fixed me with a sharp look, and said, "I want my money."

"Your money," I echoed, sounding a little stupid, even to myself. "Well . . ."

"Sure! Why do you think I came with you?"

To get away from Keeney? No, *Señora* Concepción could have had him dumped in an alley by now. Because I seemed *muy simpático*? Forget it. I was with Keeney, wasn't I? She rightly recognized me as the money man, and it was the money she was after. And why not? With a sigh, and as unobtrusively as possible, I tugged off my belt and unzipped it under the table. I pulled out some hundreds, counted off five of them, and tapped her on the knee with them. She grabbed them out of my hand as I belted up again.

"But here is only five hundred."

"Exactly as I said."

"But—"

"The information must be verified. I must find out where it takes me."

"*Señor*," she hissed emphatically, "the information I gave you may take you to your grave—and then how do I get the rest?"

"You'd better say some *avemarías* I stay alive."

"*Ay!*" She looked away angrily and began tapping on the tabletop.

"*Señorita* Alicia," I began quietly, "I asked you before if you knew where I might find Cruz-Rivera and you said no. But there was something in your eyes that said yes. I did not tell the other man my suspicion, but he evidently was also suspicious. Now that you have been paid and we understand each other better, I wish to point out to you that it is in your own interest to tell me as much as you can about this man, Cruz-Rivera, because it is only in this way that you will receive the rest of your money."

She looked at me and then looked away again. I could tell that I had gotten through to her. Sighing, she dropped her bravado at last. "Okay. Remember I said Paco had dangerous friends? That is because he is a *contrabandista*. They are all *contrabandistas*. They come down from the Sierra and throw their money around—more money in a night than I would see in a month, in a year maybe. They own Culiacan, all of Sinaloa." She was whispering now: "It's a very big business here, the drugs. Many are involved. It's not safe to talk about it. Listen, I'll tell you something. You see those two men sitting at the bar?" I turned and saw that she had nodded at the Frenchmen. "Those two have been in the city a week. They came all the way from Marseilles to buy. Everybody knows this. The girls at the Gallo know this. That bartender there, he knows this. But nobody says anything because they are afraid. I am afraid—but I *need* this money, so I tell you this: Paco comes down from the Sierra. He is always talking about the girls in Bocalobo and how ugly they are. He can be very funny sometimes, this Paco. That is as much as I can tell you about him. He talks about Bocalobo—it is not far from here in kilometers but high up in the Sierra—and so I think you will find him there, or in the vicinity."

By the time she finished, her voice had dropped so low that it was barely audible. She seemed almost physically exhausted by her speech. I reached across the table and put my hand on hers. Suddenly and quite unexpectedly, she started crying. I wasn't prepared for that—either I'd been through too much or she'd been too tough, or something. Anyway, when I saw her tears, all I had to offer her was the cocktail napkin under my Cuervo Gold. She took it, used it, and returned it, all in the course of a minute. Quite an ordinary transaction, really, but it proved very important to us, for after it was complete, I began to ask her about herself—where she had grown up and how, how long she had been at the Gallo Inmortal and why, and how it came to pass that she was obviously pregnant when *Señora* Concepción would certainly have wanted her to have an abortion. You must understand, however, that I did not interrogate her, and that all of my questions came directly from her answers. I guess I'm saying that we had our first conversation.

What I learned was this: Alicia María Ramirez y Sandoval grew up in a little fishing village just west of Culiacan. By her fifteenth year she was more or less an orphan. Her father was off someplace, but she had no idea where, or even if he was still alive. She still had family in the little town, and all of them had tried to persuade her not to go to Culiacan, but she was sure she knew what was right for her, and so she came— at age sixteen—and she cooked and waitressed and did everything but whore. Finally, it began to dawn on her that men were very interested in her. And after she had put off proposition after proposition and been deceived by a married man, she decided she might as well sell what everyone was trying to steal from her. She went to *Señora* Concepción and was hired on the spot. It had gone all right for a while—Concepción had treated her well—but after a year the life at the Gallo seemed more than she could bear. She wanted out—and then she discovered she was pregnant. Concepción tried to persuade her to have an abortion, but Alicia was determined to have the child and leave the life. The wild inflation of the last few years had reduced her small savings to practically nothing. When the reward notice came her way, it seemed like a chance—the only chance she had.

It took the better part of an hour for her to tell me all this, what with digressions, comments, and confessions, but when she had ended, I felt like I knew her pretty well. And I liked what I knew.

"What are you going to do with the money?"

"Oh," she said mysteriously, "I have a plan."

The cantina was closing. The Frenchmen had left. The bartender was polishing glasses. He smiled accommodatingly but nodded toward the door. I paid up, and we started out.

"Are you going back to the Gallo?" I asked. "He ought to be gone by now."

"In no way do I go there."

"Well, where then? I'll take you wherever you're going. I've got a car at the hotel."

"You have the money. I remain with you."

"But I'm going back to the hotel."

"Then I accompany you."

It was a logic born of desperation and difficult to argue with. Looking into her eyes outside the cantina, I saw that it was not even worth trying. "Well, come on," I said, and led her across the plaza, past the fountain, and on to the Conquistador.

We were able to get back in by the side door that I had left unlocked a couple of hours earlier. Together we climbed the stairs to the fourth floor. Out of consideration for her condition, I was prepared to stop along the way so that she might rest, but she took them without puffing or faltering. She was a tough little *chula*.

I fumbled with my key at the door, then, when I had it unlocked, suspiciously pushed it open with my foot. Motioning for Alicia to stay back, once more I tugged out the pistol from my belt, and with two bounding steps, I sailed into the middle of the hotel room. I wheeled around, covering the door. In a few seconds, I was satisfied there was no one in there with me. I switched on a light and called for Alicia to come inside.

When she did, I saw that she was a bit wide-eyed and realized only then that I still had the HK out and pointed in her direction. I put it down on the dresser and smiled. "Sorry," I said, and she answered with a shrug.

Her eyes lit up with a sudden inspiration. "You got your own bath here? A big tub? Soap? Lots of towels?"

"Sure. Serve yourself. It's behind you there."

She went to take a look and flipped on the light. The next thing I heard was an "Ay!" of mournful surprise.

In an instant I was behind her, looking down at the bathroom floor. Frank Keeney lay there, his head by the commode, his temple raw and ugly from the beating I had given him with the pistol. But that wasn't his problem. His big problem was that his throat had been cut and he was lying in a pool of his own blood. Keeney was seriously dead.

CHAPTER 7

During the next few minutes I was very busy. There were a number of things that had to be taken care of before the police got here.

"Alicia," I said, "go in there and sit down—and don't touch anything. I'm going to need your help in a moment. Will you help me?"

She nodded very solemnly and did as I told her, leaving me alone in the bathroom with what was left of Keeney. I patted him down carefully and noted that his big magnum was still tucked away under his jacket. Whoever got him did it so quickly that he had no chance to react—and it all happened right here no more than half an hour ago. At last I found what I was looking for—his wallet. I turned the body carefully and worked it out of his hip pocket. Among the credit cards in it I found an American Express card made out to Jarrett Enterprises. Then in a jacket pocket I found the letter of authorization he had flashed at the Budget girl. I kept them out. Before I put the wallet back I checked and saw there was money left in it. Whoever killed him hadn't even bothered to make it look like a robbery. All that done, I tugged his clothes back into place, stood up, and surveyed the ugly scene. It was just as we had first seen it.

Next, I went back into the room and brought the tranquilizer gun and loads out from behind the headboard and tossed the case on the bed. Alicia looked at it curiously but said nothing. Then I found the lead-cloth wrapper and made a package of the plastic case with the gun and loads, the card and letter, and finally the Heckler & Koch and its box of 9mm ammunition. This I presented to Alicia. It was big and bulky, but she would have to find some place for it.

"I want you to hide this someplace for me," I told her. "It must be someplace nearby where it can be retrieved. You find the place. It's up to you. But I want you back here in five minutes. Understood?"

"Yes, yes, and agreed."

And then I let her out the door, closing it softly behind her. Had I been stupid? Had I sent my alibi out the door with my armory? Would she come back? Not one whore in a hundred would—but in a number of ways she seemed exceptional. I trusted her. I had to.

I dug out a number from my wallet and placed my first call. It took me a good three minutes to get through to the American Embassy in Mexico City, but even so, that was good time, considering it was not Ma Bell I was dealing with. I never reached the man whose name Silverstein had given me— around midnight on a Sunday night I didn't expect to—but the Embassy duty officer took down the particulars of the problem, agreed that it was an urgent situation, and noted that I was acting here in Mexico on behalf of Seymour Silverstein of the United States State Department on a personal matter. He promised me faithfully the message would be conveyed immediately. I trusted him. I had to.

Just as I hung up, there was a quiet knock at the door. I walked over and let Alicia in. She was empty-handed. At this point that was all that mattered. I sat her down, and we rehearsed our story. That took another five minutes. Then I dialed the desk and said, "I wish to report a murder. There is a dead man here in room 411. Will you please notify the police?"

They came and went more or less in shifts. The first at the scene were, quite predictably, the uniformed cops who had answered the first call. They didn't ask any questions at all—just told us to stay where we were and took up positions, one outside the bathroom and the other in the corridor. Next came the duty detective, all alone, an older man with graying hair and moustache. He would have appeared distinguished if it weren't for the beaten look in his watery eyes. He really did little more than go through the motions, listening to our story, taking down a few notes, spending a minute or two with the body in the bathroom, emerging with Keeney's wallet, then spending a long time looking that over. It appeared to me that he was just filling time, waiting for somebody more important.

When that somebody came, he looked familiar, more than familiar. I knew I had seen him and talked with him during the few hours I had been here in Culiacan. A short, broad man with a thin, humorless mouth, he walked into the room with the almost casual air of one in authority. He glanced over at us indifferently, went to the bathroom door and leaned inside for a look, and then beckoned the older detective out into the corridor for a conference.

It wasn't until he left the room that I remembered him. He was the plainclothes cop who had looked over my papers out on the road from the airport. He was dressed differently then—he now wore a striped jacket over a blue Izod shirt—but what threw me off was the fact that he wore no sunglasses now. Those sunglasses had made quite an impression on me, hiding his eyes completely, their chrome frame dazzling me from moment to moment with light reflected from the sinking sun. He was with a uniformed Federal Judiciary Policeman then and wore the badge out on his shirt. I wondered what interest the *Féderales* had in a hotel homicide.

Hardly a word had passed between Alicia and me during all this. We exchanged looks and at one point, I reached over and gave her hand a squeeze. That seemed to help. I was relieved when the duty detective and the *Féderal* returned and it turned out that although we were to be split up—as I expected—the older man with the rheumy eyes had drawn Alicia, and I, as the star witness, was to be questioned by the officer in charge of the investigation.

As soon as we were alone, he sat down on the bed opposite me and lit a cigarette. That suddenly reminded me of Keeney. He tossed the spent match down on the carpet. That reminded me a little of Keeney, too.

"You from Los Angeles, yes?" he began in English.

"Yes."

"And so is he, the one in there, yes?"

"Yes."

"When I see you this afternoon on the road, you come from the airport then?"

"Oh, you remember me?"

"I remember you, yes. You are the North American who think he is a Mexican. Answer the question."

I answered it in Spanish, explaining that I had flown in on the Mexicana flight from Los Angeles and landed at five-forty-five, that I came as a tourist because I had heard much about this part of Mexico.

"Please respond in English. I need to practice. When I need you respond in Spanish I tell you, okay? So, this man—how you say his name? Kee-nee?—he come on the same flight. You travel with him?"

"No. We were on the same flight, but I didn't know that. I thought I recognized him at the Budget counter at the airport. I asked the girl there about him, and it turned out I knew him."

"In Los Angeles? How is it you know him?"

"We were both policemen there. I had quit five years ago to be a private investigator. That is my profession. I am licensed in the state of California."

I could tell the *Féderal* was interested in this. "And this man Keeney?"

"Officially he is still a member of the Los Angeles Police Department—or, he was—but he was on suspension."

"Why?"

"He didn't tell me that."

"You knew him before?"

"Yes." Let him try to check that one out. There was a pause at his end. Maybe he was thinking over the information I had given him, trying to decide where to go next. I decided to try to find out something: "As a former police officer, I am interested in matters of jurisdiction. How does it happen that you, a member of the Federal Judiciary Police, have taken an interest in this case?"

He looked at me a long moment, and I could tell he was not used to having questions asked of him. But he decided to answer mine: "I take interest in all matters dealing with North Americans here in Culiacan. We find that often the North Americans are in the *contrabandista* trade, you understand? Not always, but often. How you say?—we play the averages. But you tell me now, how did you meet this man Keeney here in Culiacan? Did you know he was at this hotel, too?"

"No, I didn't." True enough.

"Answer the question. You tell me how you meet him."

"On the street. Somewhere near the plaza. I should say that Frank Keeney was never a friend of mine, only somebody I knew five years ago. But when we met, we had a drink together. We talked about, well, the things that people talk about at such times—people they know, what has happened in their lives, and so on."

"He tell you why he is in Culiacan?"

"Not really. He said something like, 'Just to take a look around.' But he implied he had business here, too."

"Of what manner?"

"He didn't say. I didn't press him. To tell you the truth, I was trying to get rid of him."

"But you went together to El Gallo Inmortal."

I sighed, making a show of regret. "Yes, that was a big mistake, wasn't it? He wanted a woman. I'd heard that the Gallo was a safe place and told him so. He insisted that I take him there and then that I come inside with him and arrange things for him with *Señora* Concepción."

78

"You talk to her?"

"Yes. There was a young lady he was especially interested in. When she was brought to us, he said we should both take her together."

"And you like this idea?"

"Not exactly. But . . . I liked the girl. You've seen her."

His look told me he considered one woman the same as another. "And so you fight with Keeney over this *puta* in her room?"

I had prepared a more dramatic account, but I was willing to settle for this. I nodded.

"This Keeney, he's very big man. He had a gun, you know that?"

"No. No, I didn't."

"How you knock him out?"

"Well, he was . . . doing things to the girl, hurting her. I got very angry, and I just grabbed whatever was handy and hit him over the head."

"And what you use? What was—how you say it?—ready?"

He had me there. This was the one detail I hadn't worked out beforehand. In a panic, I flashed a mental picture of that drab, bare little room, and siezed the only possible object: "It was a crucifix. There was a large metal crucifix on the wall, probably iron. I grabbed it down and hit him over the head with it three times."

He smiled ironically at that. "Ah, that is sacrilege, I think. Very bad. Then what you do?"

"We left."

"You and the prostitute?"

"Yes."

"Why she go?"

"Well, you can ask her, but I think she was frightened at what Keeney might do to her when he came to. We went to a cantina on the plaza—the Pajaro Rojo. We were there about an hour. The bartender would remember us. We were the last to leave. Then we came here and found Keeney."

His cigarette was down to a smoking butt. I was afraid he

might grind it out on the carpet, and so I reached over and handed him an ashtray. He took it without comment, snuffed out the cigarette and lit another. All of this he did quite slowly and deliberately, taking time to consider what I had told him.

"Mr. Cervantes, I tell you what I think of the story you tell me. I think it stink. You tell it to me in Spanish, and I think it stink more. I don't know if you kill this man Keeney. I think maybe you don't. But I don't like your story. I think it stink."

He let that sink in and waited a moment to hear what I had to say. I really didn't have much to offer. It sounded weak to me, too, but under the circumstances, and in the time allotted, it was the best I could come up with. I couldn't tell him that. I couldn't think of anything to tell him, and so I just waited him out.

"I'm gonna tell you something, Mr. Cervantes," he resumed. "I don't care if you kill him or not. Is a local matter, understand? I care why you and Keeney here in Sinaloa in the first place. You know him, he know you, and you come down on the same flight—and you tell me that's an accident. You know what I think? I think you two down here to make a buy. I think you both *contrabandistas* and you fight about money or who make the deal. That sound more right, yes? Who fight over a *puta*? Is stupid to tell me that.

"I tell you what we do now. If they ever get those *médicos* out of bed and over here to get Keeney, we gonna search this place good. We gonna search you. We gonna search the room of Keeney. And we gonna find something—"

One of the two uniformed cops who had been first on the scene had come in from the corridor. Hesitantly, he signaled for the attention of the *Féderal*, then advanced close enough to whisper something in his ear.

Clearly displeased with what he had just heard, my interrogator rose abruptly from the bed, and with a warning glance at me, followed the cop out the door, leaving me wondering. He was gone not much less than five minutes. When he came back, his face was tight, and his eyes were narrow with anger. He stood over me a moment, and I tensed, waiting for that ring-studded fist he held at his side to rise and come crashing down at me.

But no. Instead, I was flooded with a stream of official-sounding Spanish: "I wish to advise you, *señor*, that there is no more need to detain you in this matter. The police of Culiacan are also satisfied and do not consider you a suspect in this homicide. In short, you are free to go—and I wish you to do that for your own safety. Since the man Keeney was assassinated in your room, it is only logical to assume that you were the desired victim. Therefore I strongly advise you to be on the morning flight to Los Angeles. You will take my advice?"

"Well, I . . ."

"Take it. We will make sure that you do. Now, there is someone outside who wishes to speak with you." With that, he wheeled sharply and left the room.

I stared after him curiously for a few moments, then got up and followed him out to the corridor just in time to see him stepping into the elevator.

"Cervantes?" Unmistakably an American voice. I turned to it and found a big, beefy, red-haired man in a light raincoat leaning against the wall. He pushed away from it and walked over to me with his hand out. "My name's Madden. In my better days I was a cop in Houston. Now I'm with the DEA."

I shook his hand gladly. Dr. Livingstone, I presume. "You mean, DEA as in Drug Enforcement Agency?"

"Yeah, that's what they tell me, but it's kind of a joke these days. I'm the liaison for the whole state of Sinaloa."

"And you got me off the hook?"

"Yeah, and you better believe it took some fancy talking to do it."

"Well, I'm grateful to you." So this was the result of my call to Mexico City. The best I'd hoped for was to have somebody show up in the morning and bail me out of jail. The way that *Féderal* was talking at the end, I had just about given up on that.

"Now, look," he said seriously, lowering his voice, "I don't want to scare you or anything, but I just don't think it's too safe for you in this place."

"So you're advising me to get out of Culiacan, too?"

"I didn't say that. I guess that's up to you. No, I mean it's not too safe for you right here and now in this hotel. What I'm telling you is you ought to get out and spend what's left of the night someplace else. I've got a house out from the center of town. It's not big, but it's way too much for me alone. Come on, and I'll put you up. It'd give me a chance to kind of explain things to you, too."

"Well, good—okay, thanks." Then, suddenly remembering: "What about the girl?"

"Oh, yeah, well, she can come too—if I can talk her loose." With that, he nodded and went off to try.

In another half-hour Madden and I were settled in his living room and Alicia was sound asleep in one of the back bedrooms. We had followed him out practically bumper-to-bumper in the Mustang and pulled up in the driveway to the barking of what sounded like a whole kennel of dogs. Madden went over to quiet them, then let us in, disconnecting a burglar alarm, then hooking it up again once we were inside. He went about it as though it were an established routine.

Now, my feet free at last of the tight boots I had bought— was it only the day before?—in Los Angeles, and a glass of Gold on the rocks in my hand, I decided to ask him about it. "You're pretty serious about security here, aren't you Madden?"

He nodded and took a sip of scotch. "I feel like I have to be. I don't trust anybody in Culiacan. Hell, I don't trust anybody in Sinaloa. I've never been in a situation like this. I'm as much a prisoner here as I am a . . . a law enforcement officer."

"What's the situation?"

"Well, Ortega—that's the boy from the Federal Judiciary

Police who was talking tough to you back at the hotel—he's run everything here for the past couple of years. The whole dope trade belongs to him. This ain't no John Wayne movie—the good guys here are the bad guys. Hell, I told my boss in Mexico City about it—that's the guy you called, in case you didn't know that. You know what he told me? 'See what you can get on him.' How do you like that? I'm supposed to build a case on a member of the goddam Federal Judiciary Police right here in his own territory." He shook his head in dismay and took a deep gulp from his glass. He seemed a little too desperate.

"Yeah, but Ortega—that's his name?—he must be doing something," I said. "The first time I saw him was when I drove in from the airport in the late afternoon. They'd shot up a truck and the two guys in it. The truck was on fire, and believe me, there was a good ton of marijuana in it. You could smell it cooking."

"Oh, you bet. I was there, too—pulled off to the side at the crossroad—and I smelled it, all right. It was a command performance—I had to be there because it was partly for my benefit. Ortega was out to show me that he really was on top of things here in Sinaloa, and that nothing escapes his eagle eye. Well, I'll tell you what that was really all about. See, those two were a couple of independents—free-lancers—and the one thing that Antonio Ortega will *not* tolerate is independent operators in his territory. He got a tip from his network that they were going to move this stuff in the daytime down the airport highway, and he made an object lesson out of those poor fuckers. He was saying, just look what happens when you don't play ball with me. He left those bodies out there past nightfall. Maybe they're still out there, I don't know."

"So he's skimming from everyone?"

"Oh, it's more than a skim. This ain't the *mordida* working. He's a full partner. He owns fields up there in the Sierra, and I don't mean fields of marijuana either. They got poppy fields up there, Cervantes. I'm talking about Mexican brown. It's in every city in the States—practically all the heroin they got on the street in East Los Angeles is Mexican brown, I hear. Listen, if it was plain old pot we were talking about, I wouldn't be so damned exercised about it."

I sipped at my Cuervo Gold and thought this over. Then I said, "That fits in with what he was trying to pin on me. He wasn't interested in the murder. He said so himself. He was interested in me because he thought I might be down to cut a deal. Evidently, what shook him up was that I wasn't on the approved list of Los Angeles dealers—and neither was Keeney. He thought I was going to make a deal that would cut him out."

"Maybe."

"What else?"

"Well, Cervantes . . . But first you've got to tell me—why *are* you down here, anyway?"

I had been pretty sketchy on the telephone to Mexico City, and he probably knew less than I had told the duty officer. And so—a confidence for a confidence—I laid it all before him. As I did it, I found it was helpful for me to have the chance to talk the thing through with somebody. I found that certain things that didn't make sense began to make sense, and that a couple of connections I hadn't even realized were there were now made clear to me. All this took a while, but Madden listened carefully, interrupting my narrative only once—and that was to refill my glass and replenish his own. When at last I finished, I shrugged and said, "Well, what do you think of it?"

"Interesting."

"Only that?"

"No. First of all, I know Paco."

"You do?"

"Oh, hell yes. Everybody does. He comes down here all the time to kick up his heels. That's his father and his uncle that he's with up in the Sierra. They're mean bastards—old *pistoleros* from way back. But Paco, he's just a big, fat overgrown kid—likes to have fun, likes to chase the girls, likes to drink—too much. He's a *borracho*, all right, and he's your man, I'm sure of it—and I'll tell you why. I happen to know he's got a Green Card. One of my informants told me he was showing it around one night at a cantina and bragging he wasn't any *alambristo*, that he could cross the border anytime he wanted to—legally. So yes, I can see him up there on the freeway, seeing triple, ramming those kids off the road. But my God, in a hearse? What's that all about?"

"Well, I don't know, but I'm beginning to get an idea."

"Uh-huh."

"And Paco and his family, they're in the trade, too?"

"Oh, you better believe it—poppies, I understand, but I can't be sure because I've never been up there. To tell you the truth, I wouldn't dare."

"Where's 'there'?"

"Just a little above Bocalobo in the Sierra. I'm not even sure it's on the map. It's at the mouth of Lobos River."

I nodded, satisfied. "Right where she said."

"Who? The little girl in the bedroom? She's a pretty little thing, though, isn't she? And you said she was in the Gallo? I guess that makes her the original rose on the dungheap, doesn't it?"

"I don't know," I said, trying to sound more indifferent than I really felt. "I guess so." I tossed back the rest of the Cuervo Gold and got up, feeling a buzz, ready at last to fall into bed.

"Just one more thing," said Madden.

"What's that?"

"Ortega is in tight with Paco and his family. It could be he knew just who you are and why you're here, and maybe he was just doing them a favor. It could be Ortega put that guy in your room who killed—what's his name? Keeney?—thinking it was you. What I'm saying is, he wouldn't hesitate. He's got a good thing going, and he isn't about to have anybody mess it up. He's got me scared shitless."

CHAPTER 8

Sometime between two, when Madden and I called it a night, and seven, when he rousted me out of bed, I had a dream. I guess you could call it a nightmare.

The way it was, I seemed to be in a room in some kind of primitive cabin or shack or something. Maybe there was only one room in the place. Brilliant sunshine was streaming in through the open door, but I was back in the room where it was dark. Between me and the door was a huge spider web, and in it a spider the shape of a black widow but the size of the biggest tarantula you can imagine—about a foot from leg to leg. I watched him as he worked spinning his web, which was a most unusual web. It was three-dimensional, an intricate, continuing geometric design of interconnecting spirals that swept around and around the room. The spider worked quickly, and I realized that the web would soon fill the entire room. I must have realized the danger, yet I could only stare on in fascination. And then I was in the web, surrounded by it, tangled in its spirals, but able to move with some difficulty. Then the spider came at me. I flailed out at it, kicked at it as its hairy legs grabbed round my boot. Somehow I pounded it down to the floor, and I was stamping on it, trying to kill the thing. But the strings of its web impeded movement, robbing each blow of force. I stamped down again and again, but that huge spider wouldn't die.

I woke up crying, "Uh-uh-uh," as I pumped my foot down again and again against the footboard of the bed. When I came to my senses and realized what I was doing, I sat up in bed, panting, and waited for my panic to subside. Day was just breaking. It must have been sometime between five and six o'clock. The ghostly gray light from the single bedroom window gave the room an eerie quality, and for a few moments it seemed as though I was still dreaming. My ribs hurt from the elbow Keeney had planted in them. When I lay back down again, my mind was still racing. Ortega kept coming back to me—that cold, brutal face of his—and that scene at the crossroads with the burning truck. With some effort, I focused my thoughts, trying to put them to work for me. I tried to figure out what my next move would be. After a few minutes of that, I went back to sleep. No more spiders.

But when Madden woke me, I had an idea. Or maybe it wasn't so much a plan as it was a scenario.

The big guy looked at me with concern. "You were sure making a lot of noise early this morning," he said. "You all right?"

"Yeah, I'm all right. Just a dream I had."

"It sure as hell must have been a bad one. I was on my way in here when you quieted down all of a sudden."

"I woke up."

"Good thing. Breakfast'll be on in half an hour. You got time to shower and shave. The maid's in, waking your girl now."

My girl? That struck me almost as funny. Alicia belonged to no one but herself. Madden had registered some slight surprise when I went to bed the night before and asked for a separate room. If one weren't available, I said I'd sleep on the couch. No need, as it turned out. Maybe he thought I was just squeamish about sharing a bed with a pregnant whore. Maybe I was.

Madden was right. I had just enough time to shower and shave—using his electric razor—then jump back into last night's clothes, when the maid knocked on my door and called in that breakfast was ready. Madden was waiting at the table, and just as I sat down, Alicia staggered in only half-awake, her eyes puffy with sleep. She collapsed into a chair and managed a *"Buenos días."* That's all.

The maid—a woman of about fifty, stolid and thick-featured—served us big platters of *huevos rancheros* in silence. When she came to Alicia, last of all, you could read stern disapproval in her face. Did she know she was a whore? Had she recognized her from around town, or did women sense these things? She grew flustered when Alicia asked her for a glass of milk and shot a sudden glance at Madden, as though to ask if it were all right, then tramped back into the kitchen and got it.

"Look," I said to Madden, "I've got an idea, a kind of an approach to the problem, I'd like to run past you."

He looked at me sharply, then glanced in the direction of the maid and put an index finger to his lips. "Well, Cervantes," he said loudly, overacting a bit, "what do you think of Culiacan? This your first visit down here?"

We continued in that vein, small-talking loudly, until we heard water running in the kitchen and pots banging. Then Madden leaned across and said, "I don't *think* she understands English, and I don't *think* she's working for Ortega, but get it out fast while she's busy."

I did, and as I talked to Madden, I noted Alicia straining forward to listen, suddenly alert, trying to pick up whatever she could from our quiet talk in English. I wondered how much she understood. It didn't matter. She would hear all about it soon enough.

When I finished, Madden leaned back and looked at me for a moment and said, "That has got to be the craziest goddam scheme I ever heard in my life."

"I thought you might say that."

"Then why did you tell me?"

"Because I want you to line up a private plane so I can fly Paco out, no questions asked, when I bring him down."

"That's *if* you bring him down."

"Whatever."

"Jesus."

The water shut off in the kitchen, and automatically Madden and I both bent to our eggs and began shoveling them in. They were good, but they were cold.

After breakfast, Alicia and I got organized for the drive back into town. Madden held a hurried, whispered conference with me, during which we settled the details of the plane, and then he sent me forth with a muttered warning.

We had a lot to do before that plane took off—Madden had said he would try to have it for eleven that night—and a lot of places to go. As we drove, Alicia directed me to a clothing store near the plaza that would be open early. I hurried her inside.

"Here," I said, peeling off fifty bucks in pesos. "Buy yourself a maternity dress that will make you look big. Out to here." I gestured descriptively in exaggeration.

"Big? I don't want to look big. I want to look pretty."

"You are pretty. But just this once I want you to look pretty and big. Understand?"

She looked at me with a frown and nodded.

"And get yourself another outfit. Something nice. Whatever you like. What you've got should cover it."

That cheered her up a little. She turned and started off. I watched her click away on spike heels and called her back. Digging into my pocket, I came up with another small handful of pesos. "Do they sell shoes here?"

"Yes, clearly." She gestured vaguely behind her.

I thrust the bills at her. "Take this and buy some sandals, *alpargatas*, anything flat. I want you to be able to walk like this." With my pelvis thrust out, I took a few steps, caricaturing the walk of a woman nine months pregnant.

She grabbed the money out of my hand, stamped her foot, and called me a *cabrón* and a couple of other things even less nice to hear. However, she went off to the women's department to do as I had told her.

For myself, I headed for the men's department and bought a shiny blue polyester suit two sizes too large in the waist off the rack. Ordinarily I wouldn't have worn it on a bet—even if it fit. And then I picked out a shirt and tie that I liked just about as well. I paid up in dollars, which the clerk accepted eagerly, and had him dump them all in a good-size shopping bag.

Next, I went back up to the front of the store and picked out a pair of cheap, horn-rimmed sunglasses from the rack and paid for them. As the cashier looked on curiously, I carefully knocked out both lenses and handed them over to her to dispose of. With a smile, I left her staring after me and headed for the women's department. There I hurried Alicia along, and with a little prodding had her out of there in five minutes.

When we hit the street it suddenly struck me. "A wig," I said, "you'll need a wig. Can you get it in the store?"

She nodded.

I handed over some more pesos. "Get it in two minutes. Nothing more. I'll bring the car around to the front right here and wait for you. Two minutes."

She couldn't have taken more than four. I had the Mustang there, idling, for about a minute when she burst through the door with a head-size square package under her arm. At least I had managed to impress upon her that we were in a hurry. Inside the car, she opened up the box and showed me what she had bought. It was blond and phony-looking, but for our purposes a wig was a wig.

"And now," I said to her, "I want to see a lawyer—and he must be a real *coyote*."

Alicia came up with a name for me immediately—Leandro Sanchez. I followed her directions—down the street two blocks and one more block to the right—and pulled up across the street from his office. I told her to wait in the car and hurried inside. It all took just fifteen minutes. Leandro Sanchez got

90

what he wanted out of me—one hundred dollars American—and I got the papers I needed from him.

There was just one last stop to make—at a *groceria*. This time I double-parked and sent Alicia inside to buy a box of cornstarch. I glanced at my watch. It was almost nine-thirty. We were still on schedule, but we didn't have time to spare. She was back with a small bag in her hand. I glanced inside to make sure she had understood me right. It's not so easy to come up with the Spanish for "cornstarch" at a moment's notice.

We entered the hotel by the side door again. There was no sign of the escort of *Féderales* that Ortega had promised—not even when we got to my room on the fourth floor. I glanced into the bathroom. The body was gone, but there was dried blood on the floor. They had left it for the maid to clean up.

What I had bought went into my suitcase along with the jeans I had on and a clean shirt. A suit I had brought with me would have to be left behind. As I stripped off my shorts and socks, I glanced up and found Alicia staring at me, a slight smile fixed on her face.

I didn't know quite what to say, whether to cover myself up, or what. "*Pues?*"

The smile disappeared. She looked me in the eyes. "It's the first time I ever saw a man like that when he wasn't going into bed with me."

"Well, turn around then, if you want to."

"No. I like looking at you."

I finished dressing, clean jeans and a shirt. Then I grabbed Alicia by the hand, and we made for the lobby. As I expected, there were two tan-uniformed *Féderales* waiting for us. One of them round and short, the other lean and mean. They looked at me carefully, nodded almost in greeting, and muttered a few words among themselves. As I checked out, the slender one stepped forward and touched his visored hat in a careless salute. He looked like the old-time actor Alfonso Bedoya—the one who played Gold Hat in *The Treasure of the Sierra Madre*.

91

"*Señor* Cervantes?"

"Yes."

"We are here to escort you to the airport."

"That's not necessary."

"Nevertheless, *señor*, we will follow you there and see you onto the plane."

"As you wish."

"Of course, *señor*," he said unpleasantly. "It will be as *we* wish."

They were out the lobby door behind us, trailing at a distance of ten to twelve feet. As we walked quickly to the Mustang, I glanced back and saw the two of them swaggering off to their marked patrol car. The one who had spoken to me at the desk caught my eye and smiled the smile of a snake.

The patrol car was right on our tail as we pulled out of the hotel parking lot. Again, I checked my watch. We had managed to pick up a few minutes in the hotel.

"*Ay!*" Alicia said, suddenly agitated. "Which way are you going?"

"To the airport."

"Well, you better stop at the Gallo Inmortal first. I gotta tell Concepción I'm all right. The way I left last night she might think I was dead or kidnapped or something."

She had me there. I certainly didn't want Concepción going to the police. With another worried glance at my watch, I took a fast turn down a side street and noted in the mirror that the *Féderales* had moved up a little closer on my tail, as though suspicious at the sudden change of route.

"Here," said Alicia, "turn right here."

I did and found it was Calle Acapulco. The Gallo Inmortal was right there on the next corner. I pulled up beside it, and the patrol car came to a halt just fifteen feet behind me. Neither of the two cops got out. They had evidently decided to wait and see what happened.

"Hurry up," I said to her. "Find her, tell her, and return. With all speed, eh?"

She nodded dutifully, jumped out, and made a great show

of running at top speed into the place. Again, she didn't take long. The only thing was that when she came back, Concepción was trailing after her, wrapped in a real old-fashioned kimono (what else would a Mexican madam wear?), and wailing out her good-bye at the top of her lungs. *¡Jesús, María y José!* I thought—more Mexican histrionics. Growing up, I'd had enough of them to last a lifetime.

Concepción wrapped her ample arms around Alicia right there in the middle of the street, as though she meant never to let go. I glanced into the mirror at the *Féderales*. They were taking it all in.

Surprise of surprises, Concepción at last let her go, and Alicia jumped into the car. But then Concepción jammed her big tearful face through the open passenger window and kissed Alicia square on the lips. Next she looked up fiercely at me and said, "*Señor*, you must take good care of my baby and her baby." What was this all about?

To Alicia: "Treasure! Daughter of my soul! I promise you one thing. When you are a big star, no one will know of your life here at the Gallo Inmortal. I will not tell! The girls will not tell! I will *kill* them if they do! Your secret is safe with us, I promise!"

With that, she kissed her again, drew back from the window, and went dramatically and tensely erect. And there, in the middle of Calle Acapulco, raising her hands to the blue sky above, Concepción let out a forlorn, bereft scream of an "*¡Aaaayyy!*" that must have been heard three blocks away in the *plaza central*. I started the engine, gunned the car, and got out of there as quickly as I could, with the *Féderales* in fast pursuit.

We were on the airport highway before I worked up courage to ask her the question that had been nagging at me ever since we left Concepción wailing in the middle of the street. I turned to Alicia. She was gazing out at the Sierra in the distance, so I reached over and gave her a tap on the shoulder. "Listen to me," I said. "What did you tell her, anyway?"

"Concepción?"

My eyes were back on the road, where they should have been. I gripped the steering wheel a little tighter. "Yes, yes, Concepción, clearly. Who else?"

"I told her you were taking me to Los Angeles with you."

Glancing over at her, I saw she was staring straight ahead and had a little smile on her face, something between angelic and smug. She was impossible! "I regret to inform you," I said, "I am *not* taking you to Los Angeles."

"We'll see."

She said it with such complete assurance that there was absolutely nothing for me to say in reply. What *could* I say? All I could do was wrap my fingers so tight around the wheel that my knuckles showed white. I waited, and I waited, and I waited, until at last the blood began circulating through my fingers again. I breathed deeply, and at last I felt myself more or less under control. Keeping my eyes on the road, I asked her, "All right, now tell me, what was that she said about 'when you are a star'?"

"Yes?" she said. "What about it?"

"What did she mean?"

"You remember I told you I had a plan? What I would do with the money?"

"Yes, yes, all right, I remember."

"Well, that is my plan."

"*What* is your plan?"

"I go to Hollywood, and I become a movie star. Hollywood is near Los Angeles, true?"

"Hollywood is *in* Los Angeles."

"You see?" She rested her case.

It was white-knuckle time again. What could I say to her? That a million girls a year come to Los Angeles with the same plan? No, I could see that it would make no impression on her at all. And so I raised a more mundane objection: "You don't even know English."

"True, but I learn quickly. I am very intelligent. You don't think I'm intelligent?" There was such intensity in that! It was hurled at me almost like an accusation.

I sighed, glanced at her, and found her frowning at me with her jaw set, looking for a fight. "I think you're intelligent," I said. It was true. I did. "I also think you're pregnant."

"That's all right. First I have the baby, and *then* I become a movie star. It's all for the baby, anyway. Not for me."

There must have been a part of her that really believed that, so who was I to challenge her? Nothing I could say would talk her out of this. I attempted to wait her out, keeping an eye on the *Féderales* in the rearview mirror. At last, I settled on something: "Well, if you become a movie star, you have to learn to act, true?"

"I know how to act. I act in bed—all the time. I say *ay*! oh!" She moaned so that for a moment I thought she was having an orgasm right then and there.

"All right, then," I said, "now comes your chance to get out of bed and act."

The airport was in sight. I squeezed down on the accelerator and covered the next quarter-mile or so at speed. The big Dodge driven by the *Féderales* kept right up with us, though. At the entrance drive, I pumped the brake sharply, downshifted, and executed a clean left. Then I slowed down immediately and looked into the mirror. I had the pleasure of seeing the escort car careen into a wild slide, almost losing it completely at the turn. But in another moment they were so close behind me I thought for a moment they were going to ram us. Maybe they wanted to, but they didn't.

I glanced at Alicia and found her looking at me with some disdain. "Games," she muttered with a show of exasperation.

When I pulled into the Budget section of the lot and into one of the assigned spaces, the Dodge stopped some distance back. The Alfonso Bedoya look-alike jumped out, and the patrol car drove on—probably to park at the entrance. If he stuck to us too closely, this was going to be tricky.

He held back, leaning against a car a few spaces away, his hand draped casually on the butt of his pistol. As I grabbed my suitcase from the back seat and handed Alicia her packages, he hailed me, "Hey, *Señor* Cervantes!"

I turned and looked. He hadn't moved. His hand was still on his gun.

"You make a joke with us back there, eh?"

"When?" I said innocently. "What do you mean?"

"Maybe you'll find out it's not so smart to joke with the *Féderales*."

"I'm learning that."

"It's a lesson to remember."

That was all. I think it was what they call a Mexican standoff: threat made, honor satisfied. I took Alicia by the hand, and we headed into the building.

At the Budget counter, I handed over the keys to the Mustang and signed out on it. I looked over and decided that my escort was out of earshot, and so I leaned over and said in English to the girl behind the counter, "I will be needing something to drive in the mountains. Something with four-wheel drive. Do you have anything like that? A Jeep? A Land Rover?"

"Our Jeeps are out now, but we do have a Toyota Land Cruiser that was just checked in. It's being serviced now."

"Well, have it brought around. I'll leave my American Express card, and you can do the paperwork on it. We'll be back to pick it up."

I found Alicia frowning, not quite understanding what was going on. She seemed about to ask, so I gave a little shake of my head, warning her not to. Then I grabbed her arm, picked up my suitcase, and swept her off to the Mexicana counter.

They found space for me on the flight to Los Angeles. I got my seat assignment—I asked for one at the back of the plane—and then there was the matter of my suitcase.

"How many pieces of luggage will you have to check, sir?"

"I just have one piece of carry-on."

The ticket agent looked dubiously through the luggage opening at my suitcase. It was designed to fit under a seat, but it was just about stuffed square. "Are you sure it will fit?" he asked.

"It always has before." That was a lie. Sometimes it did, and sometimes it didn't. But it didn't matter this time.

I drew Alicia aside then, increasing the distance between us and our police escort by a few steps. There were two of them again. Alfonso Bedoya had been joined by the rotund driver. I dipped into my pocket and came up with a wad of pesos. I handed it over to Alicia, making sure that the two *Féderales* saw me give the money to her.

"Here," I said, "take this and put it in your handbag. When I leave you, go to the ticket counter and inquire about the next flight to Mexicali. Do it immediately, so the *Féderales* see you do it."

"But I don't want to go to Mexicali. I'm going with you."

"Shhh. You're not going to Mexicali. Listen. Don't buy a ticket. Just ask. I think they'll both follow me, but I can't be sure. This ought to take care of it if one of them stays behind to check up on you."

"Okay. I do as you say."

"Then, after you've asked about the flight, just go and sit down there with your packages and wait. If one of the *Féderales* stays, just let him watch you until he leaves. If they both follow me, wait awhile, anyway. Then get up, take your packages, and go to the ladies' room. Go into one of the stalls, and change into the maternity dress I made you buy, the one that makes you look big. Understand?"

"Yes."

"I want you to look very big. I want you to look like a different person. Stuff what you're wearing and the other outfit in front. Put on the sandals and the wig, then make yourself up to look different—any way you can. Throw all the bags away, and the shoes you're wearing, too. Don't worry. I'll buy you a new pair. Then just find another place not too far from where you were sitting and wait until I come for you. Have you got all that?"

"Yes, yes. Okay."

"And now you must act. We are parting. I have promised

to meet you in Mexicali and make arrangements to take you over the border. All right. Action. Kiss me."

Suddenly there were tears in her eyes. How they got there I had no idea. She grabbed my face between her small hands, stood on her toes, and kissed me passionately on the lips.

"Ay, *mi vida! Mi amor!*" she cried out to me and to the rest of the airport. "You *promise* you will come for me in Mexicali?"

My God, I thought, it's Concepción all over again. But she had it right. I fed her a line to keep her going: "In a week, *chiquita*. You have my word . . . as a man."

"And such a man!" The tears were streaming down her cheeks. "Tell me, is Los Angeles far from Mexicali?"

"Not far. And only a week from now. I promise."

She went up on tiptoe again and covered my face with kisses. My cheeks, my nose, my mouth were wet with her tears when at last she stopped. "Then," she said, taking a single dramatic step back from me, "*hasta la vista*."

I backed off a few steps, too. "*Hasta la vista*." I turned then and started off toward the flight gate. Well, it might not play in Hollywood, but it sure played in Culiacan. She almost had me convinced, and I wrote the script. When I had covered some distance, I looked back and saw that she had gathered up her packages and was already talking to the ticket agent at the counter. I also saw that both the *Féderales* were following me.

Hurrying along, I glanced at my watch and saw I had about five minutes until boarding time. So far so good. The hardest part was coming up.

Once at the gate, I didn't bother to sit down and wait, but edged up close to the chained-off exit to the runway. I had to be among the first aboard—not, perhaps, the first; that might seem suspicious. The two officers of the Federal Judiciary Police had followed me all the way to the gate, of course, but just now were paying me no attention at all. They were exercising their prerogative of position and flirting with the Mexicana girl at the desk. The Alfonso Bedoya character—Jesus, but he was ugly!—was really coming on to her, showing his big, yellow teeth, whispering and giggling, while his partner listened closely to it all and joined in the fun.

They occupied her so completely that I was afraid she might not make the boarding call on time. The plane was on the ground, a 727 like the one I had flown down on, and I could tell it was about time to go. So could the other boarding passengers. A number of them had crowded up beside me at the chain. But at last the phone at the desk rang, and the Mexicana girl picked it up, temporarily putting a halt to the flirtatious onslaught. Then they remembered me. Without quite looking directly at them, I caught them searching the little crowd at the barrier for me. Would they come over? I hoped not. One of them did. Alfonso directed his fat young partner over toward me just as the girl at the desk made the boarding call. The door to the runway was opened, and a young man in a Mexicana uniform stepped through and let down the chain. In the general surge for the door, I took a glance back and found the fat *Féderal* hesitating at the edge of the crowd. It was his job to see that I actually got onto the plane.

Out on the runway I took my chosen place as the third in line and ascended the platform stairs ahead of about a dozen others. Once inside I could only be sure of about five minutes. Maybe longer—but I couldn't count on it. I flashed my seat assignment at the stewardess at the door and pushed past the two I had allowed to precede me, a businessman and his wife, practically pushing them over. I went at almost a run down the aisle to the back of the plane and found a stewardess blocking my way to the toilets, explaining that I would have to wait until the plane was in flight.

I put on an expression of pain and panic, trying to look as much as I could like a guy in the terminal stages of Montezuma's Revenge. *"Emergencía,"* I gasped. It must have been pretty convincing. She took another look at my face, considered the consequences, and ducked quickly out of my way.

Once inside the toilet, the door safely locked, I managed somehow to do it all. I peeled off my outer clothes in seconds, threw open the suitcase, and dressed at top speed in the things that I had bought earlier that morning. I tied the ugly tie on the brocaded shirt but waited to pull on the jacket until I had patted my hair with cornstarch to a distinguished gray. The waist of the pants was loose, as I had intended. I filled it up by stuffing the clothes I had just thrown off under the shirt, then belted the bulge tight around my middle. With the suit jacket on, I stuffed my cheeks with toilet paper, and as a final touch, pulled on the lensless glasses. I allowed myself a glance into the mirror—no more—and I had to admit that indeed I did look different. Everything loose—the box of cornstarch, the bags and wrappers, everything—went back into the suitcase. I zipped it up and unlocked the door of the toilet.

In the aisle, there were still people standing and settling in. Had I done it all in five minutes? Maybe less? I had no idea. I only knew that I had done it as quickly as I possibly could. I jammed my suitcase in the first empty spot I found. As I had hoped, the stewardess who had tried to bar my way to the toilet was now occupied seating someone, and she took no notice of my exit from the toilet. I barged past her, and snaked my way through the aisle, pushing when I had to, up to the front of the plane. There, I saw with relief that the door was still open and the platform stairs still in place. I brushed aside the objections of the front stewardess telling her that I had left something "of great importance" in the airport.

"But you'll miss the flight!" she called after me.

"Then I'll catch another," I called back from the stairs.

The ground crew was just coming to pull them away when my feet touched the runway. Were the *Féderales* watching? I hoped not. But if they were, they saw a middle-aged, overweight Mexican in an electric-blue suit leave the plane—and not me. I hurried along but tried to hurry as a heavier, older man might—swinging my arms wide, taking smaller steps, puffing from exertion.

I paused and peered inside the door through which I had exited a few minutes before. I hoped to heaven I would not see Alfonso's face peering back at me. No, but he was still there—still talking to the Mexicana girl, with his partner at his side. All three looked like they were about to leave. I ducked back, counted to 100 slowly, and took another look. They were gone. I let myself in, undid the chain barrier, and caught a glimpse of them down the corridor as they walked back together. I decided to give them a good head start. Sitting down out of view, I waited nearly five minutes and then decided I could chance it. I saw no sign of them during the long walk to the lobby.

Once I got there, I saw no sign of Alicia, either. I swept the area around the Mexicana counter, but I saw no one even resembling her. Then I realized I should be looking for a blonde—the wig, of course. There was one in the corner, but it couldn't be her . . . could it? No, this woman was older. She wore thick makeup and had a heavy, settled look as she sat there on the chair. But she was pregnant, and she was wearing the maternity dress I had bought for Alicia that very morning. So I supposed, as I came closer to her, that it really had to be Alicia.

I sat down beside the woman, still uncertain. She didn't offer me a glance. I studied the profile. It was Alicia, wasn't it? I cleared my throat and said, "*Señora* . . ."

"I am waiting for my husband," she said severely.

"Alicia?"

She turned to me, startled, and I saw that she had painted her mouth into a cupid's bow and rouged her cheeks heavily. It made her look ten or fifteen years older.

She looked at me and hesitated. "*Ay, Dios mío!*" she whispered at last. "It's you, isn't it? I didn't recognize you."

"And I didn't recognize you."

"Can we go now?"

"Yes," I said, "but slowly and very casually."

And that was how we proceeded to the Budget counter. The girl there didn't recognize me, either. She addressed me in

Spanish, and I responded in English, telling her I had come back for the Toyota Land Cruiser and my American Express card.

She stared at me. "*Señor* Cervantes? You look different."

"Yes, well, those things happen. A man can age a lifetime in minutes."

"As you say."

In another minute, I had signed out on the Toyota and had the keys. Alicia and I walked slowly and casually out the airport entrance and found the *Féderales* there, just getting into their Dodge patrol car. Alicia hesitated, but I gave her a slight jerk forward, and we resumed our leisurely gait. Neither of the two in the tan uniforms gave us a glance. As we proceeded to the Toyota, they drove away.

Once inside, she suddenly threw her arms around me and burst into a gale of laughter. Was she hysterical? amused? or simply relieved? Maybe all three. At last, her laughter subsided. She looked at me seriously then, her arms still clasping my neck. "Hey," she said, "you're pretty intelligent, too, you know that? That was a *good* plan."

I disentangled myself a little ungraciously and thanked her a little stiffly. Then I started the Toyota. I was just pulling out of the space when I was suddenly struck by a thunderbolt. I jammed on the brakes, bent my head over the steering wheel and beat the top of the dash panel with my fist. "Oh no," I wailed in English. "How in the hell could I have forgotten *that*?"

"*Qué quiere decir?*" she asked. What do you mean?

I looked at her, shaking my head at my own stupidity. "I made such a good plan that now we have to go back to the hotel. I forgot to have you pick up the guns, wherever it was you hid them."

"Oh, don't worry about that," she said with a smile. Then she dipped into her voluminous handbag and came up with the lead-cloth package I had given her the night before. "I couldn't find a good place to hide them, so I kept them."

I flipped it open. Everything was inside—the HK and ammunition, the tranquilizer gun and loads, the card and letter, all of it. I looked at her, amazed. "But didn't it occur to you they might go through your bag last night?" I asked.

She regarded me tolerantly. "Are you such a North American that you don't understand Mexican men? To them, a woman is insignificant, beneath consideration, good for only one thing. They would not think to go through a woman's handbag because a woman is of no importance."

I studied her for a moment and decided she meant what she said. There was no particular emphasis to it. She was simply explaining things to me. I put the Toyota in gear, and we started out of the airport lot, heading in the direction of the mountains.

CHAPTER 9

"I'm hungry," she said.

We had been driving a couple of hours. It was well past one-thirty, going on two, and we had climbed up and up and up into the Sierra. I had no idea where we were. The map given to us at the Budget counter lay on Alicia's lap, and she offered directions whenever they were necessary. I was only aware of the look of the country we were driving through. It wasn't quite what I had expected it to be. When I first glimpsed them from the airport, the mountains had seemed so barren and rugged that it didn't seem to me that anyone could possibly live up here. But there were houses along the way, most of them not more than shacks, primitive corrals with a burro or two inside, and occasionally a goat and some scrawny chickens. Whenever we passed a *campesino* in those little fields scratched into the mountain, he would stand and watch silently as we went by. Only one had waved. There wasn't much traffic on the road. A few rattletrap Fords had passed us coming down, as well as some pickup trucks that were so ancient and dust-covered that I couldn't even guess at year, make, or model.

"I'm hungry," she said again.

"I heard you," I said. "But I haven't noticed a lot of restaurants along the way, have you? No Burger King, no golden arches."

"What is Boorgoor Keeng?" She sounded it out with difficulty in English. "And golden arches?"

"Restaurants in the United States."

"Oh." She was quiet for just a moment. "Golden arches is Macdohnahld's, yes?"

"Yes."

"We have them in Mexico." Putting me in my place. Then: "It's not good for me to miss a meal when I have a baby inside me. And I should drink lots of milk, too. Concepción said so. Aren't *you* hungry?"

She was like a kid the way she worried away at it. She was like a kid in a lot of ways. The wig had come off as soon as we were clear of the airport, and now her dark hair billowed behind her. But she still wore the makeup, so she looked young and old at the same time.

"All right," I said at last, "I admit it. I'm hungry. But since there's nothing to do about it, I decided a long time ago not to say anything. We should have brought something to eat along with us. I didn't think of it. I'm sorry."

"Don't be sorry. Just stop at the next house. *I'll* get us something to eat."

There was one in sight. It seemed more ramshackle than any we had passed yet. Alicia looked it over and shook her head, no. "Not that one," she said. "Too poor. We'd be taking the tortillas right out of their mouths." We drove nearly ten minutes before we found a place that suited her. It was adobe, like the rest, but a little larger—probably two or three rooms. There was a horse in the corral along with two burros. And the goats and chickens around the place seemed to be in better shape than others we had seen. "Stop here," she said. "And let me talk—agreed?"

"Agreed."

She bounded out of the Toyota when we came to a halt. As she went to the door, however, I noted that she was walking back on her heels, as I told her to do in the airport. The door opened before Alicia could knock. A solid, plain woman of indeterminate age stepped out on the shaded platform that served the house for a porch. The two of them had a short conversation, none of which I caught. Alicia talked with animation, patting her abdomen, which was still padded with clothes and gesticulating in my direction. In a moment or two the woman concluded their conference with a nod, and Alicia waved me inside.

"We eat here," she said to me just outside the door. "I promised her five dollars American, and I promise *you* it will be good."

Alicia disappeared into what must have been the kitchen. I heard a pump going and water flowing, and a few minutes later she came back with her face scrubbed clean of the makeup she had put on in the airport. Now she looked her age, or a few years younger—big belly and all.

Well, the food was good, all right. Simple and good. *Señora* Benitez, the woman of the house, brought out plates heaped high with beans and a concoction of shredded beef topped with cheese and onion. I hadn't expected meat, nor much of anything, really, but it turned out that Bocalobo was just a few miles ahead and that it boasted a *carnicería*. A restaurant? No restaurant.

She served us in the shade of the patio at the back of the house, then apologetically shooed away a couple of her kids who had come to watch us. Making one last trip, she put a cup of thin, whitish liquid in front of Alicia. It didn't look like milk to me.

"What is that?" I asked.

"Goat's milk," Alicia said. "Very healthy."

To demonstrate its salutary effect, she upended the cup and took a big gulp of the stuff. She choked on it—coughing, whooping, wheezing so violently that *Señora* Benitez and her children ran out to see what was the matter. They found me pounding her on the back with one hand and offering my bottle of beer with the other. At last she took the beer, and I stopped pounding. She took it down in little, timorous sips, gasping for air between each one.

"Is she all right?" asked *Señora* Benitez.

"I believe so," I said.

Alicia nodded to reassure us, then gradually her breathing calmed, and we were truly reassured. I sat back down at the little table across from her, and the Benitez family retired to the house.

"Well," I asked her, "how do you like goat's milk?"

"It's awful," she croaked.

She collected herself and began cautiously to eat—slowly at first, but then she must have remembered how hungry she was, for in another minute or two she was shoveling down the beans and shredded beef. I did all right by mine, too. She even sipped tentatively and managed to get a little of the goat's milk down.

We had just about finished with lunch when Alicia looked up at me and said, "I like your plan, but I don't think it will work."

I had run through the script with her during our first hour on the road. She had kept nodding through it all and asked a few questions, but she had offered no criticism. Evidently she had had time to think about it and decided she didn't like it. "Well, if you don't think it's going to work," I asked, "why do you think it's a good plan?"

"Because I like my part in it."

She reminded me of actors and actresses I had heard about who only read their own lines in a script. "Have you got any better ideas?" I asked her.

"No," she said lightly, "I just think it's going to take more than that to talk Paco down from the mountain."

This had been Madden's response, too. Maybe it was a crazy idea. Maybe we ought to junk it and see what else we could come up with. "No, truly, I mean this," I said. "Do you have any better ideas?"

"No. Understand me, *Señor* Cervantes." She made a little face at that, wrinkling her nose. "*Señor* Cervantes—that sounds very formal. How do they call you, your friends?"

"Chico."

"All right, understand me, Chico. I don't think it's a *good* plan, but I think it's good enough to try. I think we should do this, and if it doesn't work, I think you should pay me my money, and I should go back to Culiacan."

I thought about that. What she was saying was that she shouldn't be expected to do more than finger Paco and play out my little scenario with him. She was probably right. All I could think of in reply was: "I thought you wanted to go to Los Angeles with me." Jesus, I thought, this is shameless. I'm making promises I won't keep.

But she regarded me frankly and put an end to that. "Only in my fantasy," she said.

"All right," I said with a sigh. "It will be as you say. We try to talk Paco down from the mountain. If that doesn't work, then I drive you back to the city, pay you off, and from there I go ahead on my own."

"You don't need to drive me. I can get a ride just walking along the road. All you have to do is pay me."

"Agreed."

If I thought what we had driven through to get to Bocalobo was rough, hostile country, I had no idea what was waiting for us when we turned off the mountain road there and headed up into the Sierra. You couldn't call what we drove a road, exactly. A mile or two out of Bocalobo, the little dirt side road we had turned onto shrank to a track as it rose steeply off to the east, up into the Sierra. The higher we went, the worse the way became. Three miles of the track yielded to two miles of what could only be called a trail. It was rock-strewn and dusty, more suitable for horse travel—although you could tell from the ruts and tire tracks along the way that it was traversed regularly by four-wheel-drive vehicles like ours.

Alicia took it pretty well. She bounced along the track in good spirits, smiling at me reassuringly when I asked if she was okay. When the track went to a trail, she simply grabbed tight to the handgrip with which Toyota had provided her and managed to suffer through it all. It was tough going, no doubt about it. Yet somehow we made it together up to the crest of the high rise ahead, and there we found a small house and somebody to ask.

Since two women were there on the porch, both of them middle-aged, I asked Alicia to get out and inquire about Paco. I couldn't hear her question or their answer, but one of them pointed higher up the mountain. She nodded her thanks to them and returned to me in the Land Cruiser.

"Up," she said with a sigh.

"Higher?" I asked.

"On top of the mountain, they said."

"Okay."

I revved the Toyota up and pushed it higher and higher up the trail to a kind of mesalike plateau. It was almost as though the peak of the mountain had been sliced off. How big? Well, it was a little larger than a football field. And there was a whole complex of buildings up—six of them, it seemed—arranged around a carefully cleared spot in the center of the area. The buildings were no more modern nor better constructed than those we had seen along the way. One of them, the main house, was larger than the rest. Around it were sheds, apparently for storage, and a barnlike building that was being used as a garage—a Land Rover peeked out of it—and finally, there was a shed that was wider and longer than the rest that must have served them as a processing factory for the poppies they grew on the other side of the mountain.

I halted the Toyota and looked from building to building, waiting for someone to appear. Alicia opened the door and started to get out. I held her back. "Just a minute," I said.

I reached behind me and hauled out the 9mm Heckler & Koch from where I had tucked it in my belt, then I dropped it in her big handbag. The tranquilizer gun was under my seat, which was a good place for it. If she was right, and they didn't search her handbag, then I'd be able to dive in after the HK, if an emergency should arise.

She saw what I did and looked up at me with a smile. "Don't worry," she said. "It's safe with me."

A man emerged from the main house. He was middle-aged, short and stocky, and in his hand he carried what seemed to be a Russian-made AK-47 assault rifle. It *was* an AK-47. I was impressed. He came across the open area in the center of things and walked straight toward us. His face wore a scowl. It looked as though we were not welcome.

"Now, remember," I said to Alicia, "just follow the script. And play it strong."

She nodded, gave me a quick smile, then bounded out of the Toyota, advancing toward the armed man almost menacingly, rocking backward on her heels with each step forward. Padded and puffed, she had certainly never looked quite so pregnant as she did at this moment. Her appearance alone was intimidating. The scowl left the man's face and was replaced by a look of uncertainty. He slowed to a stop and seemed to brace himself almost fearfully against the full force of her onslaught.

And all the while, as she advanced toward him, she was screaming out at the top of her voice: "Where is Paco? Where is that animal who has made me suffer so? You see what he has done to me? You *see*?" She thrust her padded belly out at him, practically nudging the barrel of the AK-47.

"Where is justice for a poor girl like me?" she continued relentlessly. "What is to become of me and my child? Can you tell me that?" She stood, legs wide and arms akimbo, demanding an answer from this old *pistolero*—Paco's uncle, I had decided—and yet she got none. He could only mumble and shuffle his feet.

By this time, I was out of the car myself and was walking my overweight waddle as I made my way over to them, waving a handful of papers as I came forward. "*Here* is justice! *Here!* Only by litigation will such people as these understand their duties and obligations. I say you *must* sue!"

"No, *señor abogado*," she said, "Paco is a good boy. A little careless, and sometimes he drinks too much, but fundamentally a good boy. Anyone in Culiacan will tell you that."

"Yes," agreed the uncle, "fundamentally, a good boy."

"And that's why I *insisted* that we come up here and give Paco a chance to settle out of court," she explained earnestly. "This man, my attorney, was all for filing suit today, but I said, 'Let us find Paco and appeal to his good nature, his sense of fairness.' "

"And I, like a fool, agreed to this foolish idea," I said. "I have never driven on such primitive roads. How can anyone live in such a place?"

Paco's uncle was frowning now. "Out of court is better," he said after due consideration.

"Where is Paco?" Alicia asked.

"In the big house," said the uncle. "Asleep, I think. He drank too much last night."

"Ah, that Paco," said Alicia, "he *always* drinks too much."

"But fundamentally a good boy," the uncle added.

"Get him, *señor*," I said with all the authority I could muster. "We must speak with him personally on this matter."

"I . . . I . . . I . . ." You could see the turmoil within him mirrored in his face. For a long moment, he looked undecided and unhappy. The old *pistolero*, the bad man who was used to forcing his way with a threat and a gun, was now contending with the *campesino* who lay even deeper within him and feared no man so much as a lawyer. The two were locked deep in struggle for nearly a minute. The *campesino* won: "Yes, *señor*, I will get him for you." He turned and trudged off to the main house, his AK-47 at trail arms, his head hung low.

As soon as he was out of earshot, I leaned over and whispered to Alicia, "You're doing great! Just keep it up."

She said nothing, merely nodded, and together we set out slowly after the uncle and covered the open distance to the main house at a confident amble. Once at the house, we stopped just short of the porch, and I handed Alicia some pages from the sheaf of legal papers I had gathered from Leandro

111

Sanchez. We pretended to read through them together. I pointed out phrases, words, clauses. She nodded from time to time, frowning in concentration. We kept that up for nearly five minutes, and that was how long it took for Paco's uncle to roust him out of bed, get him to pull on some clothes, and then present him to us.

Madden had Paco about right. He called him a big, fat overgrown kid, and in general he would certainly answer to that description. Something else was there, too—a glimmer of cynical intelligence, an almost crafty look in his eyes. In Los Angeles you'd say he looked street-smart. Here, where there weren't any streets, I'm not quite sure how you'd describe him, but that's what you'd mean.

"Hello, Alicia." He looked at her rather sheepishly. "What you doing here?"

"Are you called Francisco Cruz-Rivera?" I asked him. "Otherwise known as Paco?"

"Sure. Everybody knows that."

"Then we are here to serve you with papers, *señor*."

"What kind of papers?"

"Papers pertaining to the—"

"No! No!" Alicia interrupted. "Let *me* have a chance! Let *me* talk to Paco."

I looked at her in mock annoyance and then shrugged rather grandly. "As you will," I said, "but I think you are wasting your time with him." I stalked a few paces off, careful to stay within earshot of the two of them, where I returned to the pertinent legal documents. I pretended to study them, paying strict attention all the while to what was being said between Alicia and Paco.

"Why do you do this thing to me, Alicia?" he asked her suddenly. I was right. He was smart. He had taken the initiative from her.

"Do what? What do you mean?"

"My uncle says you told him I made you pregnant."

"You did! You did!"

112

"What a thing! I've never been with you. You know that. At the Gallo I only go with Pilar or Juanita. So how could I make you pregnant?"

"You forgot the one time with me, then? I'm not surprised. They were both busy, and you were so drunk you said you didn't care who, or how, or—"

"Okay," he interrupted her. "Maybe it's possible it was just the way you said. Sometimes I get pretty drunk, I don't remember. But that's just *one* time—and you been with how many other men?"

"I asked the doctor about that, and he said it could only be you. Look, for nearly a week before that night I was off with the curse. That whole day it was slow, and I was only with you. And then, the day after I got word my mother was sick, and I went back home and stayed for almost three weeks. So the doctor says you gotta be the father."

All this was pretty farfetched, I admit, but it was the best I could come up with under the circumstances. Besides, we didn't really have to win a paternity suit. We just had to get Paco to let down his guard for a little while. Then, presumably, we would have him. I give Alicia credit, though. She told her story like she really believed it. In a way, I think she did. I was sure she would want to know just who the father of her child was—even if it were someone like Paco.

"That sounds pretty crazy to me, Alicia," he said at last.

I noticed that Paco's uncle had slipped out onto the porch to listen in. He had left the rifle in the house. That was a good sign.

Alicia glared at Paco as though he had just slapped her. "That's not crazy." She breathed it forth in a dramatic stage whisper. "It's the truth. My attorney said you would doubt me, and so we have—how do you say it?—alfa-davits from all the girls at the Gallo—including Pilar and Juanita. They know what I say is so. So does the doctor. He also made an alfa-davit."

"Affidavit."

"How?"

"Affidavit. That's how you say the word. I learned it from the *gringo* lawyer in Los Angeles."

"Okay. Af-fi-da-vit." She glared at him.

There was a long pause then. I was suddenly afraid we might lose him altogether, and so I tucked the papers back under my arm and covered the few feet that separated me from them in about two steps. "Well, *Señorita* Ramirez, are you satisfied you cannot negotiate a settlement with this man? Didn't I tell you that you were wrong to think you could?"

"How much?" said Paco rather suddenly.

So suddenly that it caught both Alicia and me off guard. Finally, waving the documents at him, I managed to fumble forth an answer: "We intend to sue for eighteen million pesos, and monthly support payments of—"

"But we'll settle for fifteen hundred dollars American," said Alicia. "A thousand for me and five hundred for the *coyote*."

"*Coyote?*" I yelped indignantly. "*Señorita* Ramirez—please!"

She dismissed me with a wave of her hand. "You can pay it, Paco. You spend almost that much some nights in the city."

"Maybe not that much, but sometimes a lot," Paco agreed. "But tell me, how can I pay you when the money I have is not here?" He turned back to the porch. "Right, uncle? No money here?"

"No," said his uncle. "No money here."

"I keep mine in a special place in the city," said Paco. This was going as I hoped it might. "But you think I should pay you just so you won't sue me? Maybe my uncle or my father will kill you; then you can't sue me. They kill a lot of people, those two old men."

"You don't scare me, Paco," said Alicia.

There was a strange fluttering buzz in the air. It sounded as though we were about to be set upon by a swarm of locusts.

"Why not? I think you should be scared. Listen, *chica*, you want me to go to town and pay money, right?"

114

"Right."

The noise was louder now. I managed to place the sound—and I didn't like it.

"Well, even if I wanted to—and maybe I don't—you came on the wrong day. I gotta go away today. Maybe I pay you something when I come back in a week or two weeks. Maybe fifteen hundred, maybe more. Who knows?"

I was right. It was a helicopter—a Hughes, like the ones I had seen them testing many times before down in the marshlands around Jefferson and Lincoln, beyond the Marina. It descended almost directly down upon us. Alicia, Paco, and I ran for the nearest cover—and that was the porch of the main house, where uncle stood slouching, indifferent to the racket and the dust stirred up by the helicopter's descent. He had been through it all before. I realized too late that Alicia and I were in a very bad position, for the helicopter was settling in the large open space that we had sauntered across a few minutes before. It came down directly between us and our Toyota Land Cruiser.

The pilot cut the engine, and at last the racket subsided and stopped. The door popped open then, and the first man out was Captain Ortega of the Federal Judiciary Police.

CHAPTER 10

As Ortega's cold eyes met mine, I found myself suddenly in a state of something quite near panic. My first impulse was to make a quick grab into Alicia's big handbag for the 9mm Heckler & Koch inside it. What would I have done with it? Start potting away at Ortega? Not after I saw the two uniformed *Féderales*—Alfonso Bedoya and his plump pal—jump down from the helicopter, each with an M-16 pointed in our general direction. There was nothing for me to do then but try to talk my way out of this one.

Could I fool him with my disguise? Had I altered my appearance that much? I glanced over at Alicia and found her looking at me, her eyes big with fear. I nodded and tried to force a reassuring smile. It didn't seem to bolster her a bit. She reached across, grabbed my hand, and squeezed tight. Then she let go.

Ortega walked straight over to me, shook his finger in my face, and said in English, "Meestair Cervantes, you are an ahss hool." So much for my disguise. Chico Cervantes, man of a thousand faces. I felt like Inspector Clouseau, looking at him through my lensless glasses. Maybe he was right. Maybe I *was* an ahss hool.

"Well," I said, "I tried."

"Yes, you tried. And that is why you are an ahss hool. I gave you a chance to get out of Sinaloa. And what do you do? You spit on it. So now, what do I do? I spit on you."

He did. It was a gobbet hacked up from his throat, and

propelled across the foot or so that separated us. It landed on my cheek. I wiped it off with the sleeve of that polyester suit jacket I was wearing. Not knowing quite what to show Ortega, I looked over at Alicia and again found her looking at me. She was shocked. Hell, so was I.

This was serious. I understood that. He had insulted me grossly—and now, if I were truly a man, I was expected to defend my honor. The old macho code of course—an eye for an eye and a testicle for a testicle. Yet if I made a move against him, so much as raised my hands at this point, I would be shot down on the spot. The two uniformed *Féderales* had their M-16's raised and trained on me now, just waiting for me to make my move.

I made it the only way I could. Sucking down a wad from my sinus, I brought it up to my tongue, and launched it into Ortega's smirking face. It landed half against the bridge of his nose and half into his left eye. At this point, we were even.

He shrieked—as though what I had spat at him had been pure molten lead. He shrank from me, taking a dramatic step or two back, wiping his eye with a clean white handkerchief, then pointed me out to his men. How could there be any confusion about whom he meant? "Take him inside," he said, "and I will teach him a few things. Then you can have the *puta* for yourselves."

I don't know why I did it—there was really no point to it at all—but I tried to resist. Maybe it was that last part about the *Féderales* having their fun with Alicia. I didn't like that. I didn't like it so much that I made a dive for Ortega, trying to bring him down to the dusty ground. I caught him at the shoulders, backing away. I didn't hit him with enough force to knock him down, and he was stronger than I expected. For a moment I was crouched over him, trying to wrestle him down with one arm and trying to gouge out his eye with the other. That was when the *Féderales* fell upon me. The two of them pummeled my head and shoulders with their rifle butts. I took four or five pretty healthy blows while my thumb dug pretty firmly into Ortega's eye, but that was all I could remember for a little while.

I must not have been completely out for much more than a few minutes. They had dragged me into the house and thrown me down on something that was a little more than a bed and a little less than a sofa. It seemed I could barely move my head because of the pain in it. But shifting carefully, I got a look at the door and saw Paco's uncle there. He was back on the job now, the AK-47 cradled in his arms. I lay there simply watching for quite some time. How long it may have been I really have no clear idea. I suppose I was in a semiconscious state. I saw Paco leave, a canvas traveling bag in his hand. Out on the porch he stopped and talked in low, serious tones to Ortega, who seemed to be having trouble with his eye. It seemed they talked for only a short time. Then Paco left, and a moment later I heard the helicopter take off.

All this I saw and heard, but somehow none of it really registered. It was a little like watching television with the sound switched off. Only the sound was on, all right—I could hear what was happening; it was just that I couldn't seem to make much sense of it. *I* was switched off.

Things began to fall into place. I remembered what had happened during those minutes between the arrival of the helicopter and my coming to consciousness here in this room. There was something about this place, something familiar. What was it? Risking it all, I pushed myself up to a sitting position and found that the pain was easier that way than it was lying down. I sat blinking, and then realized that the uncle was staring at me. He smiled in a way that was distinctly unfriendly.

"Hey, *gringo*," he said to me, "the Captain is very angry at you. You gonna die, you know that?"

I said nothing. Maybe I shrugged. A few moments later, the uncle turned away from me indifferently and took a step or two out onto the porch. I looked around the room, wondering if there was a back door to the place. But before I could get up and take a look, the uncle was back in the doorway, regarding me suspiciously. "It won't be long now," he promised. "Maybe you better say your prayers, *si*?" Laughing, he stepped out again onto the porch. He would be back in a moment. I knew that.

Along with everything else, there was this room—and the odd feeling it gave me that I had seen it before, been in it before. There were three windows cut into the adobe walls, and the ceiling was low—only about eight feet up from the floor—all of which meant the room was rather dark and gloomy. Most of the light seemed to be coming in through that open doorway where my guard now stood smiling at me. That, too, seemed familiar. I glanced up at the ceiling—well, you could hardly call it that. It was a mud-caulked plank roof up there, and I was simply looking at the bare underside of the planks, unpainted and otherwise unadorned. And then I heard something—or someone—in the doorway.

It was Ortega. He held a whispered conference with the old *pistolero* and ended it by looking at his watch and saying, ". . . only an hour more—then both of you come back." That ended it. The uncle disappeared then—evidently off in search of someone. Paco's father?

Ortega entered the room at a slow, solemn pace. The pistol he held in his hand, a .357 Colt Python, was pointed down at the floor but in plain sight. He seemed to be daring me to make a move. In his hand he held an unspoken promise to blow me apart if I should try. But then, as he came closer and was no longer just a dark silhouette in the sunlit doorway, I saw plainly that he was now wearing a gauze patch over one eye. Evidently I had done some damage there. Good.

He pulled over a straight-back chair and sat down opposite me, about ten feet away.

"You're gonna die," he said with a smirk.

"So I hear."

"Real slow. I shoot you in the belly, and then you roll around on the floor. Should take about an hour. If it goes longer than that, then I shoot you in the head. I only got an hour to watch you die."

I said nothing. That annoyed him.

"The *puta*, she die, too," he added. "Vasconcelos and López, they get to have some fun with her; then it's all over for her."

That got a rise out of me. "Look," I said, "is that necessary? I mean, she didn't play any real part in this. I just talked her into coming up here with me. I paid her a little money."

"A *little* money? That thousand-dollar reward, maybe? You think I don't know about that? That's a lot of money to her."

I decided to try to keep him talking as long as I could. What choice did I have? "How did you know we'd be up here?" I asked him.

"I didn't *know* that. I figure it out. I'm a pretty good detective, huh? I go to the FBI Academy in Virginia five years ago."

"Very impressive," I agreed, "but I thought we had your two guys fooled."

"Oh, you did. Vasconcelos and López, they are pretty good boys, but not so smart, you know? It was the girl at the Budget counter. You remember her? She remembered you from yesterday when you asked her about Keeney. Then she saw in the *noticía* this man had been murdered. You come through with policemen, and then you come back in disguise without them. She make two and two together and call the Federal Judiciary Police. Is a pretty smart girl, huh?"

"Yeah," I said, "pretty smart. From now on, Avis gets all my business."

"You ain' gonna have no more business to give, Cervantes. I take care of that."

"Uh . . ." I had to think of something to do, something to ask, something to distract him. "Uh . . . But how did you know we'd be coming up here?"

"Okay," said Ortega, "I get the tip, and then I drive to the airport to talk to her—and *then* I do the detective work. The Budget girl, she say you ask for a four-wheel-drive vehicle and she give you a Toyota. I tell her you are a big *contrabandista*, and I must chase you. She say, look in the Sierra. And I think, *where* in the Sierra? And I decide it must be here."

"Why? How did you know?"

"Because Paco is here." He said it with a shrug. What could be simpler?

"But how did you know I was after Paco? You said before that you thought I was smuggling, that Keeney was involved in it, too."

He gestured carelessly with his pistol. For the time being at least, he seemed more interested in talk than in murder. "That was just to scare you into going back to Los Angeles. Why don' you do that? Much better for you. But I *knew* you were here for Paco. I hear you coming down to get him."

"You mean me, personally, by name?"

"Sure."

"But how? Who? You're moving the shit in the coffins, aren't you? Was it somebody at the funeral home?"

"Hey! You're pretty good detective, too! I respect that. If you don' hurt my eye before, maybe I let you go. But I got to look out for my honor, you know?"

"Paco always drives the hearse?"

"Always."

"But why from Ensenada? Is it always from Ensenada?"

"Always from Ensenada for special reasons. It would take too long to explain now. You don' got that much time. Paco goes there now. We put him to work again—*puerco perezoso*."

I began measuring the distance between us, hoping that I was up to another dive across the room, wondering if it would do any good, knowing that I had no other chance. All this tumbled through my mind as I tried to think of some new line of questioning that would keep him talking. He seemed to be winding down. I felt I was losing him. It was then, in this mood of desperation, that I realized just what it was that was so familiar about this room in this crude adobe house up in the Sierra. This was the place in my dream, the room

121

where the spider had spun his web. The sunlight streamed in through the open door, just as before. There I sat, immobilized as in the dream, my panic mounting by the microsecond as Ortega shifted his chair a bit toward me and brought up his pistol so that it was pointed directly at me. The spider was advancing on me now, as mean and deadly as in my dream, and I felt as helpless now as I had before.

"I think maybe we through talking now," said Ortega.

"Just one more question," I said. I *had* to think of something.

But just then from outside, there was a sudden pop. We both heard it. Although it did not sound terribly loud or lethal, we both knew it sounded like a gunshot. Ortega frowned and glanced briefly away, then came back to me, uneasy but determined to ignore it.

"Just one more question," I insisted.

"What is it?"

There were two more pops, each a little louder than the first.

I tensed, hunching forward slightly, as he glanced away again. I sensed that he might get up and walk to the door. Instead, he returned to me, this time raising the pistol to a rough sight at my middle.

"Why are you sending Paco back if you know there's a warrant out on him?"

A figure appeared in the doorway, silhouetted in the sunlight. Size—shape—skirt—Alicia. Just as I recognized her, she raised her arm, and a number of things happened at once:

Ortega turned back toward the door. She had made no noise that I had heard, but her sudden appearance must have altered the level of light in the dim room. Maybe he noticed that. Or maybe he was just uneasy. Anyway, he turned—and this time the Colt Python in his hand turned with him, moving away from me.

Alicia fired twice at Ortega from where she stood in the doorway. I heard both shots—hard, flat reports and not great roaring explosions—and I think I saw the muzzle flash on the first of them.

But I can't be sure, because by that time I had taken my leap at Ortega. He had swung his pistol in her direction. I hit him just as he fired, knocking him over and off the chair. The Colt blammed loudly. The bullet must have smacked harmlessly high into the far wall up near the ceiling.

All this happened, as I said, more or less simultaneously. And I can't tell you how long Ortega and I rolled around on the floor, fighting for his gun. It seemed like minutes, but it was probably a matter of seconds. I strained at his wrist with both hands, trying to slam down the hand that held the pistol hard enough that he would let it go. His free hand was digging into my face, his forefinger poked into my eye, his thumb in my mouth, his nail shredding my gums. Then I unclenched my teeth and bit down hard on his thumb. He shrieked, then heaved, then managed to tumble half-out from under me and swing the pistol down to where he might be able to do some harm to me. Our faces just then were very close together. I remember the intensity in his eye as he strained, and I remember the set of his jaw, that awful grimace of effort. I remember it all—just how that face looked the moment before it seemed to come apart before my eyes.

This time it *was* a roar I heard, for Alicia had leaned down over us and discharged the HK into the side of his head from a point that was about six inches from my ear.

As Ortega went limp in my arms, Alicia dropped the Heckler & Koch she had used to the floor. It was a dangerous thing to do. On one occasion I saw a pistol go off when it fell. This time we were lucky. She staggered, threw herself down on the bed-sofa where I had been sitting a few moments before, and then she began to weep uncontrollably.

Struggling a bit, I managed to extricate myself from the embrace of the corpse. Then I scrambled to my feet, picked up the HK, and carefully drew the Colt Python from Ortega's hand. I went over to Alicia.

She was disheveled, of course. Her blouse top was ripped almost from her shoulder. But her face showed a deeper hurt. Puffed, her mouth twisted in an agony of strain and shock, her eyes streaming tears, she seemed near hysteria. But I had to get her out of there. I hoped I could make her understand that.

"Alicia," I said as gently as I was able, "can you walk? I'll help you. We've got to get out of here before anybody comes. Do you hear me?"

She sobbed, gulped, and nodded.

I helped her to her feet. I tucked the Colt in my belt and held on to the HK with my right hand. With my left, I supported her as we made our way to the door.

"Quiet now." I left her a moment near the door, keeping her hand clasped in mine as I strained forward to scout the territory outside. What I saw made me jerk back quickly and hope I had not been seen.

"Go!" I whispered urgently. "Lie flat on the floor there in the corner. Now, move!" She did as she was told, and I wondered for a moment as I glanced after her if I should have given her one of the pistols. Then I immediately decided that she was in no condition to use one now, anyway.

What I had seen were two figures at the far end of the small open field near the Toyota. They were hurrying toward the house, and both were armed with long, wicked-looking assault rifles. Probably Paco's uncle and father. When I took another quick look, there was just one—and he was much, much closer now. I chose the darkest corner I could find near the door and waited. I knew I had only a few seconds.

But that few seconds stretched into nearly a minute. I waited, and then I heard from just outside the door a cautious call, "Hey, *Capitán*, you in there? Are you okay?"

Silence, followed by more silence.

Followed by a sudden stream of fire from the AK-47 on full automatic. He must have fired half a clip through the open door. But he got what he wanted: from her corner, Alicia let out a scream that ended in a whimper.

"Hey, Arcadio," he called out. "Here! They're in here!"

I looked across the room at Alicia and decided she'd be safe if she stayed where she was. He would have to lean inside to shoot in her direction. And if he did that, I had him.

Suddenly, the shuttered window on the far side of the door burst open. The barrel of the assault rifle came pushing through, and the rest of the clip was emptied blindly with no damage to anything but the adobe walls of the place.

I heard a voice, muffled and indistinct, that seemed to come from someplace above. But where?

Then, in answer, from outside the door: "No, not yet. I'm still changing the clip on this thing."

That's what he was doing, all right—I was *almost* sure. But I was unwilling to stick my head out and take a pot shot at him in order to be *absolutely* certain. They might be waiting just for that, weapons zeroed in and ready to let go at first sight. I waited.

There was a whistle then—and a short burst through the window. At the same time, I felt, rather than heard, footsteps on the roof—someone moving slowly and carefully, trying not to be heard. So that was their strategy. The one at the window would keep our heads down, while the man on the roof went for—what? A trapdoor over one of the bedrooms? A skylight someplace in back? I had to make my move quickly.

I blessed myself and inched along the wall toward the door. In that space of time, the man on the roof took three quiet steps—but not quiet enough. I knew right where he was at that moment. Standing flat against the rough, mud wall, next to the open door now, I was barely breathing as I waited for the next, and climactic, scene to begin.

When the next short burst came through the window, I leaped through the door. I had to shoot first at a specific spot—I couldn't go looking around for him. I was betting he'd be down under the window.

I landed in a crouch, and holding the HK with both arms extended, I put three rounds right below the open shutters. It was lucky for me that Paco's papa was there to take them in the neck and chest.

He slumped and never got off a shot. Was he dead? I couldn't tell—and I hadn't time to check. I grabbed the AK-47 from his arms and ran back into the house.

Standing in the center of the room, I listened for footsteps on the plank roof. Glancing over at Alicia in the corner, I saw that she was now sitting up, alert and in control. Our eyes met. She nodded solemnly and pointed to an area of the ceiling about six feet away from me. I nodded and moved to that spot on tiptoe, holding the assault rifle carefully at port arms.

As I took position, I looked back at Alicia for confirmation. I pointed above with the rifle, and she nodded. Her hands were over her ears: she knew what was coming.

Two more quiet steps above us. I tracked with them below, and realizing that in another moment they would carry me out of this room to the back of the house, I decided it was time to let go. I did—on full automatic, half a clip—up through the planks. Who could tell how many? Fifteen? Twenty? The thing did a deadly buck-dance in my hands, making a terrible racket in the enclosed space, scattering shell casings all over the floor.

At the end of the clip, as the roar echoed around us, there was an awful thud on the roof. There is no way of faking a deadfall like that. But I had to be sure. Carefully measuring off the space, I laid the AK-47 down and pulled the Colt Python out from my belt. Then I put four rounds into the ceiling just where his trunk should have been.

As it turned out, I figured it about right.

I'll tell you something. Keeney was right about me. I am gun-shy. As a matter of fact, I left the LAPD following an incident in which it was judged I had used insufficient force in making an arrest. You don't hear about cases like that so often, do you? My partner and I were making a burglary pinch. I was backing him up in a stakeout at an appliance store. The perpetrator entered through a rear window, and when he was surprised by my partner, he let him have it with the crowbar he had jimmied his way in with. I come on the scene, see him beating on my partner, and try to tackle him and wrestle him to the ground. Oh, we subdued him, all right—but my partner had a concussion and I got a broken clavicle out of it. Why didn't I just pull my trusty .38 special and fire a shot? Maybe it's because when I was young and eager, in my second year on the Force, I fired what I intended to be a warning shot at a twenty-year-old purse-snatcher and shot him in the ass, came within an inch of crippling him for life. Those things stay with you.

I guess in a situation like we had up there on the mountain, you do what you have to do. Alicia and I had no reason to celebrate. We were alive. We hadn't won. We had survived.

The body count was five. Thank God I didn't have to dispatch any wounded. I doubt that I could have done it. As I checked the two *Féderales*, and later asked Alicia a few questions, I got a picture of what had happened in that storage shed where they had taken her.

She had kept that big purse of hers firmly in hand—even held tight to it when Vasconcelos, the Alfonso Bedoya lookalike, had thrown her down on the floor of the shed, pulled up her skirt, and made ready to rape her. While he was on top of her and occupied with that, she managed to find the Heckler & Koch automatic in her handbag, and even had the presence of mind to take off the safety catch. Then, when his face came down close to hers, she eased the HK out, jammed it under his jaw, and pulled the trigger. She blew the top of his head off.

The fat *Féderal* was so amazed at what he saw when he came to the door of the shed that he was an easy target. She put two into his chest at point-blank range.

I had to admit to myself that she was really something. There weren't many other women who could have done it—

who would have even tried. She told me later that her grandfather, who was a veteran of the Obregón part of the Revolution, had taken her out a couple of times to teach her to shoot a pistol, but she hadn't liked it, so she quit. That was when she was fourteen years old. You never know when things you learn as a kid will come in handy later on.

I was quite a figure, coming out of a firefight in an overstuffed polyester suit, looking twenty years older and a quarter again my normal weight. I took off those clothes and put on the jeans and shirt I had used as padding. I told Alicia to put on the other outfit she had brought along. I dressed Paco's father in the suit and pulled him inside the big house. Then I took a fuel can from their Land Rover and spread gas through the big house and all the sheds, leaving a trail between each one. I pulled the Land Rover clear and told Alicia to get inside, then I lit the gasoline fuse I had made, and watched each building catch fire. I took the tranquilizer gun out of the Toyota, and we drove off and left the Toyota up there on the mountain. Maybe this way they would think I was dead.

By the time we reached the main road at Bocalobo, it was dark. By the time we were a mile out of town, Alicia was asleep.

CHAPTER 11

"Just what the goddam hell do you expect *me* to do about it?" Madden sounded angry. His round, red face had gone livid. But I decided that in spite of all his bluster, he was just plain scared. "You think I'm going up there on my own and just happen to 'find' the bodies? Do you?"

"Hey," I urged, "take it easy—okay? You're going to wake her up." Alicia was still fast asleep in the front seat of the Land Rover.

"I don't care if I *do*!" He practically shouted at me. "What's she done for me—except give me a whole lot more trouble than I can handle?"

Madden made a quick tour of his veranda. He jammed his hands down into his pockets as he started back again, now simply pacing about aimlessly in frustration. This had been building in him since he had opened up the peephole in his door and spotted me outside. It was dark, and it was late. When he opened the door and heard the details of what had happened up there in the Sierra, he seemed merely surprised at first. As he grasped the implications of what I told him, his surprise turned to agitation, his agitation to worry, and almost immediately his worry gave way to fear. And that was just about where we were when he began careering miserably about his front porch.

He suddenly whirled and advanced on me, shaking his finger accusingly. "You know what's going to happen, don't you?

Tomorrow—tomorrow evening at the latest—the *Féderales* are going to start wondering what happened to their boss, and they're going to fly up in that helicopter and take a look around. And you know what they're going to find."

"Yeah," I said. "Some charred remains."

"You think they won't be able to figure out what happened?"

"Well, they might think the competition moved in on them."

"Huh-uh," said Madden with a great air of finality. "There is no competition."

"Not even anybody with ambitions?"

"Not that I know of—not in Sinaloa. Besides, if it was something like that, the last thing they would have done was burn those sheds with all that unprocessed product in them."

"You think I should have *left* them? I thought you were the guy who was out to rid the world of Mexican brown."

"Well . . . no. No, of course I don't think you should have left the stuff. I'm just trying to point out to you the flaw in your thinking."

Jesus, I thought, scratch a Drug Enforcement agent, and you'll find a Washington bureaucrat. I might have burned up a year's worth of poppies in those sheds, but all that Madden was concerned about was covering his ass. He had disappointed me just a little. "Okay, look," I said to him, "I realize this leaves you in a situation that's not completely favorable. You're right. They may try to hang it on me, and they can put you with me. But they've got to explain what Ortega was doing up there in the Sierra. You think any of the young sharks here are interested in following up on these details—or will they just be out for Ortega's job?"

Madden hesitated. At last he shrugged and shook his head. "I don't know," he said. "Maybe you're right. Maybe it'll all get buried."

"And maybe I'm wrong. Listen, whatever happens, my advice to you is to jump on the first plane to Mexico City tomorrow, sit down with your boss there, and tell him all you know about this—what I told you, everything. Go on record and get transferred."

"Yeah . . . yeah, I guess you're right."

"Just one more thing I want from you."

"What's that?"

"What's the name of the pilot you lined up for me, and how do I get hold of him?"

Madden was suddenly stricken once again. "Jesus, I forgot about that completely! It's going to look like I set up your getaway."

"You did. Who is he? Where can I find him?"

I wouldn't let him off the hook. He squirmed and weaseled and even tried to talk me into driving for the border in the Land Rover. I kept after him, told him he was chickenshit, and used some other subtle psychological ploys like that. He finally relented and gave me the pilot's name and telephone number. I pushed past Madden, walked into his house, and found the phone.

The pilot's name was Anselmo. He had an old Beechcraft Bonanza, which he assured me was in good enough condition to make the border crossing anyplace from El Paso to San Diego. I told him that was fine but we would talk about destination once we were in the air. We agreed to meet in half an hour at the far end of the airport, away from the commercial traffic. That was where he kept the plane.

Madden had been watching me anxiously throughout my conversation on the telephone with the pilot. When I hung up, he clapped his hands in a kind of bluff and hearty gesture of finality. "Well," he said, "that's it, huh?" He obviously wanted to get rid of me.

That was all right with me. I had no wish to stay. "Yeah, that's it," I said. Then I wiggled my finger around the room. "At least you're not going to feel like you're a prisoner here anymore, huh?"

"No," he said glumly, "not here."

* * *

She began to stir the moment I pulled away from Madden's place. It wasn't long before she was sitting up in her seat, regarding me rather suspiciously.

"Where you going now?" Alicia asked. We had almost reached the plaza.

"Well, *I'm* going out to the airport and get a plane to Ensenada, but first I'm going to drop you off at the Gallo."

"Oh, no."

"Oh, yes. Don't worry, you'll get your money. You've . . . you've earned it." The understatement of the year.

"How you pay me now?"

"I've got a thousand in traveler's checks. I'll just sign five hundred over to you, and you can present them at the bank in the morning."

"They give me five hundred dollars American?"

"No, they'll pay you in pesos. A Mexican bank can't pay you in dollars."

"Then I wait and go to a North American bank. Pesos are like water. They run through your fingers."

So we were back to the fantasy again. I slowed at a corner and came out on the plaza. Just across it lay the Hotel Conquistador, and a couple of blocks beyond that the Gallo Inmortal on Acapulco. It was late on a Monday night—getting on toward midnight—and there was no traffic to speak of, so I simply pulled over to the curb to have this out with her. "Look," I said, "you told me yourself that Hollywood was a fantasy. You've been good. You've been wonderful. What can I say? You saved my life up there, and I thank you for that. But I've already put you in much danger, and I don't intend to put you in any more."

She studied me for a moment, and then began speaking patiently, the way you might talk to a child: "Chico, tell me this. Is there more danger for me in Ensenada—or Los Angeles, if I get that far—or *here* in Culiacan? Where is it more dangerous for me, uh? The *Féderales* know I am with you. I change five hundred dollars from your checks into pesos, and then they find what we left up in the Sierra. You think they don't bring me in to talk about that? If they bring me in, you think I come out again? You tell me Chico, where is it more dangerous for me?"

What could I say? What could I do? I sighed. If Madden was worried, and obviously he was, she had every reason to be even more concerned. Alicia Ramirez lacked the backing of the Drug Enforcement Agency and the United States government. What, really, could happen to Madden? He would get moved. Alicia might get dead. "All right," I said at last, "Ensenada it is. We'll talk about the rest of it there."

The road out to the airport was practically deserted. I had traveled it often enough in the last thirty hours that it had begun to look familiar to me. I knew, for instance, that there was a Pemex station right around the next bend, and after that I'd see the lights of the airport.

That was how it was, and the runway lights were still on. Thank God for that. I had been half-afraid that the place would be shut down for the night. Anselmo had said it would be open—and he ought to know. I followed the directions he had given me, turning in at a road beyond the entrance drive to the general aviation side. Up the road there were a few rickety hangars and what looked like a warehouse of some sort, and finally a gate in a wire fence that barred access to the runway area where the Beechcraft Bonanza was moored. I could see it there illuminated in the Land Rover's lights, just beyond the locked gate. There was something more revealed in the headlights, something that brought me suddenly aware of certain possibilities I had been offered by fate: on the other side of Anselmo's plane was a Hughes helicopter like the one that brought Ortega and his two men into the Sierra and had ferried Paco out; in fact, judging from its markings, it was the very *same* helicopter.

I glanced at my watch. We were early. Anselmo had agreed

to meet me here at the gate at midnight. That meant that if he was on time, I had ten minutes to make some repairs on that chopper.

"Wait here for me," I said to Alicia. "Just stay in the car." I dug the tool kit out of the rear—it proved just as complete as you'd expect a Land Rover's tool kit to be—and tossed it over the fence. I followed it over, managing to hook my pants leg once in the process. Then, working quickly by the lights of the car, I loosened every bolt and screw I could find in the vicinity of the helicopter's rear rotor. By the time I finished with it, I suspected the chopper would get no more than ten or twelve feet off the ground before the entire rear assembly would rattle itself apart. And that would probably give us the better part of a day's lead on them.

It was a quarter after twelve when Anselmo showed up in an old Mercedes with a teenage boy who turned out to be his son. I had advised him to bring along somebody he could trust to drive off the Land Rover and ditch it far from the airport. Alicia and I retrieved her luggage, and at the last minute I managed to remember the tranquilizer gun—again tucked under the seat. I handed over the keys to the boy, and Anselmo sent him off with a sharp admonishment not to take it out for a ride. The way that the boy grinned back at him I made a bet with myself that the Land Rover would have an empty tank when the *Féderales* found it.

"You think it will be all right?" I asked the pilot as the boy barreled off into the night. "The car is hot, worse than hot."

"The kid steals cars all the time," said Anselmo. "He'll take that one out on the back roads and try out the four-wheel drive. In his own way, he's got some sense. He knows where the cops are—and where they aren't."

I shrugged and decided to be satisfied with that.

He looked curiously at Alicia, and I mumbled some sort of introduction. She shrugged, and we followed him through the now-unlocked gate.

"You think I can get some respect from that boy? You think my own son will do what I tell him to do?" He grumbled as he snapped the padlock on the gate. "He's my oldest, too. I've got five more kids just like him. Boys or girls, it doesn't matter. You get no respect from either. I've got a bad ten years ahead of me, I'll tell you that."

"Did you file a flight plan?" I asked him.

"How not? You have to tell them you're headed someplace. I hear from Madden it's for the border. You taking the girl over? I know a good, safe field outside Douglas—if that's not too far from where you're headed."

The three of us started for the plane. He led the way.

"This reminds me of the old days," he said. "Before Ortega showed up here I used to make two, maybe three trips to the border a week. All fixed up. He comes along—no more private enterprise. He got everything sewed up."

"We're not headed for the border," I said.

"Sensemilla mostly," he continued. "The regular stuff, it's not worth putting on a plane, you know? Ah, but the money was good! Those were good times, *mano*."

Had he heard me? I wasn't sure. "We're headed for Ensenada," I said.

He opened up the Beechcraft. Alicia and I struggled inside. She sat in back with her bag, and I took the place next to the pilot. We watched him loose the moorings and kick out the wheel chocks.

"He's a strange one," said Alicia.

"A little strange," I agreed. "But you're not?"

She looked at me sharply and seemed about to say something. Then she turned away with a scowl and concentrated on Anselmo, who was now on his way back.

He jumped into the seat beside me. "You ask me," he said, "that's what's wrong with Mexico today."

He said it with such certainty and finality that I thought for a moment it should be obvious to me what was wrong with Mexico today. (What's wrong? Take your pick.) I decided at last he was looking for a straight line. "Okay," I said, "what *is* wrong?"

He started up the engine. It caught, reassuringly, on the

second try. "What's wrong with Mexico," he said, giving the engine full throttle, "is no more private enterprise. Or not enough of it. If it's not for taxes, it's for *mordida*. Do I make myself clear?"

"Oh, very."

"If it's not a government enterprise, it's somebody like Ortega, who sews everything up. In the old days, before he got here, and before the DEA came, we all had a good thing, you know? We join in the profits—a little here, a little there. Is good for the economy, true?"

"Oh, true. Without question."

Anselmo revved the engine, then began to taxi the plane forward. He flipped a switch and began talking indifferently to Culiacan tower, identifying himself, requesting permission to take off. There was a lapse in response—as though whoever was on duty in the tower was alone and half-asleep. At last the voice from the tower came through, rasping and petulant at the unexpected interruption. Permission was given to take off. A runway was designated. Reluctantly, it seemed, a safe journey was wished.

Anselmo followed instructions. We bounced for some distance over the turf and sandy soil until at last we found our way to the blacktop runway. He found his position a little ahead, came to a complete halt, revved his engine once again, and with a final word from the tower, we lurched forward, gathering speed on the blacktop, hurtling along past the runway lights.

He nosed the plane up, and suddenly the stars erupted in all their glory against the inky blue-black of that Mexican night. You can walk around all evening and never look up long enough to notice the fireworks above you, but when you're in the cabin of a light plane climbing up to five thousand feet, you can't ignore it. It's like you were blasting off for the moon, and in a minute or two more you expect to be up there among those twinkling jewels in the sky. There's nothing quite like it.

I turned back to Alicia to comment and found her white-knuckled, tense, and trembling. It hadn't occurred to me to ask, and she had said nothing, but this was obviously the first time she had flown. Would she relax? Could she? Not likely—until we had reached our flight altitude and were well on our way. I reached back, grasped her hand, and gave it a gentle squeeze. Our eyes met. There was something close to terror in hers. I gave another squeeze, and she held tight to my hand.

"Okay," said Anselmo, "where we headed?"

I was right. He hadn't heard me. He hadn't paid any attention. So what? "To Ensenada," I said. Just so he knew how to get there.

He surprised me by suddenly laughing out loud at that.

"What's so funny?" I asked.

"It's the second time today," he said, then amended that with a shrug: "Well, let's say it's the second time in twenty-four hours."

A light went off in my head. What was the best way to play this? "You don't mean to tell me," I said, after a moment's hesitation, "that you're the guy who flew Paco out there earlier today?"

"Sure," said Anselmo, "just like always."

"We're supposed to meet him there."

He glanced at me dubiously. "Really?"

"Sure. Why not?"

He shrugged, making a show of indifference. "As you say."

"When did he arrive?"

"Around seven. I had to turn right around and come back here to pick you up. I promised Madden I'd be ready for you around midnight. That's a lot of flight time for me in one day."

"Clearly. For anyone."

I glanced back at Alicia to get her reaction to this and found there was none. Still holding tight to my hand, she sat erect with her eyes now shut tight and seemed to be whispering something to herself. Of course she was praying. She didn't seem to be airsick, thank God—just terrified.

I turned back to Anselmo. He was in the process of lighting

a long, dark Havana cigar. With all the cigar smoke in this close little cabin, he might make her sick yet. I leaned toward him and said quietly, "Have you got something for her in case she should . . . you know." He glanced at me, and I mimed a gag, letting my tongue loll out.

My performance amused him. He laughed, pointing at a compartment at knee height just below the instrument panel. "Sure," he said, "you got to be prepared. Paco, he always gets sick. You never know, uh?"

I popped open the compartment door and found a package of extra-size Baggies inside. Just the thing, of course—light, strong, and easily disposed of. Taking one from the package just to have it ready, I shut the compartment back up. We had evidently reached our flight altitude. Anselmo eased the controls forward, and we leveled out. This might make things a little easier for Alicia.

"I thought back there on the ground you said Ortega had cut you off," I said. "You said it was better in the old days."

"*Hombre!*" he protested. "What can I say? He tosses me a few things now and then. Believe me, it *was* better in the old days."

"So you take Paco to Ensenada now and then?"

"As you say."

"How often? Once a month?"

"It used to be. Now not so often. It's been a couple of months since his last trip."

"That's why we're traveling there."

Anselmo looked at me curiously. "Why is that?"

"To get to Paco," I said. "We got special instructions for him from Ortega."

"You're with Ortega?"

"Clearly."

He was silent for a moment. "Two things occur to me."

"And what are they?"

"First, if you work for Ortega, why was it that the North American, Madden, set up this trip?"

"What makes you think Madden isn't working for him, too?"

"He's too worried," said Anselmo. "He's worried all the time."

"*Hombre*," I said, "tell me something."

"Anything. I am a sincere man."

"I believe it. But hear me. You say you work for Ortega yourself from time to time."

"In a small way, yes."

"Not so small, I think. You must have guessed what Paco carries with him to Ensenada."

"Well . . ."

"And you are very well paid for these trips?"

He smiled crookedly and puffed on his cigar. "Well . . ."

"You do all right. No so much action as in the old days, but the money is there, uh?"

"Well . . ." A wink.

"All right. I work for him myself at the other end in Los Angeles, so I know the answer to the question I am going to ask, but I must hear it from you. Tell me, you work for him, you are well paid, but isn't it true that he worries you?"

"Well . . ." He was uneasy now.

"He worries me. How not? He must worry you."

"All right, agreed. He worries me."

"And he also worries Madden. You agree?"

"Okay. I accept what you say."

There were suspicious noises from the seat in the rear. I glanced back at Alicia. She looked queasy.

"Then there is the second thing that occurs to me," Anselmo put in.

I handed the Baggie to her. "What is that?" I asked him.

Her eyes were open now. She took it without quite knowing why I had given it to her. Again, I mimed a gag and let my tongue loll out. She nodded. She understood.

"If you're working for Ortega, and I'm working for Ortega, then I probably said some things against him that I shouldn't have. You understand?"

"Believe me," I said reassuringly, "anybody who works for him thinks these things—and worse. He is a hard man. Don't concern yourself with what I might say to him about you. I will say nothing."

With that came the miserable sound of retching from the rear. I didn't bother to look back.

CHAPTER 12

The sky behind us was graying to dawn as we descended through the mountains to Ensenada. Ahead of us, to the west, the sky was still dark, and the ocean below it an inky and limitless expanse of black. Anselmo called into the tower and got permission to land. The airport lights, which had been visible at some distance, seemed to separate and break pattern as we drew closer and lower, until down among them, banking for our approach, they exploded around us in a sudden rush and flurry of color. It was only then, with light flooding the cabin of the plane, that Alicia began at last to stir behind me.

She had been asleep ever since being sick, almost four hours before. I had managed to grab a couple of hours sleep during the flight. Before I dropped off, Anselmo and I had talked on and off, around and about. We had a good stretch of time, so I hadn't forced it, didn't try to pump him for all he knew at once. But gradually, bit by bit, I got most of it, I think. He was bored. He wanted to talk. I wanted to listen.

Here was Anselmo Quiñones, a veteran of the Mexican Air Force, disqualified, for some uncertain reason, for employment with Mexicana. (Maybe he didn't test out right—or maybe, as he insisted, he didn't have the right connections.) He was an experienced pilot, on the scene and available when, back in the sixties, dope became the major export of the state of Sinaloa. He had been doing pretty well ever since. By his own admission, he had a Swiss bank account (small, as Swiss bank accounts go), a Porsche that he drove on weekends, and a moderately expensive mistress. If his income had declined slightly since Ortega came in with poppy seed and reorganized things, at least he was still working. Which, he assured me, was more than you could say for most of the growers up there in the Sierra that he used to do business with.

"But not for Paco—and his father and uncle?" I had put in quickly.

"*Hombre!* You make a joke, uh? Those two old *banditos*, they come out on top, no matter what! And Paco? Let me tell you something about Paco, that kid isn't so stupid!"

"Not so stupid, maybe," I said doubtfully, "but a *borracho*—or so I have heard." Let him convince me otherwise: that was my strategy.

It worked. Anselmo spent the better part of an hour telling me all about Paco. He insisted that he had come to know him well on these flights to Ensenada. Maybe he did drink a little too much, a common failing, but he was ambitious: "You give him time, and before you know it, we'll all be working for him. Don't tell Ortega what I say, though." And intelligent: "He has good English, that kid. We practice together. On this last flight—today, yesterday, I lose track—we speak only English with each other. He says he's getting ready to make his move."

All very interesting, of course, but very puzzling. If Paco knew English, then why didn't he use it that night on the Marina Freeway? Was he too drunk to remember the right words? Or was he smart enough to play dumb?

Anselmo rattled on, praising his prodigy, describing how he always reported for duty dressed in a suit, wearing a tie, looking as rich as any *Norteamericano* you ever saw. In fact, he liked to play the American at every opportunity. On a couple of occasions Anselmo had laid over in Ensenada and spent some time there with Paco, and together they played the game, putting up at a tourist hotel, making the rounds of the American bars and restaurants along Lázaro Cárdenas, smiling and flirting their way through Hussong's, even scoring with a few

California blondes. "That kid," said Anselmo, with a respectful shake of his head, "he never stops."

By the time he had finished, I had a good idea of where to look for Paco, how to approach him, in what way he might be most vulnerable. The only thing I wasn't able to squeeze from Anselmo was the name and exact location of the funeral parlor that had to be the center of the Ensenada operation. I couldn't ask him outright because I had to pretend to know it myself. About all I got out of him was a couple of veiled references to "that place up the hill."

The moment our wheels touched the ground, Alicia let out a fearful "*Ay!*" from the back of the plane.

I glanced back and saw by the weird illumination of the runway lights that her eyes were wide, but she seemed a bit more in control of herself. I nodded encouragingly. "It's all right now. We made it."

Anselmo taxied the Beechcraft in an easy route around the field. I was surprised to see that most of the planes on the ground were military aircraft, many of World War II vintage. I asked him about this.

"Sure," he said. "It's a Mexican Air Force base. It's okay for civil and commercial, though."

As if to confirm this surprising bit of news, a guard in gray-blue emerged from the terminal building as we pulled up slowly and came to a halt there. He wore a helmet and carried a carbine slung over his shoulder.

"You mean Paco moves the stuff through an Air Force base?"

"How not? As long as the way is prepared, there can be no problem."

Anselmo had another surprise for me. After I paid him the two hundred fifty dollars we had agreed upon, he announced that as soon as he gassed up the plane he would be heading back to Culiacan. With that, he reached into his flight jacket and produced a handful of capsules. "Uppers," he said in English. Only it came out something like "Ooppairs." He popped a couple into his mouth and offered the rest to me with a wink.

I took the capsules and pocketed them. Alicia stared at me with undisguised disapproval. "What's in them?" I asked.

"Two kinds of speed. My special recipe. It'll wake you up."

"I'll bet it will." I threw open the cabin door and scrambled out, assisting Alicia after me, and hauling out her bag. Then I leaned in, offering Anselmo my hand, thanking him for a safe journey.

"It's nothing. You were a good companion. Remember me to Paco."

It took the better part of an hour and five dollars to get from the airbase to the hotel—just three or four miles away. The guard assured us there were no taxis to be had at this hour, but it seemed he had a brother-in-law who had a VW. He might be persuaded, if we made it worth his while . . .

The sun was rising as we rattled along in the back of the Beetle on our way into Ensenada. At places along the way, thin men in dirty, dusty clothes, and women a bit better dressed, stood leaning in this direction and that, waiting for transportation into town. Off to the right, hanging over the horizon, was a cloud that turned out to be smog from some big smokestack operation. Even here.

We circled a statue of Lázaro Cárdenas. What had he done for Ensenada to deserve both a statue and a boulevard? But our hotel—big and sprawling in the American style—turned out to be on Avenida López Mateos. How they love their presidents, these people without politics.

The guy at the front desk didn't like us. I could tell that the moment we walked in. Not that I blamed him. Alicia looked all right—as a matter of fact, she was looking better to me each time I glanced at her—but in my jeans and shirt and straw sombrero, I must have seemed to him a little too much like those *pobrecitos* I had seen along the side of the road. He addressed me in Spanish, and I answered in English. It seemed pretty doubtful that there were any rooms left in the hotel until I produced my American Express card.

"Imprint only," I said in my gruffest and most authoritative voice. "I'll be paying in cash." I had a few things to straighten out with the Budget corporation and the Mexican police. I didn't even want to think about it now, but I knew enough not to leave a trail of charges.

"As you wish, *señor*."

Filling out the registration card, I looked up, fixed him with a severe stare, and said in that same gruff tone, "I was to meet a friend of mine here. He may have registered last night."

He dragged out the box of registration cards. "What is his name?"

"Francisco Cruz-Rivera."

"Ah, yes." He pushed the box aside. "Room 125."

He had me puzzled. "Do you know all your guests' rooms so well?"

"No, *señor*, but just an hour ago I assisted *Señor* Cruz-Rivera to his room. He was in no condition to find it alone."

I flashed Alicia a knowing look for the benefit of the desk clerk and said to her in Spanish, "Ah, that Paco. He's up to his old tricks."

"*Borracho*," she said with a show of distaste.

We were the first in the dining room for breakfast. As we ate, I told her what I had heard from Anselmo on the flight from Culiacan. She was unimpressed. "He's still a drunk," she said, dismissing him with a wave of her hand.

"But maybe he's a drunk who's smarter than most people think."

She shrugged. "Maybe."

In the room I peeled down to my shorts and climbed into one of the two double beds, determined to get some sleep. From what the desk clerk had told us, Paco would be out for half a day, anyway. The drapes were drawn. The lights were off. My eyes were shut. But nothing happened. My mind kept rerunning that firefight up in the Sierra. Jesus, Mary, and Joseph, all my years with the LAPD, and I'd never been through anything like that before—not Watts, not the SLA shootout, nothing at all like it. I'd never killed anyone before, never come so close to getting killed myself.

I became aware of Alicia moving quietly around the room. Then she sat down on the other bed. I don't know that I actually heard her. I just sensed her near me and realized she was there. Without turning to her, or opening my eyes, I said, "You ought to try to get some sleep, too. We don't know how long we'll be going once we start chasing Paco."

"I'm not sleepy. I sleep too much already."

"Yes, you've been out most of the time since . . . since the shooting." I turned over and went up on an elbow and took a look at her. As well as I could see in the half-light there in the room, she didn't appear to be nervous, just thoughtful.

"I was frightened," she said. "I've never been so frightened. I'm all right now, though."

"Yes, I can tell that." She glanced across at me. There was a slight frown on her face. "You were terrific up there," I told her quietly. "You saved my life, you know."

"I saved my own. They would have killed me, too. They were bad."

"Yes," I agreed.

With a sigh, she stood up. "I think I take a bath now. Maybe then I can sleep, too."

I felt a sudden alarm at that. Why? And then I realized what had happened the last time she went to take a bath in a hotel room.

"Hey," I called after her, "if you find any bodies in the bathroom, remember I'm trying to sleep. Just tell the manager."

"*Ay!*" she cried with a throaty laugh. "I promise."

I rolled over and played dead—but once again, it didn't really work for me. This time, instead of replaying *The Sands of Iwo Jima* or *The Wild Bunch*, or whatever the hell it was,

I got involved in reviewing the case. What a disaster! I had never worked so sloppy in my life. What was the body count so far? Five—no, six. Don't forget Keeney. And what was this "so far" business? Somehow, it was true, I sensed there would be more before it was all over. What was the matter with me? I quit reading Mickey Spillane when I was a kid.

I listened to the water running in the bathroom, gratefully distracted from my self-recriminations. Imagining her. She would be sitting on the side of the tub now, watching the water bubbling out from the faucet.

Then suddenly, though not unexpectedly, it shut off, and I was pulled into a fantasy. I saw her stripping off what she wore, piece by piece. I remembered her as I had seen her in that upstairs room in the Gallo Inmortal with Keeney. She seemed beautiful to me then, but somehow I had stopped thinking of her in quite that way. She was simply who she was—a woman I had been with constantly for how many days? how many hours? I tried to remember who there was before Alicia. There was DeeDee, of course, the night before I left and all this began, but that seemed so long ago. So much had happened since then.

To get my mind off that, I returned to the case, tossing it over in my mind, going over it again and again. There were too many unexpected developments, too many unexplained aspects to this business for me to cope with. When did I begin to suspect that this was tied up with the drug trade? When I paid that visit to the funeral parlor in Ocean Park? Or was it earlier? Something Officer Urbanski had told me that first night in Tiny Naylor's? Either way, it was early enough I could have gotten out—and I should have. I knew that now. I probably had known it then.

But who said I had to cope with anything, or anyone, but Paco? Here I was, lying in bed, supposedly resting up for this big ordeal ahead, this chase. Who said I had to chase him anywhere? He was tucked away in a room one floor below. I could just go down there, bribe a maid to let me in, and keep him on ice until I had transportation arranged. That was what I had the tranquilizer gun for, wasn't it? I had no reason to involve myself in anything except delivering Paco. That's what I was hired to do. But here I was at the bottom line, forced at last to admit to myself that I really wouldn't settle for Paco alone. I wanted them all. It seemed I wanted to put a dent in the drug trade—and please don't forget to collect your medal on the way out, Mr. Cervantes. Who was I kidding besides myself? I thought I had given up dreams of being a hero after my rookie year as a cop. Evidently not.

The bathroom door opened, sending light into the room. Alicia stepped out, leaving the light on. Caught there, nude, she stopped and looked at me sitting up in the bed.

"You couldn't sleep?"

"No."

She stayed there, continuing to look at me—and I at her. Small, rounded at the hips and the belly, but with nothing there of the high-hipped Indian build. There was a remarkable compact quality to her, as though everything was concentrated, without excess and without exaggeration.

"You want me to turn off the light?" she asked.

"No," I said, "come here."

She came. As she was about to sit down beside me, I threw back the covers, and she took her place on the sheet. We embraced. No kiss, not yet, but I felt her body with mine, and it was something I realized I had wanted to feel for many, many hours. She smelled beautiful. What was it? jasmine? gardenia? I knew it couldn't be hotel soap.

"What are you wearing? What is that smell?"

"Something a woman wears to make a man crazy."

"It makes me crazy."

"I'm glad."

Then we kissed. Long and softly, and over various parts of our bodies. There was an easy rhythm to it, as though we might continue in just this way for many hours—yet I knew we wouldn't. Gradually, the rhythm increased. We kissed and touched and squeezed as gently as loving parents—though not where parents kiss and touch and squeeze.

Then suddenly she pulled back for a moment, her eyes wide open, instantly, urgently serious. I had no idea what she would do or say.

"Chico, let me tell you something."

"Of course. Tell me."

"This is the first time I make love to a man. Truly make love. You understand what I say?"

"I understand you."

And then we resumed.

I slipped off to sleep immediately afterward. There was nothing to remember, no settling down, no line there to be crossed. Just a feeling of luxurious ease. We were holding close to one another, and then suddenly it was two hours later.

I brought myself up to wakefulness like a swimmer deep below pushing up and up and up to the surface of the water. I burst through, awake if not quite alert, aware that there were things to be done, promises to keep, miles to go before I'd sleep—again.

As gently as possible I disentangled myself from Alicia's arms, then went into the bathroom and showered. When I came out I had at least some idea of what I would do. She was stirring now and looked up at me with those dark, serious eyes of hers.

"Back to work?" she asked.

"Yes," I said, "back to work."

I dug into my wallet and came up with the telephone number that had saved me back in Culiacan. I dialed it again, right through to Mexico City. I asked for the man, and this time I got him. No Marine guard, no duty officer, not even a secretary—right through to the man. Like me, he had a Spanish name.

"Yes? Yes? Who is this?"

"Cervantes. You recognize the name?"

Silence. Then: "All right, what do you want?"

"Have you heard from Madden in Culiacan about what happened?"

"*Heard* from him? I brought him here this morning. He's scared to death."

"Have *they* found out yet what happened?"

"Not as far as I know. Not yet. Why are you calling me?" He sounded annoyed—but not scared. That, at least, was encouraging.

"I want you to back me up."

A humorless laugh erupted at the other end. "Oh, I'll bet you do. I'll bet you want me to get you right off the hook on this one. Well, let me tell you something, mister, it's not so easy."

"You don't understand."

"I think I do."

"Listen," I said, talking fast, "I think I may be able to get hold of the next shipment of brown going into Los Angeles. And not only that, I think I can give you the people at the other end. Would you be interested in that?"

There was a moment of silence at the other end of the line. He was probably trying to figure out if I was on the level. Anyway, when he came back to me, he seemed cautiously interested. "How much of the stuff are we talking about?"

I did a quick estimate. "At least fifty pounds, maybe a hundred. Maybe more."

"Uncut?"

"How do I know? I mean, sure, of course it's uncut. How else would they ship it?"

"And what about the other end?"

"Look, I propose to make the delivery myself, and you can have your guys in Los Angeles right there. They could move in as soon as the stuff is on the premises."

"Where's it going?"

Oh, no, I thought. I play my cards one by one. "I *think* I

know where—but that's not good enough. I'll let you or Los Angeles know as soon as I've got it for sure."

"How do I know you won't just make the delivery and take a payoff at the other end?"

"Because you've got Ortega on me."

He thought that over. "Okay," he said at last, "maybe we can make a deal. What do you want from me?"

"Like I said, I want you to back me up. I'll be crossing the border at Tijuana. If I get stopped—if Customs finds the stuff, I want you to tell them it's okay, that I'm working for you. And I'd like you to do what you can for me on the Ortega business."

"No problem on Customs. Just have them call me right away. As *I* said before, Ortega's not so easy." He paused. "But it's not impossible."

Good. At last I felt I had him on my side. "Oh . . . and there's a little matter with the Budget corporation. I left a Toyota Land Cruiser up there in the Sierra. I guess I was trying to make the *Féderales* think I bought it with the rest of them."

"Who knows? They might think just that. Budget I can take care of. Don't worry about that. Uh . . . Madden said you set a fire up there."

"That's right. Same reason. To make body ID more difficult."

"Did you burn the poppy crop, too?"

"Not the fields, but I burned the storage sheds. I don't know how much poppy was in them, but there was some pot. I could smell it driving down the mountain."

"Thanks, Cervantes. I mean it." He gave me the name and number of the DEA operations chief in Los Angeles and said he would tell him to expect my call. Then he wished me good luck and hung up. The rest was up to me.

A few minutes later we were dressed and ready to go. It was time to put Paco in motion. I had Alicia dial his room direct. She put on a voice and said she was the hotel operator and she had a message for him: "You are supposed to come im-

151

mediately. They say not to phone. Just come." She paused, listening to Paco, then: "No, *señor*, it seemed strange to me, but they said you would know who it was and where you were to be. That was the entire message." Another pause. "What's *that*? You think so? Well, the same to you, *señor*!"

She slammed the receiver down and let out the long, loud laugh she had been holding back. "He sounds very angry," she managed after a moment, "and still pretty drunk."

We were waiting for him in a taxi when he staggered out of the hotel ten minutes later. He looked awful and must have felt worse, but he managed to struggle into a taxi of his own, and a moment later he was off into the heavy traffic on Avenida López Mateos. We pulled out after him and managed to stay close on his tail all the way up the hill on the Avenida Espinoza until his taxi pulled up in front of the *funeraria*. This had to be the "place up on the hill" that Anselmo had mentioned. I had our driver go a block beyond it and turn around out of sight. We sat parked a half block away, waiting for Paco to reemerge. Now I had the name of the place—Funeraria Calderón—and the location, but I needed to know the name of Paco's contact there. We said nothing. I could tell the taxi driver was curious. I caught him staring at me questioningly in the rearview mirror. But not a word was spoken. I drummed impatiently on the case containing the tranquilizer gun, which sat in my lap.

But not for long. Paco came out in less than five minutes. Even at the distance from which we were watching he looked angry. Although he was weaving slightly, he seemed more erect. His arms were stiff at his sides and his hands formed fists. As he got into his taxi, our driver started his engine.

"Slowly," I cautioned him. "We're in no hurry to follow. Let a few cars get between us. He will surely go back to the hotel."

I was right. That was where he went. He was just disappearing into the entrance as we arrived. Waiting for Paco's taxi to pull away, I paid our driver and tipped him well.

"For silence," I said to him. "Understood?"

"Sí, señor, very well understood."

Alicia and I took our time. Paco would have only one destination—his room—and one thought—to get back to bed. We made no effort to keep him in sight but ambled around the lobby, looked at postcards to use up a little time. After five minutes or so, I nodded to her, and we started together out of the lobby and found our way to the corridor onto which Paco's room opened.

The corridor was empty—and a good thing, too. It was midmorning. The maids had finished their work. The tourists were out touring. The room was halfway down the hall on the right. Just outside it, I whispered into Alicia's ear what I wanted her to say, gave her the case containing the tranquilizer gun, then pulled the HK automatic out from under my shirt.

She rapped sharply on the door to room 125.

No response.

Again she knocked, louder and longer this time. And at last there was a sound from inside the room, something between a groan and a moan, long and low, then rising sharply in tone until it ended in a muffled yell of frustration: "Get away! Go!"

"*Señor! Señor* Cruz-Rivera, I have a package for you."

No response.

Alicia knocked again, making it clear she would not be sent away so easily.

A pause, faint sounds, then Paco's voice, just beyond the door: "Leave it there in the hall."

"I can't, *señor*. You have to sign for it." Her whole manner had changed. She was officious, in command, the kind of woman who could even deal with *gringos*.

Then Paco made a mistake. He unlocked the door and opened it just a crack to look out at her. A crack was all I needed. I threw myself against the door with all the strength I had, tumbled inside, and sent Paco sprawling down to the floor.

I landed on top of him, just as though I'd planned it that

way. The barrel of the pistol went up against his head. The safety was on, of course, but he didn't know that.

"Say a word and you're dead." I sounded like I meant it, even to myself.

He didn't say a word.

CHAPTER 13

We had him on the bed. There was nothing to tie him up with, or I might have done that, although it really didn't seem necessary. He was over his initial shock but still plenty scared. Lying flat on the sheet, his head on the pillow, his sallow, yellow-brown body bulged outward, and his arms, stretched straight along his sides, ended in tight little fists.

"Find his pants, Alicia," I said to her quietly. "Get his wallet out and bring it to me."

She went off, searching the room. His eyes followed her. He started to turn his head, watching her.

"Don't move, and don't say a word until I ask you a question. Is that understood? You can nod."

He wiggled his head up and down.

She returned with a thick leather packet in hand. I took it from her and handed over the Heckler & Koch. "Stand over there," I said, "and if he even twitches, shoot him in the belly."

"Good. That I can't miss." She took her place at the foot of the bed.

"I promise you, Paco, she can shoot."

Then I sat down on the other bed and started methodically through his wallet. The big bulge proved to be greenbacks, about a thousand dollars' worth, give or take fifty. I tossed them out on the bedspread. They might come in handy. And then I sorted through the cards, tossing out his California driver's license—a brand-new one in the name of Ignacio

Valdez—and a green card in the same name. But I hadn't yet found what I was really looking for. No, here it was—a folded slip of notepaper with three telephone numbers. One of them looked familiar. But dammit, no names!

I reached across the bed and hauled the Ensenada phone book from its shelf on the nightstand and confirmed what I suspected. The first of the three was the number of the Funeraria Calderón up on Avenida Espinoza.

"Paco," I said, "who's your contact at the Funeraria?"

"*Hombre,* what do you mean? I'm here on a vacation."

"Is that what Ortega told you to say? Ortega's dead."

Silence, then: "You were up there, weren't you, at the place? You were with her. You pretend to be her lawyer—it's true? I know your voice."

The man of a thousand faces strikes again—or maybe for the first time ever. I had actually fooled him for a while. That was flattering. I softened up a bit. "Paco," I said, "why don't you make it easy on yourself? Do it my way, and all you'll be up for is the manslaughter charge."

"*Hombre,* what manslaughter charge you talking about? You mean on the Freeway that night? Those two *loco* kids who chased me? That wasn't even my fault. It's all been fixed up."

"Who told you that?"

"*They* told me that, the people I work for. You don't think I'm so stupid I go back there if it's not fixed up? Maybe I'm ignorant, but I'm not stupid."

There was solid eye contact between us. He had spoken emphatically. His hand had gone up unconsciously in an earnest gesture. He wanted to be believed. I was almost convinced.

"You want me to shoot him now?" Alicia asked quite matter-of-factly. "He moved."

Panic suddenly flashed back into his eyes. He glanced back and forth wildly between the two of us.

"No, not yet," I said. "This is getting interesting." Warily, he relaxed a little—but not too much. I didn't want him too

156

relaxed. "Tell me, Paco. If it's all fixed up and safe for you now across the border, then why are you carrying a phony driver's license and green card, uh? *Señor* Ignacio Valdez?"

He frowned in concern. It wasn't as though he had been caught out—more like something was troubling him. "Ortega gave them to me," he admitted, "and I ask him the same thing. He said it's just to be safe. I don't like it, but I don't argue with him. You don't argue with Ortega."

"Not anymore," I said.

He thought about that for a moment. "You kill him for real?"

"I didn't." Then, pointing at Alicia, still there at the foot of the bed with the automatic leveled down at him: "She did."

His eyes widened at this. It was too much to believe—yet why should I lie to him? "What about my uncle? What about my father?"

This was tricky. I didn't want to lose him, so I decided to lie: "They were off someplace. Before they came back, we got away down the mountain. I set fire to the Rover so they couldn't follow."

"The *Féderales*?"

"Dead."

I could tell he was skeptical, yet here we were as proof of what I said. It was important that he take us seriously, and so I described to him in detail what had happened up there, leaving out the part about his father and uncle. He took it all in, nodding very seriously and glancing from time to time at Alicia with new respect.

"You did that?" he asked her when I finished.

"Sure, I shoot them," she said. "I shoot you, too, just to show you a woman don't have to have big *chi-chis* to pull a trigger."

"Oh, you got nice *chi-chis*, Alicia. I never thought bad about them." Suddenly solicitous, even gallant. He was trying hard to convince her.

"Enough of this shit," I said sharply. No more Mr. Nice

Guy. "Alicia, turn on the television, and turn it up loud."

"What you gonna do, *hombre*?"

"You'll find out. Turn over on your stomach, and pull down your pants."

I had gotten through to him. He was scared now, so scared that he did just as I told him, not knowing what to expect, fearing the worst. I opened up the plastic case containing the tranquilizer gun and began loading it up, the way Boomie had showed me. I went about it slowly and carefully and talked as I worked.

"Paco, there are three telephone numbers on that slip of paper you had in your wallet. I want names for all of them. Names and contacts."

"You DEA? You a Los Angeles cop? What are you, *hombre*?"

I caught him peeking at me over his forearm. "Turn your head," I instructed him. "Look the other way."

"What is that thing? What you gonna do to me?"

"Three telephone numbers, Paco." The TV was blaring loudly now. A soccer game. I almost had to shout to be heard over it. "I want the names that go with them. Okay, I'll give you a start. The first one is for Funeraria Calderón on Avenida Espinoza. I looked it up. What about the other two?"

"I can't tell you that. They kill me if I do."

"I kill you if you don't. One of them is for that other *funeraria* up in Santa Monica. Am I right?" It had to be that phone number that had looked familiar. I had found the address of the place in the phone book. I must have noticed the number.

"You know about that. You don't need me to tell you about anything then."

"What about the other number?"

"That guy, he's tough, *hombre*. He's tougher than Ortega. He kill me very slow if I tell you."

"Okay, you don't like that question; I'll ask you another. We've been speaking English for the last five minutes. You do pretty good at it for a dumb *chulo*, so how come you didn't talk *Inglés* to those cops at the accident? Were you too drunk or what?"

"*I wasn't drunk!*" Paco was shouting now, maybe because he was trying to be heard over the TV, or maybe because he wanted to be believed. "Those kids who come after me, maybe they were drunk. *Not me! I swear!*"

The tranquilizer gun was loaded now. I knew I had to shut him up or he'd have the hotel manager banging on the door. I got up and took a place beside Alicia at the foot of the bed. She still had the pistol pointed down at him. With a gesture, I signaled for her to relax, and I aimed down at him just as she had. The plump, wide cheeks of his ass were an inviting target. Alicia was right—you couldn't miss.

Paco must have sensed that I had moved, for he suddenly popped up on his elbows and began looking wildly around the room for me. And when he found me he was really in a panic.

"What you gonna do?" he yelled. "Don't shoot me with that thing."

He was starting to thrash around. I was afraid I'd lose my target. This was it. I gave the trigger a tug. There was a loud pop.

And through it all Paco kept right on shouting: "Julio! Julio's the guy at the Calderón. That's all I can tell you. I . . ."

The dart had entered his left buttock from a range of about three or four feet. There was a little blood, but not much. He went out so quickly that I was left frowning down at him, wishing he had stayed conscious a little longer. He was a bit more forthcoming there at the end. Well, I had gotten one name out of him. Maybe I could get the other two from Julio.

I glanced over at Alicia. She was looking not at me but down at Paco's inert form, which was now flattened on the bed. Her hands were clapped over her ears, as though she thought he were still shouting. She had killed three men the day before—but this horrified her.

The telephone rang.

There was a long moment while I tried to decide whether to pick it up or not. But then I made a grab for it, got Alicia's attention, and pointed to the television set.

"*Sí, sí,*" I said, "*hola. Qué quiere?*"

In Spanish: "This is the desk, *señor*. We have had a complaint from the room next to yours. They wish you to turn your television down."

By this time Alicia had switched it off. "Of course. My apologies to your guests."

After hanging up, I bent over Paco and carefully worked the tranquilizer dart out. It had gone in pretty deep. I wondered if the people next door had heard more than the soccer game on TV—and if they had, whether they had mentioned it to the desk clerk. Well, there was nothing to do about that but wait and see.

I hitched up Paco's shorts and turned him over. A stain had spread on the bed. Was it fear or the tranquilizer that made him lose control? His breathing was barely perceptible. He was certainly quiet enough—so quiet he almost seemed dead. I took his pulse. If my count was correct, then it was a trifle slow but steady. I decided uneasily that he would be all right—at least for a while.

"Alicia," I said, grabbing a fifty from the pile on the other bed, "I want you to take this and buy a bottle of tequila at the bar—Sauza, Cuervo, it doesn't matter what."

She looked astonished. "You want to drink now?"

"Never mind. Just do it. Tip the bartender the price of the bottle, and bring it right back here."

She left, taking one last look back to satisfy herself I wasn't cracking under the strain. She didn't seem reassured. Then I went to the phone, dialed the Funeraria Calderón, and asked for Julio.

As soon as he came on the line, I said, "There is a problem here."

"Just a moment. Who is this?"

"They call me Chico. Ortega sent me here to keep an eye on Paco. And Paco is the problem."

160

There was silence for a moment as he considered that. "All right," he said cautiously at last, "what's wrong?"

"You'd better come here and see for yourself. I'm here in his room at the hotel—room 125."

"It's not a good time to come. We're just finishing up now."

"All the more reason for you to get here fast."

And then I hung up on him. Let him deal with it.

There were a few minutes left, and I took them to put the room back in order. Not neat—just the way it had been when we burst into the room on Paco. I picked up a chair that had been knocked over and found Paco's pants where Alicia had tossed them when she had grabbed out his wallet. Yes, the wallet. I went to the bed, crammed the cards back inside it, and stuffed it into the pants. I pocketed the pile of fifties and the key to his room.

There was a knock at the door. Too soon for Julio. He would be calling Culiacan to check up on me. If luck held, and I had successfully sabotaged that rear rotor, then it would be well past nightfall before the *Féderales* were back from the Sierra. I had until then.

Before opening up, I made sure it was Alicia.

She handed over the bottle without a word—only a look.

"Come in here," I said. "There are a few things to settle." I grabbed out the fifties and counted off ten of them. "Here. This is what I owe you. We're paid up on Paco. Now, if I don't come back to the room or call you after two hours, you take this"—I handed her another fifty—"and check out of the hotel. If you're determined to cross over, then take a bus to Tijuana and find a *coyote*. And if you make it to Los Angeles . . ." I tucked away the depleted wad of bills, went to the pad on the nightstand, and wrote out my address and phone number. "This is how to get in touch with me there. Okay, go back to the room now and wait."

"Are you all right?" she asked. "You make me scared."

"I'm all right. Just do what I say."

She grabbed my face in her hands and kissed me quickly. Then a moment later she was gone.

And now, Paco. His breathing was light but steady. I wondered if I should do anything about that stain on the sheet. No, it would add to the effect. I took the bottle of tequila—it was Cuervo Gold, the best—and went to the bathroom and flushed half of it down the toilet. God, what a waste! Then I went back to Paco and slopped a good inch of the stuff over his face, neck, and chest. Then I wedged the bottle in between his arm and his big belly. I stepped back to the foot of the bed and checked him out. The room had already filled with pungent fumes of tequila. I was satisfied. He looked for all the world as though he were dead drunk.

I was in the bathroom and had just finished washing the smell of the stuff from my hands when a knock came at the door. That would be Julio. I opened wide and beckoned him in.

He was about sixty, with a face that was pouched and wrinkled. He was narrow-shouldered and had once been thin, but age had added inches to his middle, so that he was shaped a little like an elongated football. Julio waddled inside and took a look at Paco. *"Dios mio,"* he gasped, *"que desgracia. Puerco! Borracho!"*

"Now you understand the problem."

"This is impossible! Impossible!"

"I called him up here when I got in this morning and asked him to pick me up at the airport. I could tell he was drunk then. He never did show up, so I finally took a cab in, and this is what I found."

Julio rolled his eyes in outrage, unable to respond for a few moments. The grimace on his face said it all: he gave me to understand that he was a serious man and was deeply offended by such childish behavior. At last he calmed himself enough so that he was able to speak. "Do you know . . . do you know, *Señor* Chico, how this young pig interpreted your call from the airport? He thought that I or someone from my establishment had summoned him without explanation—demanded to see him immediately. Tell me, did you perhaps mention my establishment to him?"

I frowned for a moment, as though trying to remember. "Ah, yes! Funeraria Calderón! Captain Ortega asked me to look in on you. I believe I suggested on the phone to Paco that we stop by on the way from the airport."

"Ah-hah!" crowed Julio. "And in the drunken fantasy of this young *cabrón*, your simple and no doubt polite request was transformed into an urgent summons from me." He sighed. "As you say, *señor*, we have a problem."

The Mexican middle class is a trip. It has probably done more to put the country in its sorry state than all the *hidalgos* and *patrons* combined. I say that knowing that my father was a paid-up and fully accredited lifetime member. Yet he at least had the good sense to come north, and there in Boyle Heights and East L.A., he lost most of his pretensions and gained some sense of respect for his common countrymen. It also helped that he was a journalist and made a practice of exposing the scams perpetrated by the fortunate members of the Los Angeles Latino community upon the less fortunate.

But in Julio you had the real thing, a pure example of the deviousness and essential phoniness of the Mexican middle class. I mean, here was a man who was involved in the heroin trade, for God's sake, and look at him in his funereal black suit and tie, his starched white shirt—why, he was flapping his arms like an angry penguin, righteously indignant that one of his co-workers in the trade had proved unreliable. I could just hear him at his next confession, complaining to the priest of the burden put upon respectable people by the ignorant *Indios* and *mestizos*. He almost made me regret the shameful way I had set Paco up. Well, there were ways around such people. I decided to put him on ice.

"*Señor*," I said, "I have a confession to make."

He looked at me curiously. "Oh? And what is that?"

"Captain Ortega did not direct me to visit you. Not specifically. He was uneasy about Paco, and he sent me to keep an eye on him. It was assumed, of course, that in the course of this I would have occasion to accompany him to Funeraria Calderón. But the truth is, Señor Calderón—it is Señor Calderón, isn't it?—I was given only the name Julio."

"Si, si, Calderón."

"The truth is, I could not wait to look in on you and, I hoped, see your skilled surgical hand in action. Security in an enterprise such as ours is of the utmost importance, of course. And I hope not to be committing too great a transgression if I tell you that I am of the establishment of Turnbull and Son in Santa Monica."

"Ah!" There was a sudden glint in his eye.

I clasped my hands in what I thought would be an appropriate gesture. "We at Turnbull, all of us, *greatly* admire your work."

He puffed visibly at that. "Well," he said with a mock-modest shrug, "we do what we can. Naturally, I take a professional's pride in my work."

"A professional?" I dismissed that with a wave of my hands. "You seem to regard yourself as a simple craftsman. And that I deny. That I categorically deny! You, *señor*, are an artist of the first order."

"But you're too kind."

"Not kind enough! May I say, *señor*, that when an example of your artistry comes into our establishment, the entire staff—including young Mr. Turnbull!—gathers to applaud you. If you could hear the praise voiced by us at such moments you would not talk then of mere professionalism. We especially admire your cosmetic technique."

"I oversee that personally."

"But of course you do! You manage . . . somehow . . . to give the illusion that you have brought the poor deceased back to life. When a casket from Funeraria Calderón is opened, we almost expect its inhabitant to rise up and address us as Lazarus once addressed his mourners. You have that power, *señor*! Don't deny it!"

"Well . . ." Clearly he had no intention of doing that. His yellow, wrinkled face had colored with a blush of pride. For a long moment he was quite unable to say another word. When at last he regained his power of speech, his words came out in a rush: "I must ask—I must *insist!*—that you accompany me now to my humble little *funeraria*. We do not often have the opportunity to display our techniques to others who might appreciate them. Perhaps we could show you a few things you might make use of."

"What you suggest, *señor*—a visit to your *funeraria* with you as my guide—I would consider that an honor."

"Then it is settled. It will be my pleasure to drive you there in my air-conditioned Cadillac automobile."

"And what about him?" Reminding him of Paco there between us on the bed.

"Oh, these things work out. When true colleagues have a chance to exchange useful information, they should not allow such inconveniences as this to stop them. Shall we?"

There were a couple of surprises waiting for me at Funeraria Calderón. Julio had led me through the heavily draped anteroom and past the two chapels, which he dismissed as "the usual," and straight back to what he called his "laboratory." I don't know who he thought he was kidding. It sure wasn't spotless white tile, gurgling beakers, and smoking test tubes—just a good-size dingy room, windowless and lit only by a fluorescent rack running the length of the ceiling. The smell was what you might expect. I knew it from a few trips to the Los Angeles County Morgue. Mostly it's formaldehyde, but around the edges and in little pockets you catch a whiff of something else, a high, sweet odor that all of us recognize instinctively as the smell of death and decomposition.

Three of Julio's assistants in lab coats that might once have been white were working over two cadavers. One of the staff, a blowsy, plump female with bleached blond hair, was putting the final touches on the lips of a male corpse of about thirty-five. He could have been an American—good-size, thick-featured, maybe Jewish or Italian. The other one, still stretched out on the table, was definitely Mexican. The funny thing was, his body didn't quite match up. He was a thin, wizened character who could have been anything from fifty to seventy—but what a belly he had!

Julio led me over to him. The two male assistants had sewn him up to the sternum. They stepped away with a deferential nod to allow Don Julio to inspect their work.

He smiled with satisfaction and patted the old *campesino* on his distended midriff. "He's a lot fatter than when he came in," he said with a wink. "In death he eats more than he ever did when he was alive—and of the richest food in all Mexico."

That was surprise number one. I had assumed they were packing the glassine packets of the brown stuff into the coffin, maybe sewing them into the lining beneath the satin. But no. The meaning of Julio's little joke was unmistakable: they were cramming them into the abdominal cavity. Well, why not? A curious customs man might poke around in a casket, might even tear a little satin, but it would take more than curiosity to get him to open up a corpse.

Julio took me lightly by the elbow and led me away. "Those boys do good work," he whispered. "They learn. I teach them."

"How lucky to apprentice to such a master!" With such vanity as his there was never any possibility of laying it on too thick. He licked up each morsel of flattery, each smarmy piece of bullshit like a hungry man invited to a feast. "Tell me, *Señor* Calderón, I have often wondered, these poor unfortunates on whom you perform such artistry, from where do they come?"

"Those we ship north?"

"Yes."

"From the *Féderales*. I do not ask questions."

"Of course not."

He brought me to the man in the casket. The bleached

blonde was just standing back to look over her work. She seemed pleased with it. So did Julio.

"This one," he said, indicating the corpse whose rugged features were painted like some kewpie doll's, "he holds almost twice as much as the other one. You know those *gringos* and their bellies."

Then a look passed over his face that told me he had just remembered where I was from. "Uh . . . no offense meant, of course," he muttered.

"And none taken."

That was surprise number two. There were to be *two* caskets for this trip north. A double shipment—probably to make up for that month Paco spent hiding out in Culiacan.

"*Señora* Rodriguez, I wish to present *Señor* Chico . . . ?"

"Cervantes. Antonio Cervantes."

She smiled broadly, exposing two gold teeth, and offered me a *mucho gusto*. "You have a special interest in our work, *señor*?"

"Ah, Emilia," Julio broke in, "*Señor* Cervantes is a member of the firm of Turnbull and Son in Santa Monica, California, and he has been saying many kind things about us. In particular, he said that—"

At that he broke off suddenly, as though a thought had just struck him. He looked at me sharply, and I thought for a moment I must have gotten carried away and said something wrong. Maybe he had just put two and two together. Maybe it was all over. Without quite willing it, my hand drifted to the small of my back until it came into contact with the reassuring hardness of the Heckler & Koch beneath my shirt.

"*Señor* Cervantes," he said at last, "I believe I have solved our little problem back at the hotel. You—*you*, Chico—can take Paco's place. Obviously he is in no condition to drive and cannot be trusted. But you are here, and you certainly know the way. Why, it is as though God Himself sent you to us."

CHAPTER 14

It was well toward the middle of the afternoon before we reached Tijuana. We came down on it from a height, and as we descended, the road grew dustier and the vista more bleak. It's the border town to end all border towns. The U.S. greenback is the prevailing currency, and everybody there seems to be working some scam dedicated to accumulating as many as they can. You could call it a parasitic economy—and you'd be right—but the way they go at it in Tijuana, it's more like predatory. They figure that any *gringo* dumb enough to jump into this pool of sharks gets what he deserves.

But how dumb was I? Here I was, heading for the border with no plan in mind. I had argued with Alicia all the way from Ensenada about what we would do when we got to Tijuana. Paco was wedged between us in the cab of the hearse, still out. It hadn't been easy getting him out of the hotel, until Julio himself had come over to assure the hotel staff that everything was in order. In the end, one of the porters was detailed to help us stuff him into the hearse.

That was what got us started—Paco. I remember we were about as far as the Bajamar turnoff when Alicia suddenly leaned over so she could see me around Paco's lolling head, and said, "He stinks."

"Sure! Correct! Of course! What am I supposed to do about it?"

"He smells like tequila and peepee."

"So?"

"Also sweat."

"What can I say? You're right. He doesn't smell any better to me than he does to you."

"Why can't we put him in back?"

"Because, I told you, there probably isn't room for him there with the two coffins. And even if there were, I want him up front so I can keep an eye on him. I want to know if he starts to come around." I also wanted to know if he looked like he was starting to slip into a coma or expire altogether. But I didn't say that. "You only have to put up with him as far as Tijuana, anyway."

"So? You going to dump me out in Tijuana, uh?"

I glanced over in her direction, but she had settled back, and all I caught was her nose in profile. All right then, I'd talk to her nose. "That's ridiculous," I said. "We agreed that I'd take you as far as Tijuana. That's where you want to go, isn't it?"

"No. I want to go to Hollywood."

Oh, Jesus, Mary, and Joseph. Hollywood again. I kept forgetting that besides a drugged-out *chulo* and two corpses stuffed with heroin, I had a budding starlet on my hands.

"Anyway," she added, "you need me."

"I *need* you?" Like a hole in the head, I wanted to add, but how could I put *that* into Spanish? "All right, *why* do I need you? Just tell me that."

"You need me, if Paco wakes up, to put the gun on him. He's afraid of me. You saw him in the hotel. Anyway, you also need me for love."

"Love's got nothing to do with it," I said brusquely. "And perhaps—I say only perhaps—what you say is true. Maybe I could use some help with Paco. But there are guards at the border to keep out little girls like you who want to be movie stars."

"Only blondes, uh? If I'm blonde it's okay, I bet. Maybe I should bleach my hair like Concepción said."

"Blondes got nothing to do with it, either. Unless you've

got a green card, emigration papers, something, I don't know, there's not a chance they're going to let you across—blonde, brunette, or redhead."

"Ay, redhead! I never even thought of that! Neither did Concepción. How do you like me that way?"

I ignored her, and she fell silent for a moment. But only for a moment.

"I got an idea," she said. I glanced over. Once more she was leaning out, looking around Paco at me, smiling craftily, tapping her head, as if to point out the origin of this unexpected inspiration. Just so there would be no doubt.

In spite of myself, I smiled. What else could I do? She was funny—and funniest when she wanted to be taken seriously. "Okay, what is it?"

"You tell them at the border we got married, only you lost the papers. It's okay if we're married, yes?"

"Yes. Only no papers, no marriage."

"Oh." She disappeared behind Paco again.

From time to time, as we drove on, she would pop out with a new idea. She could be the new maid I had just hired! "No good unless you've got a green card," I assured her. Then she decided it might be best if I simply bribed them. "I won't say the *mordida* won't work," I told her, "but you've got to know in advance who will take it and who won't."

And so on. All the way to Tijuana. At one point she became angry with me and declared that I didn't *want* her to have a career, that I was just like all the other men she had ever known.

We argued about that. All the way to Tijuana. Oh, it was fun, let me tell you. By the time we reached the outskirts of the city, she was right: what I wanted to do was dump her and get over the border as quickly as I could. And she really *was* right about Paco. He did stink—of tequila, urine, and sweat. The farther we drove, the worse he smelled. I rolled down the window, but that didn't help much.

I remember we were just into the city, someplace around

Avenida de la Revolución, and I was telling her for about the third or fourth time that her only real hope was to find a good, reliable *coyote* (a reliable one? *that* was a laugh!) and go across the same way everybody else did. By that time, I had even dredged up from my memory the name of a place—*La Mariposa Negra*, the Black Butterfly—that was supposed to be the cantina where the border-crossers hung out and the deals were made.

She wasn't even listening. Somehow I knew it. She hadn't said anything for a while, and she was leaning back, hiding behind Paco. But I could tell she wasn't listening.

So I said to her, "I don't want you to be a blonde or a redhead."

"What?" That got her attention.

"I said, I don't want you to be a blonde or a redhead. I like you the way you are."

"Then why can't I come with you?"

"Do we have to go through that again?"

We had slowed to a crawl through Tijuana's afternoon traffic, and we were attracting a lot of attention. Along the way, all the local *vaqueros* and *chulos* were stopping to look, pointing us out, laughing hilariously at the sight of a hearse with no trailing cortege. Or who could tell what struck them as funny? Tijuana is a hip town, I'll give them that. You just look into those evil faces, try to halt those darting eyes, and you'll realize you've reached some lesser annex of Hollywood Boulevard or Times Square, an outer circle of hell. Down here, they're on top of it all. They know, in the immortal words of somebody or other, the price of everything and the value of nothing at all.

There really was a *Mariposa Negra*. As I said, I had only heard about the place. But here it was, looming before us at the next *alto* sign. What was it like? The sign was black, of course, but with a butterfly, outlined in three positions, fluttering in yellow neon in broad daylight. We inched forward. There was a crowd at the corner. I could hear music issuing from the place, a kind of a *salsa* Latino beat, whatever. Here they were, the wisest of the local wiseguys, doing little dances on the sidewalk in their Tony Lama boots.

As we approached the corner, just one car ahead of us, one of the group shuffled away from the rest and up to the curb. Alicia had caught his eye. "Ay, *linda*," he said, "I got a place for you inside. You wanna come and dance? I'll sing love songs to you, and you can forget about the funeral."

He looked no different from the rest. Younger, maybe, but with the same moustachioed, thin face, the same insinuating look.

"Beat it, *maricón*," I yelled at him. "We got places to go." Then I checked on the space before me, found that it was empty, and jammed down on the accelerator. After a decent interval, the huge Cadillac engine caught, and we zoomed forward, roaring through the stop sign, narrowly missing a station wagon that was just starting up on our right.

When we were clear of the corner, I glanced in her direction and found her leaning out and looking at me. "Why did you do that?" she asked. "He seemed nice."

"Nice? He was a pimp!"

"Is that so terrible? I'm a whore."

My eyes were back on the road just in time. I braked sharply and just managed to avoid rear-ending a pickup truck that had crowded in ahead of us. "I thought you gave that up," I said. "I thought you were going to be a movie star."

"You do what you have to do. It takes time."

"Fabulous," I said. "Marvelous."

She was playing me shamelessly. I knew it, but what could I say? What could I do? My mind raced through the options, instantly rejecting *La Mariposa Negra*. I couldn't send her there. I couldn't leave her here in Tijuana. And so I settled on something that under any other circumstances I wouldn't have considered. What I had told her was correct: there was no way I could talk her across the border. But it just might be possible to hide her away.

At the first opportunity, I swung up a side street and kept

an eye open for an alley, a driveway, someplace private. I found a paved space between two buildings, probably an entrance to a parking lot in back—but I didn't try to find out. I simply jammed the big hearse up far enough to get it out of sight, slammed on the brakes, and told Alicia to get out.

"You gonna leave me here?"

"Just do what I say and keep quiet for a while."

I jumped out and banged the big door shut and reluctantly she followed me around the other side to the rear of the hearse. I opened up the back door with the key Julio had provided. The coffins were piled one atop the other on two sets of rollers. There was no possibility of squeezing her in on top of them, but maybe . . .

"Look, I'll pull out the top one as far as it'll go. See if you can work your way around it and all the way to the front. There might be room enough up there for you."

She looked at me dubiously, then realized I was dead serious and nodded. I grabbed the handle of the top coffin and tugged. It pulled out easily enough on the rollers, too damned easy. It was all I could do to keep it from shooting out and crashing down on the pavement. But I stopped it, steadied it, and held it. The thing weighed a ton. I bet this was the one with the *gringo* inside.

"Come on," I gasped. "Get inside."

She did manage to squeeze in, and once past the tight spot, she was able to work her way back without much trouble as I pushed the coffin slowly back in after her. When I halted, it was projecting a little more than a foot out the door.

"How is it?" I called inside. "Can you stay there for a while?"

"I think so."

I pushed the coffin back into place.

"But only for a little while," she added.

"Yes, I promise." I slammed the back door, locked it, and turned to find that we had attracted a small crowd at the street. Five or six, mostly women, had gathered there and were staring at me curiously.

"*Vaya!*" I yelled at them. "The show is over."

173

Then back to the cab of the hearse and inside, slamming the door hard after myself. I felt angry. I don't know why. At Alicia? At Mexico? Probably just that I was wired.

I started the engine and threw the transmission lever into reverse. With just a glance into the rearview mirror, I accelerated back to the street, scattering the onlookers as I exploded past them. They yelled angrily. One shook her fist, but I kept right on going, sweeping wide in a turn-around arc there in the middle of the street. I drove back the way I had come, retracing my route on the way to the border.

Paco was now slumped on the other side, bouncing against the door where Alicia had sat a minute or two before. He, at least, remained relaxed through it all.

When there were still a couple of cars ahead of me, the border guard looked up curiously and studied the hearse for a moment. That didn't look good to me. I wondered then if it was too late to switch lines and decided that it probably was. I'd draw more attention to myself than I had already.

Now there was just one car left between me and the guard in the booth. I had chosen his line originally because he looked a little older and fatter than the rest, and a little less interested in what he was doing. But now he suddenly seemed interested, and I didn't like that at all. The car ahead of me moved on, and I crept up to the booth.

"Citizenship?"

"American."

"Got anything to prove it?"

I reached back, pulled out my wallet, and offered it to him.

He waved it off. "I don't want all that. Just show me something."

I pulled out my California driver's license and my old Army Reserve card and held them up for his inspection.

He nodded, satisfied. "What about your friend there?" pointing at Paco.

"He's drunk," I said. "Passed out."

"Well, Jesus, I can *see* that. What's his citizenship?"

"Mexican, I guess."

"You *guess*? Don't you know? Or is he just some guy you picked up along the road? I gotta see some documentation on him, or he goes right back, and maybe we hold you, too."

"Come *on*." With a great, long-suffering show of annoyance, I reached over, and with some difficulty, worked Paco's wallet out of his hip pocket. My intention was to use up as much of the guard's time and patience on Paco as I could, then maybe he'd let me go just to get rid of us. I shuffled aimlessly through his cards. "He's got a lot of stuff here," I said. "What is it you want to see?"

"His green card! Show me his fucking green card!"

After a bit more shuffling, I picked out the phony one made out to Ignacio Valdez and held it up for the guard to see. "Is this what you wanted?"

"Yes," he said, then looked at it and nodded. "Okay."

I tossed Paco's wallet and cards onto the seat next to him and threw the transmission lever into drive.

"Just a minute," said the guard.

"What is it now?"

"You got anything to declare?"

"Come *on*. What do you mean, anything to declare?"

"What I said. You know. Foodstuffs, liquor, cameras, electronic equipment—any purchases?"

"Yeah. I bought a hot new Mexican computer that runs on chili power."

"Very funny. What've you got in back?"

"What've I got in back?" This guy was far too patient to suit me. "This is a hearse. What do you think I've got in back? Two stiffs in two coffins."

"Is that all?"

"They take up a lot of room."

"I don't know." He rubbed his chin, considering. "Maybe you better pull up in line up there and let one of the inspectors take a look."

"*Maybe*? Look, I'm in a hurry. Could you . . ."

"Do it."

Shit. I eased the hearse forward in the direction of the line the guard had pointed out. For one passing second I considered swinging out around it and jamming the accelerator down to the floor. A high-speed chase down Interstate 5? How fast could a hearse haul with a full load?

I got in line just as I had been told.

After a short wait, a heavy-set young man in a lighter khaki uniform came up. He looked bored, hot, and uncomfortable.

"What's your story?" he asked. No nonsense here.

"I just came down to pick up two bodies to take them up to a funeral parlor in Santa Monica. That's all."

"Where'd you get them?"

"Ensenada."

He shrugged. There seemed nothing suspicious to him about that.

"Well," he said at last, "better open it up."

I put the key in and unlocked the door, then I tugged it open. There they were, two coffins, and nothing else to see. He seemed not in the least inclined to view the remains.

The inspector stuck his head inside and shrugged again. But then, just as he was gesturing for me to shut the hearse up, a small voice came from deep within it, asking in Spanish if it was okay to come out now.

The way I saw it, I still had a card left to play, and that was Mexico City. Alicia sat close by me in the office, across the desk from the Border Patrol captain or commander, or whatever he was. And she listened, wide-eyed, understanding little or nothing, as I argued, demanded, and then pleaded that the man in charge call the man in charge in Mexico City.

"You say he's DEA?" he asked suspiciously.

"That's right. Yes, DEA."

"What've they got to do with this?"

"He'll explain."

And so, reluctantly, he placed the call, got the Embassy, and ascertaining names and titles all along the way, at last made contact with my man in Mexico City. Briefly, the Border Patrol man gave him the situation. He named me, told him I had asked him to make the call, and said I had been picked up trying to smuggle a woman across the border in a hearse. And then he listened. He listened for a long time, nodding when it was unnecessary, saying uh-huh and yeah when some sort of assent seemed called for. I listened and waited and patted Alicia's hand more reassuringly than I had any right to.

At last the one-sided conversation ended, and I looked expectantly at the Border Patrol man. All he did was grin at me and thrust the receiver in my direction.

"Cervantes?"

"Yeah?"

"You didn't say anything about bringing this girl with you. Is she the one who was with you up there in the Sierra?"

I sighed. There was little to be gained in lying and potentially a lot to lose. "That's right. She's the one."

"Then you're . . . what? Harboring a fugitive? Aiding and abetting in unlawful flight?"

"Trying to save her neck is what I'm doing. She saved mine."

"That's nice. That's really touching, you know? Listen, Cervantes, I've thought it over and I've got a theory. I think you and that little whore have it in mind to drive up to L.A. and make your own deal for that load of brown, then just disappear with the million or so you'd get."

He paused, waiting for a ritual denial. Fuck him. Let him think what he wanted to think. Alicia was staring at me, looking scared. I must have looked pretty grim myself. I tried to reassure her with a wink.

After a moment, he resumed: "I'll give you credit, though. The Border Patrol guy said you were driving a hearse. I guess that means you got hold of the stuff. Where is it, in the coffin lining?"

"It's in the bodies," I said, "two of them."

"Jesus, that's grotesque! They really went to some trouble, didn't they?" He punctuated that with a mirthless "ha," then got back down to business: "Okay, this is the deal. Take it or leave it. You go ahead and do things just like we said. Now, I know you haven't been in contact with the Los Angeles office yet, and that makes me a little unhappy. Don't make me unhappy, Cervantes. You still got that number with you, haven't you?"

"Yeah."

"Use it. Do the deal with them. In the meantime, the Border Patrol's going to hold the girl right there in the detention pen in San Ysidro. We'll let her go with a green card as soon as the Los Angeles office tells us everything went right at their end. If we *don't* hear that, then she goes back to the Mexican police. If she means something to you, then you won't want that to happen. You got that? I figure we're holding a marker on you, Cervantes."

He hung up on me.

CHAPTER 15

"Sure, alone. I don't care," the Border Patrolman said. He looked at me and shrugged, as though he really was indifferent whether I talked to Alicia with him present or absent. "Because I'll tell you what. I'm walking out this door here, and down the hall to the can. My business there is going to take me a minute or two, so I'd say you've got maybe three minutes alone—tops. Whatever you got to say to her, you better make it fast."

With that, he turned on his heel and did just as he said he would, banging the glass door to his office behind him, pausing along the way just long enough to mutter instructions to the clerk outside to keep an eye on us.

Us. I turned to Alicia. She was still wedged into the corner where she had worked herself as I was talking on the phone to Mexico City. Hunched down in her chair, she looked at me wide-eyed.

"Alicia?"

She didn't say anything, but her solemn, dark eyes grew even wider, and she nodded.

"I'm going to get you out of here, I promise. There's another man I can call. Two men. I won't let them send you back to Culiacan. You believe me?"

Again, not a word, but once more she nodded. At that moment I flashed on our bit of theater there at the airport—the counterfeit passion, the loud pledges of love and fidelity for the benefit of Ortega's *Féderales*—and now look at us, her unable to speak and me giving assurances I had no idea I could back up. That was phony, but this was real.

I beckoned her up and toward me. She rose from the chair slowly and teetered on her spiked heels across the space that separated us. I took her into my arms and hugged her close. Without speaking we stood that way for a long moment.

And that was the way we were when the Border Patrolman returned right on schedule. Although her face was buried in my shoulder, she knew he was there. Her arms tightened around me. As he approached, he showed no sign of softening and no sympathy: he had a job to do, and that was all. Well, let him do it. I released my arms, and he grabbed her from me. He was handling her rougher than he needed to.

"Hey, take it easy on her."

"Chico, don't let them send me back."

That was all she said as he pulled her down the hall to the lockup. Those eyes of hers, *they* stayed with me for a while.

The next three hours were lost in a jumble of driving—Paco stinking in the seat beside me but still breathing steady—and telephoning. I can't say why, but at no time in that period, or for some time afterward, did it occur to me to do as I had been told by the DEA guy. I was angry. No, I was beyond anger in a cold state of sustained rage. All I could think of was Alicia held hostage back at the border, and no matter where I looked, I saw a kind of ghost image of her eyes before me—big, round, and fearful. Before I would be willing to do anything for the DEA I was determined to get her out of there.

The first call I made was from an Arco station in Chula Vista about a block from the Border Patrol station. That one was to Silverstein in Washington. I got him at home and explained the situation to him as quickly as I could, omitting a few incriminating details but making it clear that I had the man I had been sent down to get and that A. Ramirez, who had fingered him, was being held by the Border Patrol. As I talked, I could feel him fading from me. He wanted to know if the man in Mexico City knew about this.

I sighed. "Yes. Sure he does."

"And what does he say?"

"He says she stays until I conclude my business with him. You see, there's this other matter that—"

"I don't want to hear about it!"

"That's good because I don't want to tell you about it. The thing is, he's threatening to have her sent back unless—"

"Please. I *don't* want to hear about it," he repeated.

I said nothing.

"Listen," he resumed, "it's out of my hands now. You'd better do what he tells you."

I slammed the receiver down hard on Silverstein and hoped I'd popped his eardrum. He was just like Madden and all the rest of them, wasn't he? For all his concern that his daughter's killer be brought back, for all his personal questions about me, he was a bureaucrat beneath it all—unwilling to stick his neck out and lose his pension. What is it that a steady paycheck does to people?

I jumped into the hearse and got onto Interstate 5. I kept to a nice, safe 55 mph while all the time my mind was racing along at a hundred or more. After just a few minutes of that, I peeled off at a San Ysidro exit and rocked to a halt at another phone—this one stuck out in front of a Jack in the Box, next to a Chevron station and across from a Denny's.

This time I talked to Thomas Jarrett. I was dealing Paco. If Jarrett wanted him, he could have him, but my price was Alicia. I explained who she was and how she fit into the picture, where she was, and why she couldn't go back. Then I left it up to him. He certainly had the money it would take to bribe her out of detention, and presumably he also had the contacts—or could get them with a phone call or two. Was it a deal?

Jarrett was cagey: "I can't say. This is going to take time. Why don't you come here while I work on it?"

"No, thanks." I glanced from my place at the pay phone over at Paco, his big head lolling against the window on the passenger side of the hearse, and was momentarily touched by feelings of guilt. I looked away and said, "I'll talk to you about it again in an hour or two."

"All right. Where can I reach you?"

"Don't try. I'll call you back."

I hung up on him then, a little more gently than I had on Silverstein. It certainly wasn't that I liked Jarrett better, but just then we were potential business partners—or maybe partners in crime. I felt I owed him, if not respect, then at least a little courtesy.

An hour-and-a-half's drive put me just into Orange County. In fact, I was not all that far away from Jarrett's place in Newport Beach when I talked to him on the phone again.

"Saheed left to pick her up. He'll have her here in a few hours."

"I'm impressed." Jarrett was just as well connected as I had heard. Maybe all it took was a call to the White House.

"Why don't you come here? Where are you now?"

It was tempting. It seemed the reasonable thing to do. But the way I was brought up, temptation was what you resisted. "No, I don't think so. I'll call back, and we'll arrange the swap."

I started to hang up when I heard: "Cervantes."

"Yeah?"

"Uh, if you're on the Freeway, you'd better get off. You might attract attention in that thing."

A bell went off. "What thing?"

"Well . . ."

"Don't worry about me. I'll handle my end."

Then I checked Paco's wallet and got under way again. As I continued northward on 405, I kept a sharp eye on the rearview mirror, slowing down and speeding up, swinging off the Freeway and going right back on. After a little of that, I was satisfied there was nobody behind me.

* * *

By the time I pulled up to the parking facility at the John Wayne/Orange County Airport, I had a better handle on it all.

"Hey, wait a minute!" The guy at the pay booth came running over before I could grab my ticket from the automatic dispenser and zoom through the gate.

"Yeah? What's the problem?"

He was red-faced and agitated. This was a break in the routine, and he didn't like that. "Where do you think you're going to put *that*?"

"This? The hearse? In there someplace."

"You can't park a hearse here," he said.

"Why not? It's empty."

He poked his head down and almost into the window and looked at me dubiously. "You sure?"

I put on my best would-I-lie face and said, "Look, what can I do? I got to pick up a couple of stiffs off a charter flight in three hours. They won't let me park this inside the gate. They said I should put it here."

"Well . . ." He looked away uneasily. It was decision time, and he didn't like it at all. He pointed at Paco. "What about your friend?"

"What about him? He's sleeping one off."

"You going to leave him in there?"

"He's too heavy to carry."

Two cars had lined up at the pay booth. The driver of the Ford in front began honking impatiently. "Three hours, huh? Well, I guess it's okay."

He stood up and took a step back, still frowning, as I pulled the ticket and drove through the gate. That was all I needed. In seconds or so I had the hearse up near the top of the structure, all by itself, about a level and a half above the rest of the cars. For this next part I needed a little privacy.

At least one thing I told the keeper of the gate was true: Paco was too heavy to carry. Nevertheless I had to try to haul him a few steps. This I managed to do somehow, draping him over my shoulders in an awkward approximation of the fireman's carry, staggering beneath the dead weight of him to the back of the hearse. I let him down with a thud against the rear tire. He started to topple, but I righted him carefully, stepped back and took a moment to get my breath.

I heard a car on its way up through the maze of left turns that would lead straight to me, unless . . .

The car slowed and came to a halt on the level below.

It was only then that I realized I had ducked down to hide beside Paco. His breath came in deep, snoring wheezes. He smelled bad, worse than bad—awful. Yet I remained where I was during the couple of minutes it took for the driver below to alight from the car and walk to the elevator. When at last I heard the elevator doors open and shut I returned to the job at hand.

I unlocked the back door, measured the open space between the caskets and the door pessimistically and dragged Paco around to the open rear of the hearse. It took a bad five minutes to get him up and inside. He kept flopping down, and once he fell to the floor of the garage. I barely managed to catch his head with my hand and save him from a fractured skull. But after all that, I got him in, shut the door, and locked it.

Sweating and nearly exhausted, I wanted nothing more than to sit down and rest. But the back window had to be broken to give Paco some air. I looked around for something big and heavy enough to do it and settled on the tranquilizer gun. I began tapping with it on the safety glass and wound up bashing away with all my might. At last I was able to dig a hole about an inch in diameter in the shattered mess with the handle of the oversize pistol. As I was about to stow the tranquilizer gun away in its case, I thought better of it, and after taking the time and trouble to load it up, tucked it in under the driver's seat.

Then at last I shuffled off to the terminal to change out of the chauffeur's uniform and wash up, call the DEA office in Los Angeles, and rent a car. In that order.

* * *

Here I was a block away from Jarrett's place in Newport Beach, and I was about to become invisible. I parked the Avis car around a bend and out of sight. The sun was just about down, but there was half an hour of light left—and I needed that time. I put on the straw sombrero and, from the back of the car, hauled out the items I had bought in Costa Mesa at one of those huge drugstores that carry everything, even drugs— even garden tools. Just a rake and a trowel—but I thought that would be enough.

With the trowel in one hand and the rake over my shoulder, I started for Jarrett's: just your friendly neighborhood campesino, off to his last job of the day. There must have been five or ten of us in the neighborhood at that moment. From the outside there seemed nothing different about the Jarrett place. I might have walked right past it if it weren't for the *QEII* moored in the rear. There wasn't another house along the marina with a boat that big behind it. The address was right. I crossed the street and approached it cautiously, head down, sombrero forward, just shuffling along. I stayed away from the front of the house and went over to the side. There I threw down the rake, dropped to my hands and knees, and attacked the petunias with the trowel.

There were a few noises from inside the house but not many. A door opened and shut—and at one point I caught the sound of footsteps from a distant corner, maybe the second floor. I listened hard as I poked away at the flower bed, but there was nothing more to be heard. If Jarrett was in there, and I assumed he was, then he was apparently alone. Rising slowly, yet keeping my head down, I risked a quick look inside one of the windows above me. It was the living room. I recognized it. Empty now. Only a few days before I had sat there with Silverstein and Jarrett, listening to them pour out their angry tale of death on the freeway. I wondered at that moment if I should have believed either of them.

But only for that moment, for just then a big Mercedes 450 sedan pulled up in front of the house, and Jarrett's man Saheed jumped out. He threw a curious look in my direction—had he caught me looking in the window?—before opening the rear door of the car and letting Alicia out. I picked up the rake and got very busy with it, breaking down the clods of dirt I had turned up with the trowel, butchering some more petunias in the process.

From the corner of my eye I saw him hustle her toward the door. A moment later they were inside. The door slammed. There were voices—male, heavy—speaking indistinguishably. Rake in hand, I began working my way back toward the rear of the house.

But I hadn't gotten far before:

"Hey, you—you there!" It was Saheed. I hadn't even heard him leave the house.

I kept right on working with the rake.

"You! Hey! Stop!" He yelled it out. There was no ignoring him this time.

I nodded and halted my furious raking. Glancing up, I saw that he had advanced to a point about ten feet away, where he now stood and was probably looking me over. I couldn't be sure about that. The sombrero was pulled down so low that I could only see him from the chest down. But that way he couldn't see me either. I leaned on the rake and waited, ready to strike out with the first sign that he had recognized me.

"*Sí?*"

"Who told you to work here?"

"*Cómo?*"

"You people are so stupid," he sneered in exasperation. "I don't know why he puts up with you." He added something in guttural Arabic, turned away, then charged back a few steps closer. He was only five or six feet away now. My hand tensed on the rake. "You come to the wrong house," he yelled. "Wrong *casa*, understand? *Comprendo?*"

"Ah, *sí, casa!*" I pointed to the house.

"José does our work on Tuesdays and Fridays."

"Sí, José. He say."

"José told you to come? Well, you go away now. *Vaya!*"

I nodded and shuffled as though confused.

He reached into his pocket, pulled out some bills, and peeled a ten off. He thrust it toward me. "*Vaya!*"

"Ah, *sí*, okay." I took the bill and cautiously tipped my hat an inch or two. Saheed had already turned away, satisfied that he had dealt with the situation. "*Muchas gracias, señor,*" I called after him, but by then he had disappeared around the corner of the house. I heard the door slam.

I bent down and retrieved the trowel and wondered if he would be watching from the house to make sure I left. I decided he wouldn't. He was too sure of himself for that. Saheed was too sure of himself about a lot of things.

And so I tossed the rake and the trowel down in the flower bed and went toward the rear of the house. There was a redwood fence separating me from the huge boat docked in back. I took a moment to be sure that there was no one on the other side of it. Then I scaled it with no trouble at all.

I dropped down quietly onto a narrow tiled patio that faced directly onto the dock where the big boat was moored. In the fast-fading light I could only make out the size and general shape of the thing. I moved cautiously along the fence toward the light that shone through the sliding-glass door at the rear of the house.

Next to it then, just out of the light, I stood pressed against the stucco wall of the house and listened. The voices were clearer now. I could make out Saheed's and Jarrett's, but Alicia was silent. Not like her. But what could she say to them? She could only wonder at what was going on. Or maybe they had shoved her off into another room.

But no. I risked a quick peek and caught a glimpse of Jarrett standing with his back to me, and beyond him Alicia sat huddled on the couch where I had sat three days before. Back against the wall, I listened hard to what they were saying inside to see if I could make out any of it.

I couldn't. Or not much anyway. Saheed's voice, a tenor,

carried pretty well, while Jarrett's deep bass rumbled unintelligibly against the walls. The trouble was, Jarrett did all the talking, and Saheed's replies were limited to words of agreement and phrases of concern. Concentrating hard for about five minutes, I caught only one sentence that seemed to mean anything at all. After a long, deep mutter from Jarrett—I thought I caught the phrase "at the ranch"—Saheed answered very plainly, "They're always shooting coyotes up there." I'd heard enough.

I tugged the thick, blunt Heckler & Koch out from my belt and stepped in front of the glass patio doors. There I was in plain sight, but amazingly enough no one noticed me. Jarrett and Saheed were staring at each other across the room, and Alicia drooped with her head bowed, half-asleep on the sofa. I stood there a moment, posing menacingly with the pistol, my jaw set like some third-rate heavy on a TV cop show. Not even a glance. I tried the door. It was locked, as I expected. And so, having no other choice, I brought the barrel of the gun down sharply against the glass.

It didn't break. I looked down at it, puzzled, astonished, probably looking pretty foolish. I hacked down on it harder, banging loudly, but again nothing happened. Jesus, but it was thick.

They'd noticed me now, all right. Jarrett and Saheed stood gaping in surprise. Even Alicia had roused on the sofa. I grabbed the sombrero off my head and tossed it aside so they would see it was me. Saheed was suddenly furious: he knew he'd been had. But Jarrett's handsome face slowly spread into a smile. I had to do something to ruffle him, so I stepped back, slipped the safety off the pistol, took aim high up at the opposite wall, and fired.

The glass shattered but didn't break. A web of frosted glass laced out in a five-inch radius around the spot where I had aimed. I heard, rather than saw, bits of lead drop to the floor of the patio. The slug had shattered. The glass was bulletproof. Jesus, was it ever!

Jarrett turned to Saheed and said something. I couldn't catch any of it. As he looked back at me, his smile turned into a nasty grin.

Saheed went over to Alicia, reached into his coat, and pulled out the pistol I knew he carried there. He rested the barrel almost casually against her head.

And then Jarrett acted out his instructions to me, pointing at his right hand, then down at the floor. What else could I do? I bent down and set the pistol on the bricks of the patio, and then I rose with both hands open to show they were empty.

I felt like an idiot.

CHAPTER 16

I think what bothered me most was the way that Jarrett laughed at me. As Saheed unlocked the door to the patio and slid it open, Jarrett beckoned me inside—a short, quick gesture, master to servant. But stepping into the room, I ignored both of them and gave Alicia the best smile I could manage under the circumstances and a thumbs-up sign.

She jumped up excitedly and started toward me, just like I was her rescuer or something. Then Jarrett pushed her back down on the sofa, and she understood the situation a little better. *"Cabrón!"* she barked at him.

He smiled back at her and turned to me with the smile still on his face. That was when he started to laugh. That bass of his rumbled up from somewhere deep down in his flat belly in a series of groaning spasms that from any other man would have sounded like the first stages of stomach agony. The glint in his eye told me that he was really having fun. And as the corners of his mouth turned up in a grimacing smile, at last those deep rumbles rose up until they exploded forth into a long, high falsetto whinny. It was a silly laugh. You could tell he hadn't had much practice.

He went to the front window and looked out, maybe expecting that I'd been foolish enough to leave the hearse parked out in front. Returning, he had calmed down enough to tell me that I had truly amazed him. That sounded sort of flattering, but he didn't mean it that way: "What an entrance! You just keep blundering along, don't you? We gave you every opportunity to pull out of this mess, even get out with a modest profit. But you persisted—very stupidly—and you kept getting lucky. And now, it seems, you've gotten very greedy."

I only followed a fraction of that. My confusion must have been plain on my face, for he started up again: "Are you foolish, or just plain stupid? Really, Cervantes, when that Jew from Washington got suspicious and insisted we send someone down there to Culiacan, I thought he was crazy to insist on sending one of you people—one of you Mexicans. I went along with him just to keep him quiet."

"But you sent Keeney down after me just to make sure that if I did turn up something, you'd have word on it."

"Oh, yes, Keeney. Well, I am sure about him," said Jarrett with a smirk. "He was undoubtedly stupid—and just as unlucky as you turned out to be lucky. An unfortunate combination, wasn't it?"

"It was for him."

He laughed that silly whinny again. "I see what you mean. If he'd been any luckier, you'd be dead—right?"

"Something like that."

"Well, I really have to give you credit there, Cervantes. You certainly have been fortunate or lucky or whatever. Although I think that even you must admit that your luck seems to have run out now."

"Oh, I don't know," I said as coolly as I could. "I thought you might want to make a deal."

"Sit down. Let's talk about that." Jarrett gestured to the couch, a place next to Alicia. I took it, giving her a pat on the knee I meant to be reassuring.

"He's going to kill us, isn't he?" she whispered.

"Not yet."

She pushed my hand away.

Jarrett pulled a chair up and sat down. "Would you care for a drink?" He was being almost solicitous and making a show of it.

"No thanks."

"As you wish. *Now!*" He said it sharply, like he was giving some sort of signal. But no. I glanced over at Saheed who gave no response. He stood with his back against the glass door to the patio, the shattered spider-web pattern made by my bullet half-hidden by his left shoulder. The gun that he had put against Alicia's head a few moments before was still in his right hand but now tucked away beneath his left arm. He appeared relaxed, arms folded, gun out of sight, but he had his eye on me and was ready for any move I made.

"Well," I said, testing the water, "I know you want Paco."

A grin spread over Jarrett's face. "Oh, yes, Paco. Of course I want him. I've always found him an entertaining fellow. Yet we both know that you have something I want much more, don't we?"

"Oh?" I said. "What's that?"

Jarrett looked at me sharply. His face changed in an instant. Any trace of humor suddenly vanished, and he looked not quite angry but cold and very businesslike. He leaned forward and peered down at me, his face not much more than a foot from mine. "Cut the shit, Cervantes. I'm not amused. You know what we're talking about. I'm referring to that hearse you drove up here from Ensenada and what it's got inside it."

"You know all about that, huh?"

"I know all about everything."

Somehow this news failed to astonish me. I mean, here we were, after all. I'd known from the moment I stepped into the house what the stakes were in this game. The question was, why had it taken me so long to figure out his direct involvement in this business? I guess it was because I disliked the guy from the moment I met him. Any half-suspicions I may have had earlier I had put aside because of this. Didn't trust them. Too personal. But at last, during that final phone conversation out on the Interstate, bells started ringing in my brain so loud I couldn't ignore them. First of all, he was too damned worried I might get stopped by cops he hadn't bought off. Not even a guy as rich as Jarrett could pay them all off. He wouldn't have cared about any of that unless he had known what I was driving and what was in it. Then there was his phone number, too. The first time I dialed it from San Ysidro it seemed sort of familiar. It wasn't until that last time that it finally clicked. I checked, and there it was: one of the three that Paco carried on that card in his wallet.

"Why don't we just kill them both?" said Saheed. "I can find the hairse." He tossed it out as a sudden inspiration, the way you might suggest going out for dinner that night. If it didn't work out, he could always say it seemed like a good idea at the time.

Jarrett turned to him, smiling crookedly. "It's obvious to me, Saheed, that you'll never be a businessman."

Saheed frowned. "Why? Why you say that, Meester Jarrett?" I could tell he was offended. He didn't like losing face like this in front of me.

"What is the essence of business?"

"Money?"

"No. Wrong! That's the object, the goal, the jackpot. What's the heart of it? Tell me!"

Saheed raised his eyebrows and shrugged. He was trying to look bored with it all, but there was angry annoyance there as he signaled he would rather not continue this little game. He was showing more independence than I had expected.

Jarrett caught all this and didn't like it. Dismissing him, he turned back to me and fairly shouted out a single word: "*Negotiation!*"

"What?" I said. "I don't understand." I really didn't.

"Negotiation," he repeated. "That's the essence of business, the heart of it. That's deal-making, and business is one hundred percent deals."

"Negotiation?" I echoed the word, drawling it out.

"Absolutely!" It seemed to me he was acting just a little bit nuts.

"Well then, why don't we settle down and start negotiating?"

"Meester Jarrett," Saheed put in, "you make it all too complicated. I kill them both." He was a man with one idea, and he just wouldn't let go of it.

"You do that," I said, "and you'll never find out where that hearse is."

"Will you stay out of this, Saheed?" said Jarrett. "Let the man negotiate." Maybe Jarrett was a little nuts, but he was the very voice of reason compared to his Palestinian pal. "He's got something we want, and we've got something he wants."

"What's that?" I wanted to know. "What do you have that I want?"

"Why, I thought Saheed made the point pretty well. Your life, Cervantes." He smiled coldly and pointed at Alicia beside me. "And hers, too."

"Okay, let's deal."

"Very sensible. Just got in a little over your head, didn't you? Well, we can work things out, I'm sure—find some satisfactory formula by which you get what you want, I get what I want, and we're both able to retire from the field with honor."

"And alive?"

"And alive, certainly."

"It sounds to me like a Mexican standoff."

"I'm sure that's how it would sound to you, Cervantes." And he broke up laughing at his own little joke.

Alicia had watched all this and listened to it with the sort of intense concentration you give a language you don't really comprehend. So while Jarrett was still laughing, she turned to me and asked, "Chico, you do business with this man?"

I nodded.

"You know what? You're crazy—*completamente loco*."

"Quiet, Alicia, please!" I whispered. "He understands." I assumed he did, anyway. Even a total *gringo* knows what "*loco*" means.

"I won't keep quiet." She said it even louder. "This man is a shark. He'll eat you like a little fish. And me, too."

"I'll handle this"—trying to sound stern.

She threw up her hands in dismay. "You'll handle this, eh? Just like you handled things up in the Sierra! Ay, *exactamente!*"

That hurt.

"Now," said Jarrett, rubbing his hands and grinning so wide he actually did look a little like a shark, "let's get down to business."

In spite of all his talk about a formula satisfactory to both of us, it was evident when I set out with Saheed that Jarrett was holding all the cards and had every intention of keeping them. The hearse for Alicia. Where would the exchange take place? Saheed would give me directions when we got to the hearse. And that was when Saheed would hand over my pistol to me. I would drive the hearse, and he would follow me in the rental car. And so on and so on. I didn't believe a word of it, but what could I do?

Adding insult, he gave me the job of tying up Alicia so she would cause him no problems on the drive to the rendezvous point. Just imagine how she felt about that. As I tried to explain to her the arrangements we had worked out, trying hard to make them sound as reasonable as I could, she kept up a steady line of chatter—baiting me, berating me, ridiculing me.

"Tie the knots tight. Do what he tells you. Ay! You handle the rope pretty good for a little fish! How do you do that, eh? You make hands from your flippers? Very *good*, little fish!"

"Alicia, shut up and listen." I cast a quick glance over my shoulder. Jarrett was paying no attention at all. He was deep in whispered conversation with Saheed, who was keeping gun in hand and an eye on me. What were they talking about? Probably where to dispose of our bodies.

"Oh? What you have to tell me now? How everything is going to be okay? Just like in the movies?"

"No, listen to me. *I* drive the hearse. We make the switch, and you come with me."

"I won't come with you! I won't be part of your *locura!*"

So, although I hate to admit it, by the time I started off in the rental car with Saheed, it was almost a relief to get away from her. Not that he was such terrific company, but in the hours that followed he never once called me a "little fish."

He was beside me with the pistol—now it was my Heckler & Koch—held in his lap, trained on me rather casually. I was in the process of rethinking Saheed. What happened back there in the house between Jarrett and him meant that not quite all was right between them. Maybe he had been asked to clean up after the boss just once too often. Maybe he thought Jarrett took him for a fool. Or, remembering how the great man had held his first audience from his bath and Saheed had been right there with the towel, maybe there was something sexual between them. Maybe it was all of these. And any one of them meant there was a good possibility of tension between them.

"How long have you been working for him?" I asked. Just then we were turning off Balboa Island. We would soon be heading toward the freeway and on our way toward the airport. I had to stall. I had to create some kind of diversion.

"That's no matter to you," he said. "I think you should drive now and give attention to find the hairse." He spoke in a sort of indulgent way, like he was correcting a child. It occurred to me that it was just about the same tone Jarrett had used on him. "If you don't remember where you put it, then you die, and the woman dies, too. You heard what Meester Jarrett said. You should believe that."

"You believe everything he says?"

"Everything."

"Even that stuff about negotiation?" I went right in and began digging at the wound. "You want to negotiate?" I glanced over at him and found him looking at me sharply.

"You already make a deal with Meester Jarrett."

"That's right. Now maybe I want to make a deal with you."

There was a long pause. I glanced over at him, once, twice— still no reaction. Suddenly he laughed—something between a snarl and a guffaw. "You drive," he said at last.

That was what I did—for a few blocks, saying nothing. Until at last, looking straight on and studying the rear of the car just ahead, I said, "Just how much of a businessman are you? You have enterprises of your own?"

I could practically hear his temperature rise at that, but I said nothing more and continued to stare out the windshield.

At last he hissed, "Yaiss! Yaiss! I *am* a businessman. I make many deals of my own."

"With Jarrett's permission, of course."

"Some yes, some no. When I come to this Godless country I was like a beggar. I work in a gas station. I fill up their big cars. Now I have a car of my own—a big car, a Cadillac! You think I buy that on what he pays me? *Ha!* I make deals. I *negotiate!*"

I had shaken him a little, put him on the defensive. He wasn't used to having his bluff called, particularly when he had a gun in his hand.

"What kind of bargain you want to make?" he asked.

"The same one I made with your boss."

He frowned, trying to make sense of that. And then the light went on: "Ah, I understand! You wish to buy life protection."

"Insurance. I wish to buy insurance."

He looked at me with amused contempt for a long moment, reclaiming control of the situation. The hand with the pistol twitched nervously in his lap a couple of times as I waited for him to respond. Finally: "Explain."

"No need. You heard us work it out, all the details. I want everything to happen just exactly that way."

"And why you think it won't?"

"I'll feel better about it if we make our own deal."

"So? What you have to offer?"

I swerved out of traffic and over to the curb. Maybe this was really going to work. But Jesus, Mary, and Joseph, what did I have to offer? How much did I have left in traveler's checks? "Five hundred dollars?"

"Fegh!" It sounded like Yiddish to me, which, coming from him, was pretty funny.

"All right. Okay." That did seem a pretty trifling amount considering the stakes. "My car. How about my car? I'll sign that over to you."

"That little car you drive first time you came? Why do I want a little car? I have a Cadillac."

"Hey, that's an Alfa!"

"You had accident with it. I saw other kind of paint on it."

"Primer, yeah. Put a new coat on it, and you can get ten thousand anytime, anyplace."

He considered this for a moment, then shook his head. "No. You think I am Cal Worthington that I should sell used cars?"

Jesus, now I'd insulted him.

Again he laughed that nasty laugh. "Drive," he said. And just to make sure I understood, he waved the pistol at me.

I started to say something—but what? I sighed, threw the car into gear, cramped the steering wheel to the left, and was just about to move out into traffic when suddenly it hit me. The apartment—my apartment! It was the one thing I owned that might interest him—and he couldn't take it away from me without my cooperation.

"What about my apartment? You were there. You saw it. Wouldn't you like to own it?"

"Apartment?" I could tell he was intrigued. "It is yours?"

"Sure it's mine—a condo in the safest little building in West Hollywood. You'd like that, wouldn't you? I mean, you must have some life for yourself away from Jarrett—right?"

He studied me, evidently trying to weigh my question and the assumptions behind it. And at last he said, "My life is my business." Then: "You make a deal with where you live?"

"Sure. And listen, we're talking Hollywood—movie stars—Raquel Welch, uh, Goldie Hawn, John Travolta!" I tossed him in just in case what I half-suspected about Saheed and Jarrett might be true.

"Can you do this without a lawyer? Meester Jarrett always have a lawyer."

"Sure I can. Only . . ."

"Only . . . what?"

"Well, I can write up the deed on anything, the back of an envelope—it doesn't matter. I sign it, and the place is yours—all completely legal. But I'm not writing up anything, and I'm not signing anything until the girl and I are out of this."

"We work out the details. Now you drive."

And drive I did, back along the route I had come from the Orange County Airport. On the way up the short Newport Freeway, I saw the blinking lights that marked the field some distance ahead. I tried to work out in my mind just how far and how long I could string Saheed along with the promise I had made to sign over the apartment. It seemed oddly like a mathematical problem—the kind that begins with thirty-seven barrels of nails on one side of the river and a boat that will only carry three. How many lies would I have to tell? What kind? How many times would Saheed wave the gun under my nose? How many times would he pull the trigger? Because, as I was sure, he must be working at the same problem from the other end, we made most of the ride to the airport in silence. By the time we were close, I had decided all I could do was to take it one step at a time. Why kid myself? It was all just a stall, anyway.

"I knew you leave it here." It was Saheed. If a wolf could smile, he would have looked like Saheed did just then.

"Yeah, you said you were pretty sure you knew where it was."

"I know."

"Are you a gambler?"

"Am I a gambler? I have gambled many times with my life. I am not afraid to take a chance with my life, if you mean that."

"No, I mean, would you like to make a bet?" I never met

an Arab who wouldn't. "You find the hearse. Tell me where you want me to go."

"What you bet?"

"That five hundred?"

"Sure. I bet."

We were just about there. A little action on the side—why not? It might keep him diverted, amused, interested enough to play the same game with me for a bigger payoff.

He tapped me on the shoulder with the barrel of the pistol as we approached the turn into the airport and indicated I should take it. It looked like he had me cold, until a couple of hundred yards down the road he made his mistake.

"Turn left," he said.

"You're sure? Left? Not right?"

He gave me that wolfman look again. "Left."

I did as he said and saw by the signs posted along the way that we were headed toward the cargo area. Good bet—safe, logical . . . but wrong.

There was a small parking lot just in front of the long, low warehouse structure. He had me stop there, jumped halfway out of the car and scanned the area. No hearse. He dropped back into the seat beside me and snarled something unintelligible. Probably Arabic.

I'd really rather he had won. The idea was to keep him interested—not get him pissed off at me, but he was pissed off now, all right. I glanced over at him and saw that the hand that held the gun was shaking—and he had his finger just about on the trigger. Was the safety on? I was afraid the thing might go off by accident. Then where would we be?

But for our dealings in the future it seemed important that he be reminded of the rules. So I reminded him. "You lose," I said.

Then, just as suddenly as the fit of temper had siezed him, it vanished. Not that he was suddenly calm—but at least his shaking stopped. His eyes narrowed, and he jumped out of the car again, looking farther and wider this time. He had another idea.

Back in the car, he slammed the door. "Turn around," he ordered.

"Hey, wait a minute. Admit it. You owe me five hundred."

"*Turn around!*"

Well, sure I did it. Wouldn't you, with your own HK nudging you in the ribs?

This time Saheed got it right, sending me directly to the parking structure and inside, and every foot of the way up the ramp I'm arguing with him, telling him that he's got some nerve if he thinks he can welsh on a bet. And so on. I sounded obnoxious even to myself—but getting him to admit he owed me five hundred had suddenly become very important to me. It's funny that in tight situations you can sometimes become obsessed by matters that are, to say the most, of secondary importance.

"Stop," said Saheed.

Somehow it didn't register. "Huh?"

"I said, *stop!*" He jammed the pistol so sharply into my side that it hurt.

That registered. I slammed on the brakes, throwing him up against the windshield and jarring loose a stream of curses in Arabic nasty enough to shock his imam back in Jerusalem.

I looked around, and there we were, just opposite the hearse.

"There. You see?" He pointed with the pistol.

"All I see is you owe me. Admit it."

"I knew you would leave it at the airport."

"Close doesn't count."

He looked at me sourly and seemed about to say something. Instead he simply motioned me out of the car. With a shrug and a sigh, I opened the door and climbed out. For some reason, he chose to follow me out on my side and was just struggling out from under the steering wheel when, without looking, I almost slammed the door on him. Well, I did slam the door on him—but it didn't shut because his ankle got in the way.

Two things happened simultaneously. He let out a howl— of anger? pain? It didn't matter. That I would have expected.

But at the same time, he fired a shot from the Heckler & Koch, my pistol. I didn't know whether to run or hit the deck. Instead I just stood there, frozen, listening to him growl out another string of Arabic curses.

He hadn't aimed it at me. In fact, he hadn't aimed it at all. The thing just went off from a reflexive squeeze on the trigger when the door hit his ankle. The shot pierced the side window and left a little ring of shattered glass. It must have traveled up on an angle away from me. Maybe I heard it ricochet. I'm not sure.

But one thing I was sure about now—and that was that he had the safety off. Then and there I gave up all hope of making that swap Jarrett had worked out in such detail. He probably told him just to leave me in the trunk of the car I'd rented. What could be neater? I began tingling a little. Not shaking—tingling. My nerves began telling me to do something. Anything.

"You try to hurt me? Or you just stupid?"

"Just stupid, I guess."

"Fegh!"

He pushed out of the car and limped around a few steps, testing his ankle. Satisfied it would support him he waved at the hearse. "Open it up," he said.

I felt for the keys in my pocket and, with them in hand, stepped slowly to the rear door of the hearse, still tingling.

"A moment," said Saheed. "Wait."

I looked back at him questioningly, and he limped over toward me.

"I think you make out the paper now."

"What paper?"

"The one that says I have your apartment."

It seemed to me then that if I did that I was as good as dead. "Bullshit. You know the deal. This is when you hand over the pistol." Fat chance.

"Write it out . . . *now*. You have paper? An envelope? I have a pen." He reached into the inside pocket of his jacket.

"No! Bullshit!" Keep him occupied. I turned around and jammed the key into the rear door of the hearse, pulled on the handle, and flung the door open.

It's difficult to describe just what happened then—partly because I didn't see quite all of it. As I pulled open the door, I stepped back and held it so that it was between me and the open rear of the hearse. And a damned good thing I did.

There was a sudden movement on the other side of the door. I don't know if I saw something, heard it, or simply sensed it. But there it was—there *he* was—*Paco!*

He fairly exploded from that space in the rear of the hearse where I had worked so hard to stuff him. With a scream, he leaped into Saheed, slamming into him as though he hadn't known he was there. He probably didn't.

Saheed flopped onto the floor of the garage, down on his shoulder so that his arm went out at a crazy angle and his head hit the cement with a loud, nasty crack.

Paco? He didn't even bother to look around. He ran down the long ramp, his arms flailing wildly as he staggered down the double line of cars. And with each step he took, he let out a scream or a sob. He went like that, howling into the night.

Then I remembered poor Paco had been shot through with PCP. That boy was having one hell of a bad trip.

I stepped around the door and knelt down beside Saheed. He was not only unconscious, judging from his crooked posture he must also have broken his arm or dislocated it at the shoulder.

I looked around near him and saw what I wanted—the pistol, my HK automatic. I picked it up and tucked it into my belt. Saheed was in pretty bad shape. His head was bleeding onto the slick cement. I felt around just below his ear until I found his pulse. And there I sat, counting it, while I tried to figure out what I was going to do now.

CHAPTER 17

I was sitting in the waiting room of the Costa Mesa Medical Center emergency ward, and it reminded me of when I was a cop. Got any idea how much time cops spend in emergency rooms? Bringing in the wounded, taking statements from the dying, or maybe just waiting around for their partners to get bandaged up before they go out on the street again. A lot of time, believe me.

I even met my ex-wife in an emergency room. That was my second year on the LAPD. Me and my partner—back then, it was a very crusty redneck type named Breckenridge—we picked up a woman, about thirty, on Normandie who came staggering out into the middle of the street, waved us down, and said she'd been raped and robbed. Her face was cut, and she was drunk—but drunk women get raped too. We took her to the nearest hospital, which was a Kaiser Permanente, a lot like this place, and after they had done whatever they do, I went in and took her statement while Breckenridge waited outside in the lobby. The nurse was just finishing up with her—a blonde, kind of petite, not big and tough the way a lot of nurses are. That was Gloria. She sort of hung around while I talked to the woman, and she told me afterward she admired my professional manner. That was nice. I told her I thought hers was okay, too. One thing led to another, and before you knew it, I had her phone number and had asked her out to lunch the next day. The woman on the table looked at us like she couldn't believe it. She gets raped, and we're hitting away on each other like a couple of college kids at the spring mixer. I understand her confusion.

But, like the song says, that was another time and another place. So here I am waiting, remembering how it was when I was a cop and how I met my ex-wife. From time to time I glance over at the only other person in the room, a middle-aged woman who brought in her husband a half-hour ago with an asthma attack. She's reading a magazine like she's been through it all before. I've been here about an hour myself. Not that I spent it all sitting. It seemed like I'd been on the phone about half that time—but probably only five minutes or so. First I called Jarrett's place and got his answering service. No, Mr. Jarrett was not in now—or at any rate he was not taking calls. The ranch? No sir, we don't give out any of Mr. Jarrett's other numbers. Your best bet is to leave your number. You'd rather not do that? Is there a message?

"Yes," I said, "tell Mr. Jarrett that there's been an accident. Saheed's out of it. But I've got two stiffs stuffed with Mexican brown, and I'm still ready to deal."

There was a long pause at the other end of the line. Finally: "I'll tell him that, sir. Just as soon as he calls in."

I hung up. Then I paced the waiting room, back and forth, two or three times, trying to make up my mind what to do next. I knew I needed help, and so I decided to try to get it from the only other place it might be available. I went back to the telephone and called the DEA in Los Angeles.

I identified myself.

"We'd about given up on you," came the response.

"Well, uh, I've had some problems."

"Tell me about them."

I did, about as quickly as I could, casting looks over my shoulder from time to time as I did to make sure nobody was near enough to hear what I was saying. But there was only one interruption, and that came from my contact at the DEA.

"Wait a minute," he said. "You say this man's name is Jarrett?"

"That's right."

"I've heard of him." Only that. No exclamation of surprise and no long, low whistle. He had just heard of him, that was all.

I pushed the story to a quick conclusion with a brief description of what had happened in the parking garage, where I had left the hearse, and I told him where I was right at that moment. It all took about four or five minutes of fast talking. When at last I finished, there was a moment's pause while I caught my breath and let what I had said sink in.

At last he said, "So?"

This guy was really trying my patience. "Whatta you mean, 'So?' "

"I mean, so what? Look, Cervantes or whatever your name is, none of this is any good to us unless you show up with the hearse at that funeral parlor on Ocean Park. That's where we got our search warrant. That's what we were set up to hit. We've been sitting here in the office half the night waiting for you to call. So now you do call, and you tell us, forget about the funeral parlor and come on up and nail Jarrett with the stuff, only you're not quite sure where he is right now, and you'll call and let us know just as soon as you find out. Isn't that what you're saying?"

I sighed. "More or less."

"Well, forget it. You want to bring Jarrett in on it, then you get him down to Ocean Park because that's the address on the fucking warrant. You got that?"

Pause. Never mind what I was thinking. "Yeah."

"Another thing. I had a pretty good team assembled for this operation, and all they been doing is sitting around here tonight pulling their dicks and piling up comp time. I'm sending them home. There's no way I can be sure when you're going to show up—or if you're going to show up at all. But I'll tell you what I'll do. I got two pretty good men out there on stakeout right now. I'll do you a favor. I'll leave them out there. That's your backup. Lotsa luck."

He hung up on me. People had been doing that a lot lately.

Not long afterward the lady with the asthmatic husband came in. The nurses came and went. There was nothing else I could do. I settled down to wait.

"Your friend can talk to you now."

It was a nurse—the bossy one who had taken over when I ran into the emergency room and told them I had an unconscious man in the car. She came out with two orderlies and a gurney and sped Saheed off into the curtained interior of the place. They even managed to be reasonably careful when I told them about his arm.

I looked at her. "My friend? Oh . . . yes."

I followed her past the desk, through a door into the treatment section.

The nurse glanced back at me. "That must have been quite some fall he took," she said rather pointedly.

"What? Oh, yeah. It was."

"How did it happen?"

"In a parking garage."

"That's where, not how." She stopped and confronted me.

"Uh, he was looking at some stuff on the back of my pickup. He lost his balance and fell off the tailgate."

She looked at me, nodded at last, then turned and led the way into the emergency ward. I wondered if the nurse had asked Saheed the same question. Probably. If she had gotten any answer at all out of him, then it had to be different from the one I had just given her. She was suspicious, that was certain. The last thing I wanted was local cops in on this. What could I say to set her at ease? Not much.

Down the aisle and to a curtained area of about eight square feet. She threw back the curtain, and there was Saheed.

He was off the gurney and on a kind of high cot now, not exactly a hospital bed. The nurse stood back by the curtain—watching us closely, I was sure. As I approached, Saheed looked at me but said nothing. His head was bandaged, and there was a cast on his left arm.

"Well, uh, how you feeling?" I asked, pretending sympathy I certainly didn't feel.

Saheed still said nothing. He simply watched me as I hovered awkwardly at the foot of the cot.

"Can you talk?"

"I . . . can . . . talk." But not without some difficulty.

I turned to the nurse. "I wonder if you'd mind leaving us alone for a few minutes?"

Obviously she did mind. She stood there and looked at me and then at Saheed. And after nearly a minute, she turned and bustled away without a word.

I moved up close to him on the side with the cast. I bent close to him and said, "You're in deep shit."

He stared at me. "Paco . . . with you. He die . . . too." Then a pause and a slurred "Messkins," followed by a word or two in Arabic.

"Never mind that. Listen. You're out of it. You're out of the game. What I want from you is the location of Jarrett's ranch, if that's where he is, and the goddam phone number."

His answer was in Arabic. It sounded scatological. But so does the whole language.

"I'm still dealing. I want the girl. Jarrett wants the hearse. He's left his house. You two were talking about a ranch. Is that where he is?"

This time he didn't say anything at all. He just stared at me.

I looked around to make sure the nurse wasn't back watching us. Satisfied we were alone, I gave him a short, hard jab on the cast where I thought it would hurt most. The cast was still soft. I felt it give under the force of my fist. It must have hurt plenty, but he didn't cry out, thank God. He just gritted his teeth and let out a sharp groan.

"I'll keep it up," I promised him. "And if this doesn't work, I'll start on your head."

I got through to him. I must have looked a little crazy because that's how I felt. Anyway, he began to take me seriously. He got his voice back at last. "We make a deal."

"What kind of deal?"

"Same deal . . . apartment . . . paper."

Jesus, never underestimate the power of avarice. Here I am trying to save Alicia's life, if she still had a life left to save, and he's in the market for real estate. I couldn't believe it.

I stared at him, and he stared back. At last I patted around my pockets and pulled out a ballpoint and a memo pad. I hastily wrote out something with a lot of "whereases" and an "in return for certain considerations." But I purposely put down the wrong number on the address—not that a document that had been extorted like this one would ever stand up, but just to be safe. I dated it, signed my name, and added, "under duress" in parentheses, assuming the phrase would only look like so much legalese to him.

I held it up for him, and he read it with difficulty. He moved my hand back and forth until he could find a point where his eyes could focus. Not quite satisfied, he pointed to the final phrase in parentheses. "What . . . means this?" he asked.

"Under duress? It means the sale is final. You know, for the duration of our lives or something."

He nodded, satisfied, and tried to pull the paper from my hand. I pulled it back. "Can you write?" I asked.

Again he nodded. I handed him the pen and notebook. "Address and phone number," I insisted.

With a shaking hand, barely under control, he scrawled something down on the pad.

I didn't have a chance to read it, for just at that moment the nurse showed up with a cop. He was young but he was big, and he came at me like he was expecting trouble.

"Sir, I wonder if you'd mind stepping out into the lobby and answering a few questions." The way the cop put it, it was an order and not a request. There didn't seem to be any point in arguing with him.

As I turned to go with the cop, Saheed grabbed out of my hand the bit of paper on which I had signed my apartment over to him "in return for certain considerations." I looked at Saheed, and I looked at the cop. I decided this wasn't the time to fight him for it. A lot of good it would do him, anyway. With a shrug, I pocketed the notebook and followed them out to the lobby.

"I don't mind telling you," the nurse said, practically shaking her finger at me, "I think there's something very suspicious going on here."

"I'll handle this, ma'am," the cop said.

"Look, this is very easily explained." I was speaking with an exaggerated calm. "The man simply fell off the back of my pickup truck."

"That's what he said before," the nurse snapped. "Didn't believe him then, don't believe him now."

"Was the truck moving, sir?"

"No, of course not. It was parked."

"Where?"

"Look," I challenged them both, "would I have brought him here if I did all that to him?"

"I'm going to ask you again, sir, where was the truck parked?" He was what you might call insistent.

"It was in the parking garage at the airport."

"Which airport, sir? The John Wayne Airport?"

This guy was beginning to annoy me. "The Orange County Airport."

"Well, sir," he said, "I'm not sure they allow trucks in there."

"They allowed mine."

"Well, I'll tell you, sir—" he moved toward me like he might be measuring me up for a choke hold. "I think maybe we ought to go back and talk to the man back there in—"

There was a sudden commotion at the entrance. Screams, cries, yells, curses—and two other local cops exploded through the automatic doors with a very reluctant patient. It was Paco,

210

wild-eyed and barely under control—howling, kicking, flailing, and, just inside the door, almost shaking loose.

"Hold him! Shit!" one of the cops yelled. "Dortmunder, give us a hand with this guy! He's fucking crazy."

Dortmunder—my cop—looked at me, looked at them, and turned back to me. "Uh, I'll be right with you, sir," he said, and then ran over to help. Polite to a fault.

I sort of faded slowly around them, giving them a lot of space as they pushed, shoved and pulled poor Paco in a direction he obviously didn't want to go.

The nurse noticed me just about the time I reached the door.

"Hey! You! Stop!" she yelled. "Officer, he's getting away."

Dortmunder let go of Paco and started after me. Just then Paco kicked out wildly and landed one on Dortmunder's knee, sending him sprawling to the floor.

I was through the door. Into the rental car. And out of there.

It wasn't until I was back inside the parking garage and sitting behind the wheel of the hearse that I pulled out the notebook to see where I was headed. When I saw what Saheed had written, I was ready to bang my head against the nearest concrete pillar.

Of course! There, in scrawled block letters, was the address of the funeral home on Ocean Park and underneath it the telephone number of the place. That settled it. He must certainly have had orders to leave me in the trunk of the rental car and drive the hearse straight to Santa Monica. With me out of the way, of course there would be no need to adjourn to neutral ground to make any sort of exchange. With me out of the way, there would be no need to keep Alicia alive.

I got out of Costa Mesa just as quickly as I could, half-expecting Officer Dortmunder to show up on my tail, dome-lights flashing, until I got onto the 405. Once on the freeway, I thought hard, trying to work out some sort of plan. Nothing came to mind. The trouble was, I was going in there blind. I had no idea whether the two DEA guys would be there, or where. And I couldn't figure out how I could sucker Jarrett out to do business. If I got too close to him, then he'd have me for sure. Like that big spider in my dream.

Add to that, I was exhausted. Whatever adrenalin I had left had been used up getting away from the hospital. As I settled in for the long drive to Santa Monica, the crushing weight of all those hours without sleep pressed down on me like some huge, shapeless mass. The steady flow of lights from the onrushing traffic in the southbound lanes lulled me hypnotically, trailing sizzling streams of yellow-white. And the haloed red taillights of the cars ahead danced weirdly, stuttering up and down, shimmying back and forth. I had a firm hold on the wheel, but I was afraid that in another moment or two I'd start drifting out of my lane, or begin hallucinating, or maybe just pass out altogether.

"Jesus!" I yelled out loud. "Get hold of yourself, man!" That helped. The sound of my own voice in my ears roused me momentarily—enough, anyway, to remember those uppers Anselmo had presented to me when we left him back in Ensenada. I rummaged through my pockets and found I had a few. I popped one, and then I thought, what the hell, and popped another.

Then I started yelling again—hooting, hollering—anything to have some noise in my ears. High school cheers, half-remembered songs from the sixties. Anything. Noise.

I'm not sure how long I kept that up, but by the time I'd grown hoarse, I was feeling slightly nauseated from the capsules and suddenly alert, more than alert—brilliantly, precisely, completely in command. In other words, I had speed-balled my way into a state of screwball euphoria. Which was terrific for getting me where I wanted to go—but probably not so good once I got there. I drove.

Me worry? My luck had held out this far, hadn't it?

Was it at that precise moment that the lights of the CHP

cruiser began flashing in my rearview mirror? No, farther on, I think. It was just that time had telescoped while I was flying along on that mix of speed. Not exactly a dreamy state—completely the opposite, in fact—but the clarity and precision with which I seemed to be experiencing everything had reality slowed to half-speed or less. Or really, the passage of time wasn't a factor at all. Each instant was complete in itself, as though I was moving along outside of time.

That was the state I was in when those lights suddenly exploded behind me. I admired them in the rearview mirror. It had never before struck me how completely that revolving pattern of red and blue could fill the night. Terrific. Like a light show from the sixties.

The speedometer said I was doing seventy-five miles an hour. That surprised me. I had bet a few hours ago that this old hearse wouldn't do more than fifty-five, and I had been careful enough then not to try to find out. Now I began to wonder just how fast it really would go.

We were somewhere near the airport—probably just about at the Imperial Highway exit—which also surprised me. Had I really come so far? I eased over to the right, one lane at a time, slowing down as I went. At last the hearse moved over to the shoulder lane, and I let it coast to a halt. The CHP cruiser stopped behind me—close but not too close.

I sat tapping the wheel triple-time, trying to decide what to do. I should probably get out and walk back to the cruiser. I tugged the automatic out of my belt and tucked it down under the seat next to the tranquilizer gun. A lot of good that would do. If they wanted to, they'd find some excuse to go through the car, and they would want to. A jumpy joker like me, trying to prove he's a private detective licensed in the state of California? Questions, check it out on the radio, and then more questions. I could see the entire scenario reel out before me, and it looked like it would take an hour or more. Maybe all night if they checked with Orange County. Under the circumstances, I couldn't let that happen.

They had red and white sidelights on me now. I watched in the rearview as one of the two cops inside the cruiser opened his door, got out slowly and stiffly, tucked in his baton, and began lumbering toward me.

Then. Just then I suddenly saw it all—what would happen next and what would happen after that. Man, I was totally in control of events. This was my scenario, and I would make it happen my way by force of will. (Look, I know how this sounds, but I was still sailing.)

I let the cop get close—oh, very close, right up to the door, in fact. Then just as he was about to lean in the window, I jammed my foot down on the accelerator. And would you believe it? That hearse peeled rubber. The cop jumped clear—and I was *gone*!

There was something under the hood that wasn't stock. The boys in Tijuana had worked this one over so that it roared out, fairly fishtailing along the shoulder lane, streaking beside the flow of traffic that had slowed to form a sort of mini-gaper's block. It was all I could do to control the wheel for a moment, then just as it looked like I was going to sideswipe a gleaming Mercedes, the driver panicked and screeched to a full halt, giving me the gap I needed. I swung through it, intimidated the driver of a pickup truck in the next lane over and was suddenly free of the crowd. The speedometer needle climbed steadily. I stopped looking when it hit eighty. I had to. I had to pick my way through the field of cars ahead. A couple of them saw me coming and made way. Smart. A few others must have wished they had as I rocked on by them. I was doing a great job getting away from the CHP.

But hey! I was doing *too* well. I shot a glance into the rearview and caught a glimpse of flashing domelights far behind: the cruiser was still fighting to get clear and out in full pursuit. This wasn't part of the plan. I wanted them right on my tail. I eased off a little, and for a long instant took my foot off the accelerator until I saw them trailing directly behind and beginning to close the gap between us. Then I hit the gas again and kept them right back where I wanted them.

Look sharp now. Don't miss the turn. I was all the way to La Tijera. I worked my way back over to the right. They'd see that, wouldn't they? Just to make sure they didn't miss my intentions I hit the brakes a couple of times, pumping hard for that long, sweeping down-and-up curve that shoots you out onto the Marina Freeway. Even so, I hit the curve pretty fast—too fast—and almost lost it there among the pillars under the 405. But somehow I held on, somehow I steered through, and I wished the boys behind me the same good luck. I needed them.

Once out there on the Marina Freeway I got a very funny feeling. It must have been when I saw the Centinela exit flashing by. That was when I realized that it was here that Paul Jarrett and Sarah Silverstein went over the side trying to cut off Paco. That happened right here—and I was driving the hearse now. I looked up and found the CHP moving up on me in the rearview. As I jammed the accelerator down the fraction of an inch that separated it from the floor, I suddenly lost a lane. Jesus! That was how it must have happened with those two kids. I swung left sharply, cursing myself for not remembering the freeway layout but managing to keep the big boat on even keel as I swept past three cars in quick succession.

We were down to two lanes now, and the END OF FREEWAY sign was flashing dead ahead. I barreled through Culver, and then Alla, and the cops behind me were really getting close as I approached Mindanao. Now I'd see if those guys in Tijuana had done more than crank up the engine on this machine. Let's check out the suspension. I hung back to the last possible moment and then some, then slammed down hard on the brake pedal twice and twisted the wheel to the left.

Somehow it all hung together, and I made it around the corner on to Mindanao—which is more than I could say for the CHP guys behind me. They must have fishtailed and overshot it a good fifty feet—not that I looked close and counted—but they were just getting untangled when I shot across Lincoln and began looking for the Sheriff's cops who would be waiting for me around Admiralty Way. Marina del Rey was their territory, and its main drag was a speed trap. They had to be around here somewhere.

Yeah, there. As I careened right onto Admiralty Way, a black-and-white roared out of the shopping plaza parking lot in hot pursuit. Now I had two of them behind me, and with any luck I might pick up a third. The trick from now on was just to keep my lead on them for the rest of the run.

I worked my way onto Washington Boulevard, still ahead of the pack. They would expect me to continue right on down to Pacific—but no, I drifted left and swung right suddenly onto a sidestreet—Dell—knowing that what lay ahead might break the hearse into a smoking pile of nuts, bolts, rods, and springs. In the two blocks I had left before the big crunch I let the hearse slow down to about fifty or fifty-five. The flashing lights were gaining on me fast. Over the roar of the big Cadillac engine I could hear the wail of their sirens. Let them come. If they didn't know what was just ahead of them, they'd slow down quick enough when they found out.

As everybody and his aunt and uncle must know by now, Venice began life during the early years of this century as a real estate development modeled after the other Venice, the one with the pigeons and canals and gondoliers. They threw up a few houses and dug some canals before the development failed. Now there are many houses, including the few originals, and there are still the canals which are fed by seawater from the ocean. And over the canals there are bridges. The four bridges on Dell that pass over the four parallel branches of the Grand Canal are not much more than ten or fifteen yards apart. They hump over the water suddenly, rising a uniform three feet above street level, one after the other. Moving at a reasonable speed over them is a little like going slowly over a roller coaster. But hitting them at 55 mph is a little like . . .

Well, it was a lot like flying. Oh, I landed, all right—hard—four times, but at the crest of each successive hillock I soared out into the next with all four wheels off the ground. Nothing like that ever happened to me before, and I hope it never does again. The repeated explosion of tires on tar rattled my teeth and shook my bones and wrenched the steering wheel viciously in my hands. All I could do was fight to hold on and pray that the hearse held together. It did, finally bottoming out badly as it landed the last time on the unyielding pavement with a great WHAM.

Onto Venice Boulevard, only then risking a look back. They were a long time coming. I was a good block on my way to Pacific before the Sheriff's car wobbled out with the CHP close behind. I eased off a little to keep them in sight. Then, as I turned north on Pacific, there was a sudden, eerie light from above, and I realized there was no danger of the cops losing me. A police helicopter was up there just above me, shining its searchlight down. I would have heard him except for the roar of the hearse's engine. I rode into, and out of, and then back into the beam of light. The pilot was doing a good job of staying on top of me.

Maybe I was starting to come down a little bit from those two speed caps I popped. Or maybe this wild ride I had taken had scared a little sense into me. Anyway, I was no longer quite so confident. What seemed like a terrific idea when I took off and left that cop staring after me on the freeway now seemed kind of doubtful. It appeared simple enough at the time: if the DEA wouldn't provide me with backup, then I'd have to bring my own. I was still hoping to pick up another cruiser along the way.

I got my wish when I turned up Ocean Park and headed for the funeral parlor. The lights were still flashing behind me, and the Sheriff's car was moving along just fast enough to keep the CHP from cutting around it. It was all I could do not to leave them behind. The helicopter had pulled behind me. I could see its light playing down on the street ahead—and a bit of the thing itself, low, at the top of my windshield.

I hit the intersection of Ocean Park and Main doing sixty

and probably less—and I almost slammed into another cruiser right there at the corner. This one was white with blue markings—Santa Monica Police responding to radio call. The dome lights saved me. I caught a glimpse of them just as I entered the intersection and swerved hard left by pure reflex, just managing to avoid it. The Santa Monica car squealed to a full halt. Although I felt my right front wheel lift off the pavement, I managed to get back on course for those last few blocks.

God, where was it? That big old Victorian structure ought to be visible for a quarter-mile at least. But no, of course—it was just east of the overpass. There were three cars behind me now, back just where I wanted them—Santa Monica Police, Sheriff's cops, and CHP. Not much of a strike force, but they were what I had.

There it was on the corner, Turnbull and Son. The lights were on. I drew a bead on the funeral parlor, picturing the layout of the place, knowing that the big garage was right at the corner. I slowed, pulled the hearse up to the ramp, and backed it as far as I could. Then I came to a complete halt. The caravan of police cars had stopped to see what I was up to. The helicopter hovered directly overhead, its eye in the sky lighting my target. I had the hearse in neutral and revved that big Caddy engine up as high as it would go. When I threw it into drive, the big thing hurtled forward like some big, black cannon shell.

All I remembered then was crashing through that garage door.

CHAPTER 18

My head had hit the windshield. But I was out—completely out—for less than a minute. It couldn't have been more than that because as I struggled back to consciousness and peered through the windshield I had cracked, I saw a door open at the other end of the big room and two men come running inside. The open door threw light enough inside for me to see that I had crashed completely through the outside garage door and slammed into their hearse. The two Cadillac hoods had become one big, continuous crumpled mass.

Where were the cops? I scrambled to get out and found the door on my side wouldn't budge. A figure loomed before me—wild-eyed, moustached Mexican. He held a pistol pointed at me and waved excitedly for me to get out. Where were those cops?

"Hey! Put that gun away, mister. This guy belongs to us." The voice came from behind me, just about where the door should have been. My backup had arrived at last.

The Mexican looked around and yelled, "Ramon! *Policía!*"

With that, Ramon let go with a burst from an automatic weapon of some sort. I dove down, hugging the seat as my hand explored the space underneath for the pistol I had stashed there. I hoped I hadn't managed to get a cop killed.

My fingers touched something, found the pistol grip and closed around it. I opened the door on the passenger side and rolled out onto the floor of the garage.

"You're under arrest, mister." I knew the voice. It belonged to that cop they had shot at. "You have the right to remain—"

Ramon fired another burst, shattering the windows and windshield above us.

"Shut up," I whispered to the cop. "They can hear us."

He was one of Santa Monica's finest, young, about twenty-five, and probably a rookie. He nodded obediently. The kid knew how to follow orders.

"Where are all the rest of you guys?" I whispered.

"Well, they said it was our jurisdiction and they'd cover the back. My partner's calling for backup." So much for the CHP and the Sheriff's cops.

"And they sent you in alone?"

He nodded. He knew how to follow orders, all right.

I heard some shuffling around the other hearse, raised the pistol in my hand, and only then discovered that in my confusion I had grabbed the tranquilizer gun. Idiot! I laid it down, pointed, made a pistol with my hand, and wiggled my thumb. Again the kid nodded. And again there was the sound of movement. He jumped up into a crouch and pulled off two rounds through the windows of the hearse. I jerked him back down again—and a good thing, too, because Ramon got off a short burst of three.

"Who are those guys?"

"Shhh. Heroin."

He nodded. I had a pretty good idea where Ramon was. If I could get around the other hearse, I'd have an angle on him. I mimed out what I wanted the young cop to do: count off ten seconds, then give me some cover—bang-bang. I picked up the tranquilizer gun and began crawling forward as quietly and quickly as I could. At about the count of nine I had reached the point I was headed for. Which gave me one second to set up. Not enough time.

But when the rookie shot twice into the corner, it was the guy with the pistol who shot back—from over near the door where I had no chance at all. It looked like they might be edging their way out.

"Hey, Callagy, you need help?" Another voice from behind me—evidently the rookie's partner—reinforcements at last. Ramon must not have liked that because he let loose another burst.

"Jesus!"

I caught the muzzle flashes about where I expected them to be. But a moment later I saw a bulky figure, all but lost in the shadows, moving cautiously from that point toward the door. If he got much closer I would have lost my shot at him. Did I have a shot at him? Would the tranquilizer gun propel a dart across a space of thirty feet? Only one way to find out. I lined up on the shadowy target, resting the barrel on the bumper of the hearse, and then squeezed the trigger.

The noise of it was as before not quite as loud as a shot, more like the loud pop a BB gun makes. Who knows if Ramon even heard it? He went down in slow stages. First there was the clatter of his weapon, followed a couple of seconds later by the muffled clump of his body hitting the floor, and then almost simultaneously the nasty crack of his head on the concrete.

"Ramon? *Qué pasa contigo?*"

The rookie's partner fired at the sound of the voice—twice—with a pump gun. It reverberated off the walls of the garage like a couple of rounds of artillery. That was all it took.

"I geev," came the shout from near the door. "I geev op!" It was followed by the sound of his pistol skittering across the floor. A pause. Then: "Okay?"

"Okay," the rookie shouted, taking command at last. "Come out slow with your hands open and away from your body."

That's what he did, arms high above his head, a very serious and unhappy expression on his face.

The cop with the pump gun advanced carefully toward him, bent to pick up the pistol from the floor, and looked around.

"Callagy," he said to the rookie, "go check on the other guy." The kid went off and did as he was told.

I came out from behind the hearse and started over to the partner. He swung the shotgun in my direction. "Hold it right there," he said, "and drop that weapon."

"It's not really a gun. Well . . . it's sort of a gun."

"Drop it."

I bent down and carefully set it on the floor.

"This guy's out," the rookie called. He was kneeling over Ramon's body on the floor. He tugged him over onto his back. "It's like he's dead, only he's breathing—you know?"

"Tranquilized. He's going to have bad dreams."

The cop waved the shotgun in my direction again. "Now who the fuck are you?" he asked. "And what's this all about?"

There were four of us in the reception area of Turnbull and Son—Alicia and I sitting together, holding hands, and to hell with what anyone thought; young Mr. Turnbull, whom I'd met once before in this room, trying hard to look bored but sniffing nervously; and Thomas Jarrett, making no pretense to be anything but what he was as he paced the tight space—agitated and angry. His fury was so obviously aimed in my direction that the CHP cop at the door got edgy each time he came close to me.

"Mister," said the cop. "I think you better sit down."

"I won't sit down," said Jarrett. "I have no intention of sitting down."

The cop looked at him, weighing the situation, trying to decide if this guy really was as important as he claimed to be and if, under the circumstances, it really mattered. In the end, he decided it wouldn't be worth it to press the point. He shrugged. "Well, keep your hands to yourself. No trouble, understand?"

"You don't have a thing to worry about," Jarrett said dramatically. "I wouldn't dream of touching this . . . this . . ."

"Spoilsport?" I suggested.

That was as close as he ever came to leaping on me and throttling me. Maybe I should have kept my mouth shut. It would have been easier for both of us if I did. Just then I was more interested in getting an answer to a question than I was in maintaining the fragile truce between us.

They had rounded us up one by one from various points around the funeral home. By the time they marched me through the shattered door and out of the garage, there were two more Santa Monica squad cars on the scene. Their radios crackled. Their lights were on. Even at this time of night—it was close to 3:00 A.M.—the sudden police invasion and the sounds of battle had roused half the neighborhood from their beds. The helicopter still hovered above, throwing its light down on the small crowd of people in robes and pajamas, others in jeans and T-shirts. They stood conferring and staring at us across Ocean Park, which was as close as the cops would let them come. The partner with the riot gun walked me around the corner to the entrance of the funeral home. He was strutting with self-importance. "We got the guy," he called out. Why not? He had barely listened when I tried to explain the situation to him, only showing some interest when I told him the two bodies in the hearse were packed with Mexican heroin.

"The one you were driving?"

"Yeah. The one I was driving."

That settled it. They got the guy. Never mind the two who were doing all the shooting in the garage.

But at the entrance to Turnbull and Son, who should be there to greet me but Thomas Jarrett? Only he didn't say hello, he turned to the CHP guys who had him in tow and said, "That's the man. That's the one I told you about. He's a dangerous criminal."

They weren't buying it. At least not for the moment. They had picked him up as he made a hasty exit out the back when the shooting started, and it seemed they were getting a little tired of listening to him tell them what a terrible mistake they had made.

There were two guys in zip-jackets with some kind of badges pinned on who said they wanted to talk to me. They pulled me aside. When the Santa Monica cop started to argue, the shorter one pointed to the badge and said, "DEA. Agents Rossi and Sepulkis."

"Well . . ." The cop lowered his riot gun and looked from one to the other in confusion.

"He's ours," the short one said, "and we're going to talk to him."

"Well . . ." the cop repeated uncertainly.

The larger of the two agents, and this guy was plenty big, grabbed me by the arm, pulled me to an unmarked car close by, and shoved me into the back seat. Then he squeezed in beside me. The other one got in front. The interior of the car was unadorned federal. These guys seemed like the real thing. I hoped to hell they were.

Then the one in the front seat, Rossi, lit up a cigarette and said, "Okay. Tell us about it."

I did, and it took almost five minutes, blurting out the deal I had made with Jarrett, and what their boss had told me on the phone at the hospital, and the wild ride here from the freeway. I figured they knew the rest—or didn't need to know.

"That sounds like him, doesn't it?" said the big guy beside me. "Especially that part about 'piling up comp time.' Shit."

" 'I got two pretty good men on stakeout. They're your backup.' Oh, that's nice. That's real nice." Then to me: "You know what he told us? He said it was off. We should just hang around and note arrivals and departures. Well, we noted your arrival. Maybe we should note your departure."

"Huh?"

"He's on his way down. Let him sort through it without you. We'll make it right with the locals. You wanta walk, you can walk. Just be where we can find you." He looked back at the big guy who answered with an affirmative nod.

That was all I needed. I had my hand on the door handle—

and then I hesitated and pushed back in the seat. "I can't," I said.

"How come?"

"The girl's in there, at least I hope she is—the one that Jarrett had. The deal was, I go through with this and she gets to stay."

"The deal with Jarrett?"

"No, the deal with you guys. Maybe she's dead, I don't know. But look for her, okay? No telling what else you'll find if you do."

What they found was a regular little chemistry shop set up in the attic for processing raw heroin. In the showroom on the first floor, they found young Mr. Turnbull hiding in one of the coffins, a deluxe model with a lot of bronze and gilt trim over solid oak; he had propped the lid open with his cigarette lighter for air, and Sepulkis, the big guy, happened to notice. Finally, in a back office on the first floor, they had discovered Alicia tied to a chair, gagged and unhappy.

They brought her down to the reception area, which I was sharing with Turnbull. She ran to me and threw her arms around me. Nice. That felt good. Now the question was whether I could get her out of here. I asked her if she was okay.

"Sure, sure—but all these police . . ."

"We'll work it out."

"They don't even speak Spanish. I talk clear and very slow for them, but it does no good. They don't understand nothing."

Just then the CHP guys brought Jarrett in, and Alicia flew out of my arms at him. It was all I could do to grab her back.

"You!" she screamed at him. "If I had Chico's pistol I would shoot you. Chico, give me your gun and let me kill him!"

Jarrett understood perfectly well what she had said. And for all of his show of composure, he knew she meant it. "Take her away," he said to the CHP cop at the door. "I absolutely refuse to share the same space with her . . . or with him," pointing at us.

"Can't do that, sir. You're all supposed to stay right here."

I pulled Alicia back and seated her forcefully in a chair and pulled another one next to it. Then I sat down and grabbed her hand.

That's when Jarrett started pacing the room, losing his cool with each step he took. And in five minutes he had taken a lot of them.

"Look, Jarrett," I said, "why don't you just relax and accept the inevitable? You've had it. You're through. Not even Saheed's around to help you now."

He stopped suddenly and looked at me. "Yes, I'd like to hear about that. I'd like to know what you did with him."

"I put him in the hospital." Technically, that was true.

"I don't believe you."

"Costa Mesa Medical Center. Call them up and check."

His face seemed to crumple a little. "They won't let me use the phone," he confessed. The pacing started again.

"Aw, too bad. Can't get on the phone and fix this one, huh?"

"Hey, you two," the cop at the door called. "You shut up."

"Listen to what he's got to say," I called back. "You might learn something."

Then Jarrett turned to me and pointed again, just so I'd know he was talking to me. "I'm warning you, Cervantes."

I stood up and took a step toward him. "Okay, what's the warning?" I was daring him, baiting him.

"Sit down, you two—both of you. I mean it!"

"What does he say, Chico?" Alicia asked. She meant Jarrett.

"He says he killed his son," I said in Spanish, then repeated in English: "He had his own son killed." I didn't believe it for a minute, but I figured it might get a rise out of him.

"He did this thing?" She jumped up in outrage, then advanced toward Jarrett, shaking her finger at him as she said, "Let me tell you something, mister. You are an animal, a snake. No, snakes protect their babies. You are an insect, like a spider." She was the very picture of outraged motherhood. "You kill your own!"

The cop was in to separate us. He was pushing at Jarrett, trying to force him into a neutral corner. "I *didn't* kill him," Jarrett yelled at me. "The kid just got in the way. He found out about the schedule from Junior Turnbull here, who happened to be his fraternity brother. He showed up with that little Jewish bitch the night Paco made the last run. He started to lecture me—his own father! Trying to tell me what was right and wrong. While he was doing that, Paco got away, but they caught up with him, and they tried to knock him off the road. You know what happened then."

By that time the cop had wrestled him into a chair. Jarrett was panting from exhaustion—emotional, not physical. He looked for a moment like he might start to cry.

"Uh, Mr. Jarrett . . ."

There was a stranger in the doorway—a man about fifty dressed in a suit and tie with a badge on his lapel that looked like the ones Rossi and Sepulkis had on. He had to be their boss. "If I could have a word with you in private?"

The cop looked around in annoyance as Jarrett jumped up and smirked at me. "Certainly," he said and walked out with the man from the Drug Enforcement Agency.

"Okay, you two"—the cop suddenly turned on Alicia and me—"sit down and shut up."

That was the last I saw of Thomas Jarrett. It seemed that even though Jarrett had been denied access to a telephone, a few calls had been made in his behalf. I got this a week later when agent Rossi agreed to meet me at Barney's Beanery, and we wound up feeling so sorry for ourselves that we drank too much. He had to crash at my place around the corner. Come to think of it, that's the last I saw of Rossi, too.

Anyway, the DEA agent told me the night we got together that when his boss had heard somebody as big as Thomas Jarrett was involved, he got cold feet, and that was why he had called off the operation and sent the team home. Besides, he didn't really think I'd make it to Turnbull and Son. But just in case, he had kept Rossi and Sepulkis on the scene, knowing I had no way to communicate with them and that I would really be on my own. He didn't count on me making the entrance I did. And he wasn't prepared when he heard that Thomas Jarrett had been picked up making a swift exit out the back of the funeral home. He got on the telephone to Washington, asking his own bosses what he ought to do. By the time he got to Turnbull and Son, he had his instructions.

After Jarrett left, there was another wait of fifteen minutes or so. Turnbull was called out and didn't come back. At last the DEA man came back and beckoned to me. I left Alicia with a pat on the knee.

He wore a sour expression as he led me back to one of the offices. Nodding me inside, he stepped in behind me and slammed the door. "Well," he snapped, "you certainly screwed things up, didn't you?"

But I stood my ground: "I did just what I said I was going to do."

"Oh, sure," he sneered, "but the way you did it! You brought everybody in on it. I'm surprised you didn't call the newspapers, too."

"I would if I'd thought of it."

He gave me a disgusted look. "I'd like to remind you, Cervantes, this was supposed to be a DEA operation. You made a deal with us. We had a search warrant for this place. We had a team assembled."

"And you sent them home."

"Never mind what I did. Look what you did. You came crashing in with a parade of cops behind you. The deal was, you were supposed to be let in, and we'd come in after you and find the stuff in their possession."

"Tell that to Rossi and Sepulkis."

He glared at me. "Turnbull's saying now he never heard of you, doesn't know anything about any bodies coming up from Baja, and his night watchmen were just protecting the premises. In other words, we haven't got a case. Legally, the heroin's still in your possession."

I didn't like the sound of that. He seemed to have me measured to take the fall. "Yeah?" I blustered out at last. "Well, what does Jarrett have to say about it? He's in this up to his ears. He ran the whole operation."

That was when he dropped it on me at last. "Who's Jarrett? I never heard of Thomas Jarrett, and neither have you. If you ever get confused about that and think you have, then just remember that Mexican brown out there belongs to you. We're willing to forget that as long as you're willing to forget some things, too."

So that was the new deal. I didn't like it, but it looked like I would have to live with it. I put one last squeeze on him and got the green card that had been promised for Alicia. But that was where negotiations came to a halt.

I found her in the reception room where I had left her. She came when I waved her over, and without a word we walked past the CHP cop at the door. He gave me kind of a funny look. When we stepped outside we found a cab waiting for us, courtesy of the DEA. I gave the driver my address in West Hollywood. As we pulled away down Ocean Park, I noticed that the crowd that had turned out to watch the show had disappeared. They had all gone back to bed.

CHAPTER 19

The next couple of weeks were a mess. There were forms to be filled out for Budget Rent-a-Car of Mexico, S.A. I kept the details sketchy and suggested that further information could be supplied by William Madden of Culiacan in the state of Sinaloa. That was the last I heard from Budget. It was fixed.

I sent Silverstein a long letter explaining as well as I could just what had happened and managed to do it without once mentioning Jarrett by name. I believe I referred to him as "the other party to our agreement" and thereafter as "the other party." Which was pretty awkward, but I felt I had to give Silverstein a more exact explanation of the death of his daughter and Paul Jarrett. I asked him to destroy the letter after he had read it and said that I could only be more specific face-to-face. Under the circumstances, I didn't have the nerve to bill him for any more money. After all, I hadn't brought in Paco. Nevertheless, by return mail, I received a formal little note thanking me for services rendered and enclosing a check for five thousand dollars. I held it for a few days debating with myself whether to send it back. In the end I deposited it.

No, I didn't bring in Paco. Both he and Saheed disappeared from the hospital the next day. Paco was probably back in Mexico, and so were those two *pistoleros* who had shot up the Turnbull garage. The Santa Monica cops arrested them for assault with a deadly weapon, assault with intent to kill, and resisting arrest. All that got knocked down at arraignment to discharging firearms within the city limits, which was certainly a bailable offense. They walked and were last seen in a fast car headed south.

Turnbull and Son was closed for repairs and never reopened. The huge, old turreted structure stands vacant now, plywood patching covering the hole I put in the garage door. I drove out to Santa Monica one day with Alicia and asked around the neighborhood one day, but nobody seems to remember much about that night with all the fireworks.

None of this exactly astonished me—but I was in for a couple of surprises. The first one started with a telephone call.

"Mr. Cervantes?" It was a woman's voice—crisp, clear, and commanding.

"All right. Who's this?"

"Grace Jarrett. We have a mutual friend—*not* my ex-husband."

"Who then?"

"That nice Mr. Silverstein. We've been talking about you—and my ex-husband."

"Talking long-distance, I assume."

"No. He came out here last weekend to do a little investigating on his own."

"Oh?" I was surprised and a little disappointed. I had hoped to have the chance to give the details.

"I think he understood your situation better than you realize," she said in answer to my unasked question. "He thought it might be better if I talked to you . . . privately."

That led to an invitation to come by the next day for lunch at her home in San Marino. Alicia was a problem. Except for that night with Rossi, I hadn't left her alone, and I didn't want to. I explained to Mrs. Jarrett.

"Certainly I understand. Bring her along. I've heard a little about her, and of course I'd like to meet her."

That was how it happened that Alicia and I traveled to San Marino one Tuesday, making a stop on the way at Bullocks Wilshire's maternity shop to pick up something appropriate for the occasion. When we left, she was wearing a simple black frock with an ample drape that covered her rounding form discreetly, white gloves, and a white purse. She looked lovely, take my word for it. She was very quiet. As we settled in the car, Alicia leaned over and kissed me softly on the cheek. "No matter what happens, I'll always remember what you do for me, Chico. Only you have been so good to me."

After that, we were both pretty quiet on that drive out to meet Mrs. Jarrett. At one point, probably on the Pasadena Freeway, Alicia said, "This place we go to—San Marino? It's a Spanish name. Are there Spanish people there? Mexicans?"

"Not in San Marino."

Of course there were—gardeners, servants of every sort— and as a matter of fact, the woman who greeted us at the door was unmistakably Mexican. Alicia made the mistake of trying to engage her in conversation, asking her where she was from and who her people were. Probably she was lonely and bored, cooped up with me day and night. The maid handled the situation gingerly and with dispatch, answering her questions directly, then depositing us in the living room before fleeing off to another part of the huge house.

Grace Jarrett swept in, fluttering chiffon with each sure step she took. Alicia was intimidated. "She looks like she is in a movie," she whispered to me, and she was right. The house and its mistress had a perfection you don't associate with real life.

Mrs. Jarrett shook her hand and said very solemnly, "I'm glad to meet you. You're a very brave girl."

Alicia looked at me. "¿Cómo?"

"She says you're very brave."

That pleased her so much that she smiled and didn't say a word for the next hour or so—a personal record.

"Well, first things first," said Grace Jarrett, then strode over to a secretary where she sat down and wrote out a check for five thousand dollars. "Consider this my contribution. I'm used to paying my ex-husband's debts. The trouble you caused him is worth far more than this to me. You may need it, so please take it."

I did and thanked her. She made no attempt at small talk but plunged right into the matter at hand: "I want to hear how my son died."

As I told her, she listened carefully, not putting in a word or a question, her face gradually taking on the look of a mask as she refused to let go a tear.

When I finished, she nodded, sighed, and said, "I think Pilar is ready with lunch." She rose and led the way into a sunny nook off the living room. "I thought it would be much pleasanter out here."

When she sat us down, she went to a bar in the corner and poured herself a very stiff whiskey. "I need this. I think you'll find the wine much nicer." She pushed her plate aside and took a deep gulp. For the next couple of minutes I played with my food—some sort of avocado and shrimp salad—as she sipped silently at her glass. I'm sure she was right: the wine was much nicer.

"You know," she said at last, "I blame myself in a way. I had the money, and I managed to keep it. We old-timers are good at that. If I'd let Tom walk off with a little, he might not have gotten involved in what he did."

"Maybe," I said. "Maybe not."

She nodded. "Maybe not. Paul must have been terribly ashamed of him. Well, we must talk about you. Mr. Silverstein feels you're in at least some potential danger. He's going to do what he can at his end, and I'm going to do what I can. But there's something you must do to protect yourself from Tom."

"What's that?"

"I want you to write out a full account of this, all this, from start to finish—and do it as quickly as you can. When you finish, send Tom a photocopy by messenger so that he has to sign for it. Then place the original, with your signature on each page, somewhere he can't get hold of it—a safety deposit box, with your lawyer if he has a good safe, but somewhere that it will be read in the event of your death."

"All right," I said. It seemed like a good idea to me.

"Good," said Grace Jarrett. "I'll let Tom know it's on the way."

And that's how I came to write this. It hasn't been easy because Alicia can be kind of a pain in the ass sometimes. She wants attention and can't understand why I've been banging away on the typewriter night and day. I told her this is our insurance policy—but that makes no sense to her.

The second surprise came just today, as I was finishing this up. The doorbell rang. Because it was a woman who answered down below in broken and barely understandable English I buzzed her in. Big mistake. But I took the precaution of tucking my old .38 into my belt and going out into the hall with my hand on the grip.

There was a lot of noise on the stairs. A lot of noisy discussion in a guttural language that sounded to me like Arabic.

"Meester! Meester! We move in now please. You go away." The woman led the way, struggling up the stairs, hauling a suitcase and two boxes, while behind her trailed a procession of people, male and female, of a variety of ages and sizes. There must have been six or eight of them. A very extended family.

"Stop!" I said and displayed the old Smith and Wesson. They were impressed. They stopped. "Now what in the hell is this all about?"

"We move in. You go away," the woman repeated. She was about forty, dark and determined. An older man farther down yelled something up at her, and she yelled something back.

"No," I said. "This place isn't for rent. I own it, and I don't intend to leave."

"But we have paper!" she wailed and waved it at me. It looked familiar. "Mr. Saheed sell it to us. You go away."

"*You* go away!" I aimed the gun like I intended to use it. They turned and stampeded back down the stairs.

234

"We have paper!" the woman shrieked at me. "We come back!"

My lawyer assures me we can beat it, but it's going to take a little time and money. How much? Well, Rome wasn't built in a day, Chico.

THE MEASURE OF A MAN IS HOW WELL HE SURVIVES LIFE'S MEAN STREETS

BOLD NEW CRIME NOVELS BY TODAY'S HOTTEST TALENTS

BAD GUYS
Eugene Izzi
_____ 91493-8 $3.95 U.S.   _____ 91494-6 $4.95 Can.

CAJUN NIGHTS
D.J. Donaldson
_____ 91610-8 $3.95 U.S.   _____ 91611-6 $4.95 Can.

MICHIGAN ROLL
Tom Kakonis
_____ 91684-1 $3.95 U.S.   _____ 91686-8 $4.95 Can.

SUDDEN ICE
Jim Leeke
_____ 91620-5 $3.95 U.S.   _____ 91621-3 $4.95 Can.

DROP-OFF
Ken Grissom
_____ 91616-7 $3.95 U.S.   _____ 91617-5 $4.95 Can.

A CALL FROM L.A.
Arthur Hansl
_____ 91618-3 $3.95 U.S.   _____ 91619-1 $4.95 Can.

Publishers Book and Audio Mailing Service
P.O. Box 120159, Staten Island, NY 10312-0004

Please send me the book(s) I have checked above. I am enclosing $_____ (please add $1.25 for the first book, and $.25 for each additional book to cover postage and handling. Send check or money order only—no CODs.)

Name _____

Address _____

City _____ State/Zip _____

Please allow six weeks for delivery. Prices subject to change without notice.

MS 9/89

RESCUE AT GUNPOINT

Alicia fired twice at Ortega from where she stood in the doorway. He swung his pistol in her direction. I hit him just as he fired, knocking him over and off the chair. The Colt blammed loudly.

I can't tell how long Ortega and I rolled around on the floor, fighting for his gun. His free hand was digging into my face, his forefinger poked into my eye, his thumb in my mouth, his nail shredding my gums. Then I clenched my teeth and bit down hard on his thumb. He shrieked, then heaved, then managed to tumble half-out from under me. Our faces just then were very close together. I remember it all—just how that face looked the moment before it seemed to come apart before my eyes—for Alicia had leaned down over us and discharged the HK into the side of his head from about six inches from my ear...

"A STANDOUT...The plot is tight, with hairpin turns and hairbreadth escapes. The action is almost nonstop."
— *Washington Post Book World*

"FAST-PACED...Cervantes is an appealing character."
— *Chicago Tribune*

"GRIPPING AND COLORFUL!"
— *Detroit News*